"Because I was the darkest of the children, it was always understood that I would receive the most education and would rise highest in the state."

It's five hundred years after the nuclear war which destroyed the world as we know it. The elite black society thought they were the only survivors, until evidence of the existence of others turned up. The others were white, and their society was patterned after the beehive, with a queen and workers and drones.

In this incredible adventure, a research team from the black world saves a condemned drone from death, and learns from him the amazing facts of their own survival.

the day of the drones

by A. M. Lightner

BANTAM BOOKS · TORONTO · NEW YORK · LONDON

THE DAY OF THE DRONES
*A Bantam Book / published by arrangement with
Grosset & Dunlap, Inc.*

PRINTING HISTORY
*W. W. Norton edition published February 1969
Bantam edition published December 1970
2nd printing
3rd printing*

For Christopher

The
Day of the
Drones

PART ONE

Chapter One

Because I was the darkest of the children, it was always understood that I would receive the most education and would rise highest in the state. Fortunately for the expectations and hopes of my parents, and later of my teachers, I had a quick mind and a fair amount of ability, and I adapted easily to the tasks set before me. When I left home at the age of twelve to enter the school of the Medics at Har, I had no trouble adjusting to the strict rules and discipline.

Each year, when the rains were over and the roads passable again, I was allowed to go home for a short visit with my family. And each year the report I brought with me was stamped with the coveted words, "Recommended for Higher Training." Father would kiss me and say there was no telling how high I would go. Mother would say it was only to be expected, that I was sure to go all the way to the top, and that it was time the Wasan should be a woman again. The people had been ruled long enough by a man.

In those days all this meant very little to me. I was still a child and glad to be home and to escape as soon as possible from the grownup talk into the happy world of children. We were a large tribe and I not only had many brothers and sisters, but a whole flock of cousins to play with—and the beautiful wilderness of jungle, lakes, and mountains in which to play. We had been trained from childhood to avoid the dangers, and we knew and respected the boundaries beyond which it might be hazardous to stray. Nobody watched or governed us. We were on our own.

On these treasured visits, my first thought was to find my cousin N'Gobi. He was three years younger than I but he never seemed younger to me. He could always run faster and was more agile and sure-footed in climbing tree or mountain than any of the others. As far back as I can remember, he learned everything twice as fast as I did. I looked forward to the year he would be twelve and could join me in the halls of learning at Har. It seemed obvious to me that if I had done well, N'Gobi was sure to do better. The year I was fifteen I came home after the rains, expecting to find preparations under way for his departure. They would be arranging the proper rituals. In two weeks he and I would return together.

To my surprise there was no sign of N'Gobi about the compound. Two of my cousins and a younger sister were being made ready, but I could have told the elders ahead of time that these children would last only a year or two with the Medics and that each would then be sent back to fit into his destined niche in life. They were not made for the higher learning.

When I could not find N'Gobi, I went in search of Mother. She looked at me strangely.

"You must realize you're growing up, Amhara," she told me in a tone that I at once recognized as the beginning of a parental lecture. "N'Gobi is growing up, too. I know he's only twelve, but he's advanced for his age and it's time he began to learn a trade. He's been working in the forest for several months now."

I looked at her, dumbfounded.

Mother had always been able to guess my thoughts. "Surely you did not expect him to be one of the chosen?" she demanded. "After all the teaching you've had!"

Only then did I understand, so differently does the eye of childhood look on the workings of authority. N'Gobi was lighter than I. He was not one or two shades lighter; he was a great many shades lighter. I guess he was the lightest skinned of all the children in our tribal group at that time. He used to admire my glistening black skin. Like ebony, he would say. When he was little he would spend a lot of time in the sun, trying to get really black. Once he had almost had sunstroke. All he could achieve was a dark brown. I thought he looked very handsome, but the other children laughed at his efforts and when he grew older he gave up trying.

Now, for the first time, I failed to adapt to the laws and ideals of the Medics. In fact, I rebelled. I stormed and cried.

"It's not fair!" I shouted. "It's absurd—stupid—ridiculous! He has the best mind and the most ability. He'd be a far better Medic than I! It's senseless and wasteful!"

Fortunately, I was at home with my family. Mother shut all the doors and pulled the curtains and set about putting me straight. Otherwise, I hate to think what might have happened to me.

"Who do you think you are, Amhara?" she demanded. "Who are you to judge? A young girl only on the threshold of learning! You should thank fortune for your color that made it possible for you to be chosen and for your good mind that lets you learn quickly. Though after this silly scene, I wonder if you've learned anything at all. Haven't they taught you history? Don't they make you learn the Sacred Laws anymore? Go on and repeat them so I'll know you haven't forgotten."

"Yes, of course," I persisted. "But that hasn't anything to do. . . ."

I had learned the Sacred Laws in early childhood. They were always with us, recited on every possible occasion. Like most children, I took them for granted and never applied them to the life around me.

"Go ahead," said Mother, "repeat them for me."

"In the beginning there was a great Disaster," I sing-songed. "And fire on land and death in the sea and the air. And the cities were destroyed and the people were annihilated and the lands were made desolate.

"And everything that went before was lost to man, in building and learning and knowledge.

"And this crime against God and man was committed by the white people. They were the rulers of the world. They had built great nations and learned all knowledge, and they used it to destroy the world and themselves

5

therein. And their name is forever accursed.

"And the only people saved from destruction were a few of the black race. And they had struggled with the little that is left and have walked humbly with God.

"And our duty is to cherish the little world we have. To preserve it and husband it and to keep ourselves clean of the white plague."

"Well, you still remember it," Mother said, "but apparently it means nothing to you."

"But I've never seen a white man," I cried. "N'Gobi isn't white. He's brown. When he's been in the sun he's almost dark brown. Is that what they mean by white? Someone who's just brown?"

"No, of course not," Mother said. "White people were really white. Some more and some less, I suppose. And there were some that were yellow. All kinds. There are pictures. I'm sure they'd show you at school if you asked. It must have been very different in the old days, before the Disaster. What you've got to realize is that N'Gobi is very lucky that he was born now. A hundred, or even fifty, years ago he wouldn't have been allowed to grow up. As soon as his coloring was apparent, he would have been liquidated. But things are getting easier. He was Aunt Dessie's only child. Her husband died before he was born and everyone felt sorry for her. Of course, she married again later and had all those little children, but nobody could have predicted it. And she cried so none of us had the heart. Still, N'Gobi is lucky to be alive at all."

I looked at her in horror.

"But N'Gobi's the best swimmer," I cried, "and the best runner and the best shot—and he knows more already than any boy his age!"

"A hundred years ago we would never have known it," Mother said. "A hundred years from now he might be able to go on to higher learning or even become the Wasan. But he's living right now and so are we, and you'd better get used to the idea. I think you'll find he has. If you want to see him, he's working over by Lake Wala."

I went away in a rebellious mood, but Mother was quite right about N'Gobi. I found him at work in the woods along the lake shore, and he was not nearly as angry about things as I was.

N'Gobi had grown up a lot since I last saw him. He was only a little more than twelve, but he was taller than I and easily looked fifteen. He was going through the forest, inspecting the trees and marking them as he had been taught by the forester. He was delighted to see me and stopped work at once. We went down to the lake and sat on a flat rock under some overhanging trees, the sort of spot where we used to fish together. We stared into the limpid, shifting colors of the depths and we said all the foolish, polite things we always said when I returned and we were getting used to one another again.

Finally I told him about my scene with Mother. It was impossible for me to keep anything from him for long, and I was still seething with disappointment and revolt. N'Gobi seemed quite calm about it.

"Of course your mother is right," he said. "I never expected to go. For a long time I've known that I could not hope to be chosen. And your mother is right that I'm lucky to be alive. Also to be allowed this work. Suppose I were sent to the mines, like some of the boys. Or trained for service. No, this is my meat—the woods, the jungles, the rivers, the birds, and the animals. If I can't go on to the higher learning, I can learn a lot from the forester I work with. He's been trained up there, and I'll learn from him. He says you can even rise from the ranks, and by the time I grow up there may be less prejudice."

I was silent a long time and I guess he knew I was not convinced. Like Mother, he could almost read my thoughts.

"There's one thing you might do," he said at last. "When you get done studying a book, don't return it right away. Pretend you want it for more study or you lost it or something. Send it to me and let me read it. That way I'll learn almost as much as you do. That is, if you think it's safe. I wouldn't want you to get into trouble."

"It's a wonderful idea!" I cried. "Of course I'll do it. Nobody needs to know a thing about it. When you're done with them, give them back and then I'll turn them in. I'll pretend it's getting harder for me to remember it all."

N'Gobi laughed and that broke the spell and my cross feelings vanished. We peered into the dark waters together and he pointed out a new little fish that I had never seen before.

"Do you see that?" he asked. "That's something called a trout. They were supposed to be extinct, but they're coming back. We're taking special care of them, watching their food and predators. We may try to get eggs for the hatcheries soon. They're the best eating fish, but the Disaster almost finished them off. Nobody knows where they've come back from. You know, those white people not only blew up the world, they were killing off all the animals. Even the fish in their rivers were dying off, long before the Disaster. I'm glad I'm not white. I'm really lucky when you think about it."

I went back to Har with the new students when the time for visiting was at an end. I stopped worrying about N'Gobi, since he seemed to be happy. I never forgot my promise to him that day by the lakeside. Each year when I returned after the rains, I brought a huge parcel of books. I pretended I had to study them, but I slipped them to N'Gobi as soon as possible. No matter how many I brought, he would have read and practically memorized them all by the time I was due to leave. Between my yearly visits, I found the opportunity to send him a parcel now and then by someone traveling in that direction. He always returned them promptly, and we were never caught in this subterfuge. Probably it did not occur to our elders that such a situation could arise. Everybody was carefully tested and graded by the Medics according to his interests and abilities and consequently everyone was supposed to be happy in the work and station finally assigned to him. Perhaps the problem of a really light-skinned individual with remarkable abilities had never come up before.

It was the year I was eighteen that we began to run into difficulties, not from the authorities but between the two of us. We discovered a difference in interests. N'Gobi was disappointed with the books I brought back that summer.

He looked over the history and the literature, the books on philosophy and language—for even then I was beginning the study of ancient Anglic, and was looking forward to reading Shakespeare in the original.

"All very good," he said, turning the pages rapidly, "but I don't see any science or math. Don't you get to mechanics pretty soon?"

"I'm not going to do any more science," I replied. "I'm going to specialize in what they call the social sciences."

"But how can you do that? Nothing's as interesting as science!"

"It may be interesting, but it's awfully hard," I said. "I wouldn't have passed last year if you hadn't helped me when I came home. And anyhow, you know they don't teach science beyond the eighth form. It's taboo, unless you're awfully good and are going to be a top Medic. I never could do that in science, but I can make it this way."

N'Gobi looked very disappointed. "I was afraid of this," he said. "I could see it coming, though I tried hard to coach you. I thought you were doing pretty well last year."

"You're a wonderful help," I told him. "I don't think I'd have gotten through last year without it. I might even have been sent back without a recommendation this year. Maybe it would have been better at that. I really like home better than Har. And I'd see you more than once a year."

"You wouldn't like it better." His tone had a savage quality. "You think you would, but you wouldn't. Nobody with your mind would like to stand still for the rest of her life."

For the first time I realized what N'Gobi must really feel. He had concealed it so well until now. He had seemed to accept his rating without question. Now I could sense his pain and disappointment, and my own feeling of revolt began to boil up in sympathy.

"But you've been standing still all these years!" I cried.

"Not really. Not with your help. Don't think I don't appreciate all you've done. I know what things would

9

have been like without it. But now, well, give me what books you have. I'll read them anyhow."

"Perhaps I can get some science books from someone at school who's studying it. Perhaps even mechanics, though that's really taboo." My mind was running over all the possibilities.

"You'd have to know the person awfully well," he said doubtfully. "You'd have to be much more careful."

"There's my brother," I offered. "Tadessa. You know, he's ninth form and he's science special."

"I don't think you should trust him," N'Gobi objected. "He's never liked me. He's a one-man man, meaning for Tadessa only."

"You just think that because he's older and didn't grow up with us."

"That's my opinion," he insisted. "If you get any books out of him, don't let him know what you want them for."

When I got back to Har that summer I began to cultivate Tadessa. He was five years older than I and had already been initiated into the lower order of Medics. I had seen very little of him up to now, as students kept pretty closely to their age groups. That year he began to teach in the lower school, and when I called myself to his attention, he responded kindly and soon began to make much of me. Perhaps he found it useful to have a younger sister with a rating like mine, who was expected to go far.

Tadessa was going to be a doctor. This was the science with the highest rating and also with the largest student body. It was generally admitted that but for the doctors among the early Medics, the race might have completely died out. Certainly it would have deteriorated and all civilization would have been lost. And so doctors were encouraged at all levels. However, doctors were not likely to use the kind of books I knew N'Gobi wanted. The study of medicine demanded books on chemistry, and these he accepted when I passed them on to him. To his urgent demands for books on mechanics, I had no answer. The ancient science of physics had been taboo for hundreds of years. The few remaining books were kept in secret places, and only the highest among the Medics might read them.

All this I came to realize gradually, for I had no bent for science myself and my time was spent studying such things as history, government, the arrangement of our tribes and laws, and—my favorite—the ancient languages and arts, such as were left to us since the Disaster.

Every year, as the time came for me to visit my home, I began to think what books I might take back to N'Gobi that he would like best. This year I made a special visit to Tadessa's rooms to see if I might borrow something from him. Tadessa had become used to my unusual interest in his field of study, but he never failed to tease me about it.

"Don't you ever go home with the idea of a holiday?" he asked. "A few days to forget all this, to enjoy the fields and the woods and perhaps ride a horse? Last time I was home I was hardly out of the saddle."

"You don't need to study extra," I told him. "The only way I've gotten anywhere is by hard work and lots of it."

"But you don't need to study this," he said, handing me the books I wanted. "However, I suppose the future Wasan has to know everything."

I looked at the floor and giggled. He knew I didn't like him to call me the "future Wasan." I felt he was not only making fun of me, but also of our mother's dreams. She had never hoped he would be "Wasan." At this moment I thought for the first time that he might be jealous. It did not seem worthy of him, and to hide my confusion I grabbed the book—a simple text on rocks and minerals, with a chapter on volcanoes that I thought might interest N'Gobi—and hurried to the door. He called me back.

"As long as you're making free with my books," he said, "you might run an errand for me. This has to go back to the library. I promised to take it for a friend who lives over in C compound, but I haven't been near the place. You go right past it."

"Of course," I said. "And thanks for yours. I'll bring it back when I return."

"Oh, and take my greetings to our parents," he added as an afterthought. "Tell them to stay well until I come home at the year's end. After that they needn't worry.

They'll have me around to keep them well."

I stopped at the door, barely able to believe my ears. "You mean you're going home to stay?"

"Surely, you must have heard. I've been assigned to our tribe. Have to start working sometime, and old Doc Ato's getting pretty feeble. More people than he can handle. It's a good spot, and there'll be time left over for horses."

So Tadessa had reached his level. He was assigned his niche. No more study. No higher to go. Second-degree Medic, probably. No wonder he was jealous. I knew he'd expected to go much higher. Perhaps someday I myself would face this destiny. How would I feel about it then?

My mind raced in confusion as I slipped out into the hall; and it wasn't until I was crossing the larger courtyard that I thought to look at the book Tadessa had given me to return to the library. Then I stopped and stared at it in disbelief. It was a very old book and had been tenderly cared for with a special cover to protect it. It was written in ancient Anglic and I could see that I would have to translate it for N'Gobi. But when I looked at the drawings and diagrams, I knew he would be wild to understand the sense of it. It was called *The Internal Combustion Engine*.

As I stared at the book in my hand and wondered if I had the courage to "borrow" anything as valuable as this, even for N'Gobi, I heard a low cough at my elbow, no more than a clearing of the throat, but I knew that the hand that was placed upon my arm must belong to my teacher, Don Ylma.

"What a beautiful old book," she said softly. "How should a young student like you be reading it? Or are you going to translate it? I believe you could, my dear. I believe you know the ancient tongue as well as I do already. And I suppose some handsome young expert, who never took the trouble to learn Anglic, has persuaded you to do it for him?"

I stammered at her close perception of the truth. "My brother gave it to me," I said, "to return to the library. I was going that way."

"Then I'll go along with you," she said. "I've an errand there myself. And perhaps on the way you'll tell me what you think of the machines you see described in there."

I was glad enough to get the subject away from why I had the book, even if only to discuss the book itself. For of that I could frankly say I knew nothing at all.

"It seems a very obscure and ancient subject," I said, "and one not easy for me to understand."

"But surely you must realize," persisted Don Ylma, "from the reading and studying you've already done, that machines like those described here were once the accepted mode of travel. There were hundreds and thousands of them. Everybody had one. You can still see the ruins of the old roads, though our country had far fewer of them than the rest of the world. They were once smooth and unending ribbons across the land, and the motorcars ran upon them at unheard of speeds."

She went on to describe the life of the old days and let her imagination play upon the idea of what it must have been like to drive one of those motorcars. I followed behind her all the way to the library, thinking of how almost any student would give his right hand to hear this discourse by Don Ylma, whereas all I could think of was how thankful I was to have got off the subject of what I had been doing with the book.

Then, under her watchful eye, I duly handed it to the librarian, knowing that now N'Gobi would never read about the combustion engine and that I must not tell him of it and make him sad.

Don Ylma was watching me curiously. "My rooms are only a little farther in the inner court," she said. "I'd be happy if you'd come with me for some refreshment."

It was an invitation I could hardly ignore, although at the moment my one desire was to escape from my teacher's attention. I followed her along the unfamiliar paths of the inner court. It was unusual for the younger students to be invited to the private dwellings of the Dons, and I had never been so honored before. I should have felt it a step forward in my career, that I was now progressing from the stage of pupil to candidate. I was still worrying about my intended theft of the book and my near escape from discovery, however, and it was with reluctance that I stooped through the door and into Don Ylma's room.

I was struck at once by a riot of light, color, shapes,

and objects. The Don's rooms had none of the monastic simplicity and tidiness that were fostered in the students from the first day at Har. I had heard gossip that the Dons did themselves well in their own quarters, but I had never given the matter much thought. There was a strict code that kept the students to their own compounds until they had reached the coveted rank of candidate to the Medics.

Don Ylma's floor was carpeted with heavy blankets woven by the highland tribes in typical geometric patterns and rich browns and reds. The walls were hung with paintings of animals from our forests and jungles, both the living and the extinct. The room glowed in the bright sunlight that came through the wide windows and doors opening on the garden at the back. Everywhere there were books and papers. Papers on the desk, books on the chairs and the couches and the tables. To one who had been taught that books were sacred and often taboo, and that each bit of paper must be prized and husbanded, this prodigality was startling. Through a side door I glimpsed Don Ylma's bedroom, a corner of her bed, and more rows of books around the wall.

I followed her timidly into the room as my eyes took stock of what was later to become an accustomed sight. Then I became aware that we were not alone. A man was lounging on a chair in the corner. He was turning the pages of a book of drawings that appeared to be maps.

"Come in. Come in!" said Don Ylma. "Here's Don Woldi waiting to have tea with us. You've come for cakes and tea, I presume, Woldi? I've brought young Amhara along from the library, so you'll have to talk to her, too."

She clapped her hands and a maid-servant appeared and began setting the table for tea. I noticed that Don Ylma's ceramics were of the best, chosen for excellence in color and design. Were these also things that went with the higher learning? I had never considered this before. My mother had emphasized hard work and study, duty and devotion to the state. She had never mentioned the best of ceramics, a lionskin on the wall, or a garden of one's own. I began to have dreams and resolved to study twice as hard in the future.

Then I heard Don Woldi saying, "And what was the

14

young lady doing in the library? Should she not be ending her studies and returning home for the time of rest?"

"She was bringing back a book that her brother had given her," Don Ylma answered, as she poured out the tea. "A most unusual book about the internal-combustion engine."

"So. And she did return it? She didn't want to take it with her, as she has done with so many books in the past?"

I nearly dropped the cup that Don Ylma was handing me. Only the realization that it bore a unique tiger design that could hardly be replaced made me hang on for dear life.

"Oh, I made her return it," Don Ylma replied coolly. "It had been given her by her brother. You know, young Tadessa. I thought it best that he have no reason to question her. But she looked so disappointed! Amhara, my dear, if you really want that book, I'll get it back for you. But I don't believe you'd understand a word of it."

"The question is, who does understand?" said Woldi. "Who reads the books you take home with you every year?"

I had the teacup now safely on the table. I clutched the edge of my reed chair and tried to sound casual.

"Why, I do, of course. I don't want to forget . . . to get behind. I wouldn't be without books."

"Amhara, my dear," Don Ylma said softly, "why do you think I made you return the book? And why do you think I brought you here now? You must realize you're about to become a candidate for the Medics. Next term you will study with Don Woldi, too."

"What you probably don't realize," put in Don Woldi, "is that your brother is not to be trusted. Now he cannot say that he gave you the book and you did not return it to the library."

"When you become a Medic or even a candidate," continued Ylma, "you are no longer of your family. You are one of us. Surely you see that you must trust us."

"Who is it that reads your books, Amhara?" asked Woldi.

"Well," I said, "perhaps I've done wrong and you won't

want me as a candidate. But it's better to know now. If you don't want me, you can send me home for good." Suddenly I was in a great hurry to tell them everything and be done with it. "It's my cousin, N'Gobi," I said. "He always wanted to study and he had no chance. He's with the Forest Service now, but he was the best at everything, the best runner, the best swimmer, the quickest to learn." I described N'Gobi as I had always seen him, the victor at all games, the guardian of animals, quick of eye and ear in the jungle.

"And why," asked Don Woldi, when I drew breath, "was not this paragon of children sent to us for teaching?"

I looked at the floor. I realized that I had forgotten to mention the one important aspect of N'Gobi.

"Because he is light of skin," I whispered. "The clan would not send him."

I saw my teachers look at each other and heard their quick intake of breath.

"How light?" demanded Woldi. "As light as I? You see, I am lighter than you or Don Ylma."

I shook my head. "No. Lighter."

"As light as the maid who was here just now?"

"Lighter . . . lighter."

"Well, how light? He's not really white, is he?"

I shook my head. "I don't know. How can a man be really white? I don't know what a white man looks like."

Don Woldi laughed. "Neither do I, nor any man living. But the literature describes them and we have pictures. Have you any here, Ylma?"

"I think so. Let me see."

Don Ylma went into her bedroom and rummaged. I looked up at Don Woldi and my fear and misery must have been in my eyes, for he spoke kindly.

"Don't worry, little one," he said. "We're not inquisitors. Only old teachers who still want to learn. Now drink your tea and eat one of Ylma's cakes."

I did as he said, and presently Don Ylma came back with several large, flat books in heavy bindings that looked extremely old. She spread them out on the table and we all bent over them while she turned the pages. A strange world was revealed to me, with unfamiliar buildings, queer machines, and odd costumes.

"Now, this is all material you'll study when you have me next term in Pre-Disaster Civilization," said Don Woldi. "But observe the lightness of skin in this woman and the yellow hair in this color print. Hard to imagine, isn't it? And the thinness of features. Even with the faded colors. And although this man is obviously sunburned. And here, the unusual hair on the face. A different race. A totally different race. And gone forever by their own doing."

He turned the pages as I stared, fascinated, at the alien people. The sharp, hawklike faces repelled me, the white skin looked sickeningly like something brought up from the bottom of the lake.

"Well, what do you think? See your cousin there?" asked Woldi. "Any of them look like N'Gobi?"

"Oh, no!" I cried, recoiling in horror. "No, no! He's like one of us!" But as I said it, I thought about the time N'Gobi had gotten so sunburned. And there was that picture of the sunburned man. But the face was different. Entirely different. I continued to shake my head.

Woldi sighed. "Just local prejudice, it seems," he said. "I thought perhaps an interesting throwback."

"It's just as well," Ylma said. "What could you do with such a case?"

"Might be a mechanical genius if it bred true to form."

"In which case it would be our duty to blot it out."

"Oh, yes, our duty. But since the young man obviously isn't a mechanical genius or a resurrected white man, but only Amhara's cousin, I see no reason why he shouldn't read a few books. Do you?"

"No reason at all if the two of them continue to be as discreet as they have been. Come back before you leave tomorrow, my dear, and I'll have that book for you. The library will list it to my name."

Don Woldi closed the picture books with a snap. "I'll look forward to seeing you next term, Amhara. I'll leave you now, Ylma. And you might get that boy a good physics text while you're about it. I imagine that should interest him, too."

When he had gone, Don Ylma looked at me. "You must realize," she said, "that we Dons are not of the Medics entirely. We do not govern. We teach and we advise. And we look to the future. Don Woldi thinks that someday we may need people like your cousin. And I think he may be right."

The next day she gave me the books as she had promised, and I went home to N'Gobi with a light heart. I would not be exaggerating to say he almost ate them up. In fact, before I returned to Har, he had copied all the drawings about the internal-combustion engine.

"I never thought such books existed," he said. "Don't let those teachers up there forget about me."

"I don't imagine they will," I said. "I wonder if I should tell them that you copied the drawings."

We worried about it for a while, but in the end I decided it was best to tell them everything. If I was going to be a Don and a Medic, those were the people I would have to trust. I had told N'Gobi what they had said about Tadessa and warned him never to let Tadessa know of the books and drawings. My brother seemed far too busy learning the local medical practice from old Doc Ato and in building up a string of racing ponies. An occasional distant hail was all I heard from him. I wondered if he had checked with the library on my return of his book.

Chapter
Two

From that time on I had no more trouble supplying N'Gobi with books. In fact, I had the help of both Don Ylma and Don Woldi in selecting the subject matter and acquiring the texts. N'Gobi began to get an education in the fields of his choice.

At the same time I was treated to my first contact with the brilliant mind of Don Woldi. To my surprise, I was put at once into his advanced class. When I stammered my thanks, he replied blandly, "Why should you bother with the beginners? Anyone with your experience and attitude does not need an introduction to the universality of minds —what used to be called the brotherhood of man. I take it for granted you know the history of the last five hundred years. Our little, cramped history since the Disaster. Don Ylma speaks highly of your ability in her field, so you should have no trouble reading the ancient manuscripts. Perhaps some students require indoctrination into the theory that what we now see around us is *not* the be-all and end-all of existence. But not you and your interesting cousin who reads books!" He looked at me with his sidelong glance that I later realized was typical of him when waiting to see how a student would receive a new idea.

That year was my happiest and the most intensely interesting of my years at Har. It was also my last, though at the time I did not know it. Under Don Woldi's hand, the curtain of the past was pushed aside, and the picture of a vanished civilization, as much as could be seen from

the ancient manuscripts, was spread before our eyes
There were a bare dozen of us in his class, but we all fel
the fascination. Of course, we struggled with the eterna
questions in our minds.

"Why?" my classmates demanded, one after the other
"Why can't we do that now? Surely we could learn agair
from the books? Why can't we fly again? Why can't we
have motors and machines and huge buildings and cit
ies?"

To each question, Woldi replied, "Taboo."

He told us, "You are only studying these taboo subject
because you will one day become Medics and leaders o
the people. And who knows? In your time some of these
things may cease to be taboo. Not all, but some. It is goo
for you to know they existed. You must also learn why
they are taboo. We must not make the same mistakes over
again. Before you finish here you will have a more thor
ough study of the Disaster itself. Much more thorough
What it did and what it implies. After that there will no
be so many questions."

Another time he said, "It is not only the machines that
are taboo. Remember that the minds of men were responsible for the machines and the destruction they made
That is why each of us must be fitted to his life and hi
way of life fitted to him. The greatest taboo is against
interfamily quarrels, inter-tribal strife. We have prohibite
any war of clan against clan, race against race. But we are
struggling to build a new world for man, and in our little
space of five hundred years we have been . . . somewha
successful!"

I sat in my corner and I thought about Tadessa. Did he
feel fitted to his life as it had been decided for him? In the
old world he could have gone away and built his life i
some other country if he did not like it here. Now there
was nowhere else for him to go. No known part of the
world had remained livable outside our little haven in the
mountains of Africa. A student across the room felt some
questioning like mine.

"But how can there be any war of race against race?"
he asked. "We are the only race left on earth."

Don Woldi regarded him with a sidelong glance. "How do you know?" he asked softly.

"But . . . but . . . we just learned it in last year's history, and all the years before that!"

Don Woldi smiled. "Now that you have arrived at the advanced pinnacle of my class, you will begin to question everything. Oh, not outside the classroom, please. But here, where we are training leaders for the future, we have to consider what the future may bring. It is true that at the time of the disaster all communication with the outside world ceased. No ships came into our ports. In fact, our ports were destroyed and only generations later did we venture back to the sea for food, and that was of dubious value. The wonderful communication instrument that the ancients called radio did not bring our ancestors any word, for the simple reason that there was no one at the other end to communicate. But we must not imagine that anything in the world stands still. We have only to look at ourselves. From conditions of panic and chaos, the original Medics began to build the society we know today. Around us we perceive that the scorched and desert regions are slowly retreating. It may well be that within your lifetime we will see a new age of discovery. As our population increases and as the distant areas of the earth are possibly cleansed of their poisons, our Wasan may see the wisdom of and the need for expansion. At such a time we must have leaders who are aware of both the perils and the possibilities of that world of the distant past, to guide us skillfully to greater glories without the disasters."

After a lecture like this, I left Don Woldi's class with a feeling that great things were just around the corner. If I thought I would be welcome, I would stop in Don Ylma's rooms, more for the chance to discuss the new ideas I had just encountered than to sample her delicious cakes and tea. Sometimes Don Woldi followed me there, and then I had the special pleasure of curling up in a corner to listen to them argue and discuss their pet theories about the world of the past and how we should develop our world of the future.

Among other subjects, Don Ylma taught the culture of the past and the art of digging up or excavating for further

21

knowledge of it. She had a special interest of her own i[n] an ancient writer or poet called Shakespeare; and alread[y] I had read several times the three books on the subjec[t] that were kept under lock and key in her room. Ther[e] were so many references to this poet in all the ancien[t] books and manuscripts that she was sure he must hav[e] been far more important than was indicated by the tw[o] plays and several fragmentary verses and quotation[s] known to us.

Don Woldi, who thought there were more importan[t] things in the world than poets, used to tease her about it[.] He insisted that probably there had been no such perso[n] as Shakespeare, but that it was a common name given t[o] many writers, which would account for the many differen[t] references and quotations from dates apparently severa[l] hundred years apart. In fact, there was a school o[f] thought at Har that insisted that Shakespeare's works ha[d] really been written by another man, known as BernShaw[.] When it was pointed out that this writer had supposedly lived some three hundred years later than Shakespeare, they claimed that no one would be performing plays that were three hundred years old. Consequently, they must have been written by BernShaw, under the other name, of course, as the two styles were so different. Since the plays of Shakespeare and BernShaw were all being performed right up until the Disaster, it was obvious that the two men must have been contemporaries.

Don Ylma would get angry when people set forth these ideas. It was one of the few things that could rouse her wrath. Her eyes would flash as she declared that no one who had read both Shakespeare and BernShaw could possibly maintain that they were written by one and the same man. This did not keep the argument from flourishing, especially among those who had never read either of the writers, except perhaps in a poor translation.

The day I heard Don Woldi give his "Age of Discovery" lecture, I walked out of the classroom in a daze. Perhaps some of these things would come to pass within my own lifetime. I wandered through the courts and found myself, without thinking, at Don Ylma's door. She beckoned me in and as the weather was fine we went out

22

into her garden. I had hardly started to describe my excitement at Don Woldi's lecture, when that teacher, himself, came through the rooms and joined us in the garden.

"Well, I see my pearls of wisdom fell on fertile ground in at least one case," he said. "Are you going to feed us, Ylma? And do we have to stand in the hot sun to get it?"

"Sit in the shade then," she replied, and clapped for the servant to bring tea. "I find the sun pleasant after all the rain."

Don Woldi lost no time in making himself at home. "Now tell me, what did you like most about my lecture?"

"The idea that we might be able to discover more things," I said promptly. "Go out into the world and dig up the record of the past."

"Oh, dig, dig! She's just like you!" cried Woldi. "Might well have been your daughter. No wonder she's your protégé. Now, for me, I would like to have one of those air machines of the past. To be able to fly all over the world and look down on the sites of the ancient cities. Then you could pick out the best spots to dig. Then you'd know what you were doing."

"But we don't have an air machine," Ylma said, "or the tools to make it, or the fuel to fly it. So we aren't going to know what we're doing, and the only way to get anywhere is hit or miss."

"I fear you're right," said Woldi, stuffing a cake into his mouth. "And it usually turns out to be miss, which is why all this digging is so useless. You know why she wants to do it, Amhara? She thinks she'll be able to settle this silly argument about Shakespeare and BernShaw, whereas if she ever *does* get anywhere, it will probably only be to prove that the Shakespeare-is-Shaw advocates are right after all! So you'd do better to leave the matter alone, my dear."

"Oh, you!" cried Ylma. "I don't know why I let you come to tea and eat up all my cakes!"

"Why, because I'm speaking for exploration and excavation, and you know the Wasan will listen to me—someday, perhaps."

"Perhaps," said Ylma, and her anger had suddenly

disappeared. "But we will be too old. Even you, Wold Others will have to do it."

"That's understood," he said. "Let's hope they do bette than we did. Did you know we went on an expeditio once, Amhara? Yes, it was thirty years ago and we wer both very young, and we didn't find very much. All w found was a great deal of poisoned planet. And that's wh Ylma is always looking for a daughter among the stu dents. She never had any of her own."

Ylma put down her cup with a clatter that ignored th exquisite ceramic.

"You needn't have brought that up," she said. "Don' discourage the young. It was an accident probably, a piec of bad luck."

"And all exploration was stopped as a consequence But it's a good thing to bring it up. We must all profit b the mistakes of the past. Perhaps it would be better t build an air machine after all, even though it seems to b impossible."

He sat, turning his cup in his hands, looking at the geometric design as though he could trace the fate of mar therein. The argument seemed over, and Ylma made nc pretense that it had not been disagreeable to her. I crep out of the garden and through the rooms, and the follow ing day I left Har to go to my home.

That was the vacation that marked the turning point of our lives. I arrived, much as usual, at the end of the rains when the rivers were beginning to dry up and the heat to become intolerable. I was received with praise and kisses by my parents and with what I noticed as growing respect by the elders of our clan. The girls and boys who had played with me as children were mostly married with babies of their own now. They followed me into my parents' house, all eager to ask my advice about something or to hear news of friends and relatives at Har. Even Tadessa asked me to look at his horses and give my opinion of his breeding program.

All this time I was waiting for my chance to get away and look for N'Gobi. He was probably at the forest sta- tion, and I would have to wait till the morning to take him the books I had brought from Har. I stood impatiently by the fence and watched Tadessa showing off his favorite mare. His powerful, stocky figure sat easily upon the high-spirited pony, moving in rhythm as though he were a part of the animal. Of course, I told myself, it was the other way around. The mare was moving in rhythm with the mind behind that impassive face. Horse and man might seem as one, but the commands originated in Tadessa's brain and were communicated in some invisible way to the animal. Certainly, it was only on rare occasions that even his best friends saw behind the façade of his countenance.

The dust was in my throat and the sun in my eyes, and I wondered if I had come all this distance only for a demonstration of horsemanship when out of the corner of my eye I saw N'Gobi among the shadows by the stable.

I knew at once that something unusual had happened for him to come this way to me. After I had showered Tadessa with all the compliments at my command, I took the path back through the forest toward my house. I felt rather than heard the movement of branches at my back as N'Gobi caught up with me.

"Are you so anxious to see what I brought you this time?" I teased him.

"That can wait till tomorrow," he said. "I've something to show you. It's at my hut. Come along before the sun is down."

If N'Gobi was in no hurry for the books, neither was I anxious to return to my parents' house and the demanding throngs of relatives. I followed him down the path to the lake and along the water's edge to the round, thatched ranger's hut that had been assigned to him. We went inside and N'Gobi at once opened a box in the corner. He took out a small bundle and handed it to me, and I saw it was a little duck of a kind that occasionally feeds upon our lake. It was so well preserved that it appeared almost to be alive, and I thought that N'Gobi wanted me to admire his skill in preparing a specimen.

"It's a beautiful job," I told him. "All you have to do is mount it and it will be a decoration worthy of any chief's house."

"Is that all you see?" he asked. "You're not very observant. And if you think I'd hurry you down here just to look at the mounting of a bird. . . ."

I looked closer. "Well, it's not a very common species," I ventured. "You know I've not spent much study on these things and I'm away at Har so much of the time now. . . ."

I could see he was frowning at me. Apparently, I was making a fool of myself. There was something about that duck. . . . I looked closer and then I noticed that there was a string of some sort hanging from its foot. A noose.

"You caught it in a snare!" I cried. "You've invented a new trap!"

N'Gobi snorted. "That is not my snare," he said. "I shot it with an arrow. That noose was on its foot when I killed it. Does that mean anything to you?"

"Oh, of course, it means it was caught in a snare and then it got away and later you shot it. Is that what you mean?"

"That's what I mean. Only it isn't *our* snare. Look at the knot. I never saw a knot like that. And look at the string. Here, feel it. Did you ever feel anything like that? Try to break it."

I took hold of the string. It was extremely fine and of a peculiar texture. The first thing to come to my mind was a spider's web. Pull as I might, I could not break it. I let go of it with distaste. There was a strange, sticky feeling about it that made my skin crawl. It reminded me of running through the woods as a child and feeling the web of insects upon my hair and face.

"Where did it come from?" I asked.

"That's what I'd like to know," N'Gobi said. "I'm sure it's not from around here. Neither the snare nor the way it's tied. In fact, I wonder how the bird got loose at all once it was caught in that."

"Perhaps it slipped from the hunter's fingers after the snare had been loosed from whatever it was tied to."

"That's what I thought," he said. "But what hunter and where? There are not many of these birds on our lakes, and they do not breed here. They come here when it is winter in the north and they return to their northern homes to build their nests. I know they are very good eating. But where they go and how far they fly is a mystery. The forester says that in the old days these things had been mapped out and the trails of the birds were known. But now it is forgotten. Besides, where could a bird fly that is not poisoned desert?"

Then I remembered Don Woldi's words and I told N'Gobi about it and about that last evening in Don Ylma's garden.

"He said he would like to have one of the ancient air machines and fly all over the world and pick out the best spots. But don't you see, N'Gobi, a bird *is* an air machine. It can fly over the desert and pick out the good, clean spots."

"There's more than that. Don't forget this." He let the strange slender snare run through his fingers. "Don't you see what this means?"

I looked at him as understanding flooded through me. "It means," I whispered, "that we are not alone." But I was still quite unable to believe what I said.

We sat beside the lake until twilight had deepened into night, and we both thought about the meaning of those words. We decided the best thing would be for me to take the bird, with the snare still on its leg, back to Har when I returned. Perhaps there would be a book among the treasures of the library that could tell us where such birds flew when they returned to their ancient breeding grounds. Perhaps we could find a clue, though it might also be that these birds had changed their habits and nesting sites since the Disaster had polluted their world.

Two weeks later I carried the little duck back to Har, carefully wrapped against loss or injury, and took it at once for my teachers' inspection and opinions.

I expected the bird to arouse interest, but I was unprepared for the sensation it created. I had gone to Don Ylma's rooms on the first evening of the new term. There were several other students who had come to pay their respects, candidates of many years' work, and some, like myself, who had just been elevated to that grade. I had to wait to a late hour till they had departed.

I could see that Ylma was tired and expected me to go

too, but I could not hope for a better opportunity to exhibit our discovery.

"Before I go, I have something to show you," I said.

Ylma stifled a yawn. "Oh, very well, but why at this late hour? I have a lecture tomorrow, as you know."

"I thought you'd want to see it alone." I was dismayed to see I was annoying her, but I would not be put off. I began to unwrap the box. "I brought this from home. It was found by N'Gobi, my cousin."

"Yes, I know. The one that reads the books. Has he begun to make things with his learning?"

"He didn't make it. He found it. Look." I held the bird out to her with the noose hanging. I disliked touching that because of the queer feeling.

She came close and peered at it in the candlelight. "A duck. Only a little stuffed duck. If your cousin mounted it, he did a good job. But what's this? A string? A snare of some sort? And what a strange kind of string!"

She did not hesitate to hold the string as I had.

"These knots are different. Do your tribe make knots like this?"

"No," I replied. "Nothing like that. And N'Gobi says the duck is rare on our lake. It does not nest there and comes only when it is winter in the north. He shot it with an arrow and found the snare on its leg."

"One thing at a time," said Ylma. "You'll overwhelm me with information. Wait here a moment."

She left me suddenly and went out through the garden to the servant's quarters, and I heard her rousing her maid.

"Go quickly," she said, "and bring Don Woldi here. Tell him I don't care how late it is. He must come at once."

Then she came back and lit more lamps in her study and examined the duck and the string from every angle. When Don Woldi arrived, his hair uncombed and looking as though he had been dragged out of bed, Don Ylma was poring over a book about birds, comparing every picture of a duck with the one she held in her hands.

I had to tell the story all over again for Don Woldi, and

then he looked at the bird pictures, too. However, he was even more interested in the snare.

"Your cousin is right," he said, looking sidewise at me in his speculative manner. "This is certainly not a knot or snare made by any of our tribes. If I should guess, I'd say it was like the old seamen's knots, from the times when there were men of the sea. And the string itself. I've never seen anything like it. Indeed, I've never felt anything like it before."

"It must come from a great distance, don't you think?" said Ylma.

"So I would imagine. But the question is, how great a distance? We know that all around our little country we are surrounded by deserts and polluted regions. But how far it extends and where there is any safe ground . . . ?" He spread his hands in a gesture of ignorance.

"It's a pity," he continued, "that your cousin killed the bird. Otherwise, we might have attached a message of some kind and let it return whence it came. How would that be, Ylma? Like a carrier pigeon. Almost as good as a flying machine to cross the desert!"

"Well, it is dead, and you don't have a flying machine. And who would read a message in any case?"

"Don't be obtuse, Ylma. You know as well as I do that this proves it. This should be the bomb to get things going, the lever to pry loose the Wasan. Somewhere in the world there are others besides ourselves. Somewhere there was a little pocket, like the one here. Perhaps several little pockets, where men were able to live and survive the Disaster. All this time we've been separated from each other. They don't know about us and we don't know about them. And a lot can happen in five hundred years."

"We'll have to tell the Wasan," Ylma mused. "What do you think he'll do?"

"We'll tell the Wasan," said Don Woldi, "but in our own good time. First of all we must prepare matters. Amhara must send for her cousin. It will be a good excuse to get the boy here, and put an end to this ridiculous waste of talent. Then we must try to get some idea as to where this bird may have come from—at least the general direction—and over what areas it might fly. First thing

29

tomorrow morning, we'll dig out every book the library has on migration. There used to be a lot of work done on that subject. At least some of it should have survived."

In the end I left the bird with Don Ylma, who locked in her cabinet with the pictures and books about the ancient world. Both my teachers urged me to say nothing about this to my friends and classmates at Har, and to pursue my studies as though nothing had happened. All that was easier said than done. I found that my mind was seldom on my work during the weeks that followed. I knew that Don Ylma had shut herself up in her quarters with some of the most taboo books from the library and was busily making maps and drawings of the ancient world, with all manner of migration routes marked on them in a variety of colors.

More than that, I knew Don Woldi had sent a hurried messenger to my tribe and village, ordering that N'Gobi be brought to Har with all possible speed.

Chapter
Three

I did not see N'Gobi when he first came to Har. He was taken to Don Woldi's quarters and remained there in seclusion. The first suspicion I had of his arrival was when Don Ylma sent for me and told me to get ready to go before the Wasan.

"Now? Today?" I stammered. "I thought we were to wait till N'Gobi could come from the village?"

"And what else have we been waiting for?" she said with a smile. "Now get ready quickly. Put on your best kente skirt, the one you save for rituals. Hurry, for you must look your best and must not keep the Wasan waiting."

I hurried. My classmates helped me to comb my hair and plait it into many well-oiled braids and to pile it around my head in the intricate patterns prescribed by the modern style. They helped to wind the kente under my arms and I could read the envy in their eyes that so young a student as I was to have her first interview with the Wasan. But as I dressed and then walked toward the inner courts, all I thought was that soon I should see N'Gobi.

The inner courts at Har were laid out as small apartments and gardens for the Medics, none over two stories high. Behind them all, isolated and guarded by walls and gates, was the hostel of the Wasan. That one building towered above all of Har, with its own separate courts and corridors, its halls and living quarters for the Wasan's guards. It had been the brain and nerve center that had ruled Afria for the five hundred years since the Great Disaster—the high place of the Medics who had brought us slowly back from savagery and destruction to a peaceful civilization. Here all laws were promulgated and order issued, and here was the only armed force, the Wasan's guards, that carried out those laws and orders throughout the whole of Afria.

As I followed Don Ylma through the inner courts and up to that forbidding gate, my heart turned over with apprehension and excitement. I knew that out of this meeting must come a development of profound and unknown proportions that would in all probability affect my whole life.

The Wasan held his interviews in the largest room in Har. It was a long hall, the only windows high up among smoky rafters. That morning, when I was led into the Presence, the sunlight sifted down upon the rows and rows of tall, black warriors and their mysterious, shiny weapons. I knew these men had all been picked for size, physique, and unquestioning loyalty to our ideals. In most cases their heredity had been checked for imperfection three generations back. They were the Wasan's guard, the army and police, the real force that ruled Afria. They were the only men drilled in the use of the weapons of lightning, the only ones permitted to use or possess the arms of our remote ancestors. Only in this way, it was believed, could we hope to prevent the wars and disasters that had almost annihilated the entire race of man.

I had seen the Wasan's Guards on duty about the country or striding through the streets of Har. (They were not allowed in the courts of the Dons, who policed and disciplined the university themselves.) Never had I seen so many drawn up in one place at one time.

As we walked down the hall between the lines of guards, I saw that we were approaching a throne set upon a small platform several steps above the floor of the hall, and I knew that the man sitting on that throne was the Wasan. He sat cross-legged with his feet drawn up under him, and to my apprehensive eye he appeared to have nothing on, but I knew that his drawn-up knees must conceal his black shorts. The whole effect was of very

32

black, glistening skin outlined against the crimson upholstery of the throne. To me he appeared very old, with scant hair and gnarled and protruding features. Nevertheless, he was probably not much over fifty years of age.

When we were directly in front of the throne, Don Ylma dropped to a kneeling position; and mindful of what my mother had taught me of how to behave in the Wasan's presence, I also fell upon my knees and pressed my head to the floor. I was conscious of the power of life and death which this man held over all of us. I had been taught that he ruled only for our best interests, but now that I saw him for the first time, I was not at all sure I would agree with what he considered best.

Then I heard Don Ylma addressing the Wasan. She was telling him my name and tribe and the location of my village, giving him a glowing account of my abilities as a student. I realized that she had risen from her knees, and I ventured to sit back on my heels and look around me.

The Wasan was coming down the steps of his throne, right toward me. When he stood and spoke, I could see that although he was small and thin and a poor physical specimen compared to any one of his guards, he nevertheless conveyed an amazing amount of dignity in his carriage and in the power of his voice.

"So this is the young student I have been hearing about for several years," he said. "Stand up, my dear, and let me see you. Yes, a fine young woman. You say her mental abilities are of an equally high order?"

Hearing this, I hung my head in confusion and heard Don Ylma answer. "I could not ask for a better student," she said. "Works much harder than I did at her age."

"And what is this remarkable thing she has to show me? You know I like to see what the new generation is doing, but you sent word this was something special."

"Sire," said Ylma, "what she brought me was remarkable, and Don Woldi and I thought it should be brought to you at once. But she did not find it herself. It was found by her friend and cousin near her native village. In order that you might learn all the facts, we believed you should have the boy to question also."

"Very good," said the Wasan. "Is the boy here?"

"He is coming with Don Woldi," Ylma said. "In the meantime, here is what they have brought for your decision." She held out the box containing the wild duck.

The Wasan took it and inspected the duck with interest, handling it with the greatest care.

"I have seen these birds before," he said. "I used to shoot them when I was a young man. Before I learned the use of a gun, I shot them with old-fashioned arrows. They are very good eating. I see the young man knows how to prepare a skin. But what is this hanging from its foot?"

"That," said Ylma, "is the crux of the matter. I must ask you, Sire, not to remove the string or snare, for that is the evidence we want you to consider."

"I see. A very pretty piece of evidence," said the Wasan, as he fingered the string and examined the knots. I could see that he at once comprehended all the possibilities that we had considered in many hours of discussion.

"And now this boy, Woldi? The one that shot the bird!"

At that moment I was aware that Don Woldi had come in through a side door. I had been so fascinated with watching the Wasan that I had not noticed. But there was Don Woldi with someone behind him, and as he stepped aside for the Wasan to see, I realized that man was N'Gobi.

He stood there, staring at the Wasan for a full minute and I thought that even in his homemade, country kente he was more handsome than anyone in the room. He stood straight and agile, as I had seen him walk in confidence through the forest, his hazel eyes noting and understanding everything in his surroundings. This was the first time he had been out of those forests and in such a place as Har. In the Wasan's presence, with the many guards lining the wall, he must suddenly have lost confidence and remembered how he should act, for he fell on his knees and with lowered head muttered, "Your servant, Sire."

The Wasan walked over to N'Gobi and stared as if fascinated. I thought he must feel as I did the exceptional beauty of his chiseled features, his bronzed skin and the straight brown hair that he tied with a thong at the back of his neck. Then I heard him say to Don Woldi, "Where did you get this anachronism?" Without waiting for an answer, he suddenly shouted, "Lights! Torches!"

Then, as it apparently struck him that torches at midday were a little silly, he cried, "Bring him over here where the light falls from the window!"

Two guards seized N'Gobi by either arm and dragged him across the floor to a spot of sunlight. It all happened so fast I could only gasp, and in that second Don Ylma pushed me behind her and hissed through clenched teeth, "Not a word! Not a sound! I promise he'll be all right."

It didn't look all right at all to me. The Wasan had followed along and was examining N'Gobi as though he were as extraordinary as the bird that Ylma had just given him.

"He's at least six shades lighter than the prescribed limit. You mean to say you didn't notice, Woldi? And look at his hair! Absolutely straight. Definitely a throwback. What I'd like to know is how he got by the birth inspection. Somebody's going to do a lot of explaining!"

Don Woldi's face wore a strained but patient look. After the first shock, when the guards had grabbed him, N'Gobi had frozen into stolid apathy. I knew he must be aware of my presence, but to all appearance he was unconscious of us all.

Don Woldi was pursuing his stubborn argument. "You're quite right about the color gradient, Sire," he said. "Only that was some thirty years ago. They've relaxed the standard since then."

"Not this much, Woldi. Not this much! The boy must have been born at least twenty years ago."

"Eighteen, I believe," said Woldi. "I understand there were mitigating circumstances. And a very good thing, too. The state would have lost an outstanding citizen. However, N'Gobi is not the remarkable discovery that we have for you. He merely implemented it. What we want you to consider is that duck."

The Wasan transferred his attention from N'Gobi to the duck. "Ah, yes. The duck. And the remarkable snare on its leg. Am I to understand, young man, that the snare was on the duck when you shot it?"

N'Gobi brought his gaze back from some distant point

in the rafters and stared at the Wasan. He did not open his mouth to speak. He merely bowed his head. I could see that they were going about everything wrong with N'Gobi. He was beginning to get stubborn. Pretty soon he wouldn't even bow his head. But I had figured without the Wasan. He merely looked at the two guards, and they jerked N'Gobi up and backwards. There was some twist to the arms as they did it and I heard him gasp as the pain hit him. He stared at the Wasan with a look of outraged disgust such as I had never seen on him before.

"I shot it," he said.

"And how do I know you aren't lying?" the Wasan asked. "No doubt you shot the bird. But you could have tied the knots and brought it to these impressionable Dons just to gain some attention. To be brought to Har and make a name for yourself. Isn't that how it was?"

The guards gave another twist and N'Gobi bit his lip. He only said, "I shot the bird. I couldn't tie the knots. I don't know how it's done. And I never saw string like that in my life."

For a long moment the Wasan stared at N'Gobi, and N'Gobi stared right back. I saw Don Woldi making covert motions behind the Wasan's back, but he might as well not have been there for all the effect it had on N'Gobi. If Don Ylma had not laid a firm hand on my arm, I might have spoken myself and been sorry afterwards. At last the Wasan spoke.

"We have only your word for all this. And how much trust can be put in the word of a boy of your color, I would not be too sure. It's obvious to me that there has been great laxity in the Committee on Race Purity in your part of the country. You, of course, are not to blame in that. But somewhere in your heredity is a strong strain of the white madmen who almost destroyed this earth and us with it. I will have your genetic line traced, if it is not already in the records. Perhaps you will find that this scheme to advance yourself at Har has not been as successful as you had expected. Perhaps it will turn out that having let you grow to maturity, we should at least take steps to ensure that this undesirable strain will not be handed down to future generations. Take him away and keep him under guard till there's a decision!"

The guards removed N'Gobi before I could do more than catch the stricken look upon his face. I wanted to cry out in protest, but the horror implied in the Wasan's words kept me frozen to the spot. As a good citizen I should have agreed with him, but if this was what went on at Har, I wanted no more of it. If I could just get N'Gobi out of the clutches of the guard, I'd willingly return with him to the village for the rest of my life. Let them keep their education and learning and honors. I wanted none of them. Behind these thoughts, although I would not admit it to myself, I knew that return or escape was impossible. The whole of my world was in the power of this man and the state he represented. Beyond the borders of our state there was nothing but the poisoned lands: the deserts and jungles inimical to life and harboring unknown danger and death. There was no flight possible and no escape, and N'Gobi would be lucky if he came out of this with his life.

Then, gradually, I noticed that Woldi and Ylma were arguing with the Wasan. He had returned to his chair and they had left me to go and stand on either side of him and to talk in low, murmuring tones. The Wasan had the duck in his hands, and every once in a while he held it up to look at the snare on its leg.

"Just feel that string," Don Woldi was saying. "Have you ever felt anything like that strange stickiness? And so light weight. Probably never interfered with the bird's flight. Yet it's very strong. I've been unable to break it with my hands, and I have very strong fingers."

"It's certainly strange," the Wasan admitted. "Perhaps in the mountain tribes. A new discovery. We might send a messenger to inquire."

"By all means send the messenger," said Woldi, "but I doubt that you'll find knots like these. I spent some time with the mountain tribes when I was studying our desert fringes, and I never saw string or knots like this, and I don't believe they could have developed a thing like this in the last ten years without our knowing about it."

"Then what do you think?" demanded the Wasan. "I know you've got an opinion that you're waiting to express."

"On the contrary, I don't know what to think. But I do think we should find out about it."

"And how, my dear Woldi, do you propose to do that?"

"Sire," interrupted Don Ylma. "If you will look at these pictures, I believe I may have a lead on the knots."

She handed him one of the books she had brought with her, holding it open at the page she wanted. The Wasan bent over it and then straightened up with a look of intense amazement.

"Yes. The picture at the lower right," he said. "It's very like the knots here. Almost identical. What book is this? Is it taboo?"

Don Ylma nodded. "It's from the secret archives. These were knots used by the white English navy. They were a specialty of seafaring folk."

"In other words, they're pre-Disaster. They're the taboo science of the extinct white race. Everything you've shown me is very disturbing. It's taboo knowledge and brought here by a taboo boy who should never have been allowed to grow up!"

"Sire," interrupted Ylma, "he did not tie those knots! I'll swear to it. And suppose he did? Suppose, as you would imagine, some inherited instinct caused him to tie them? What about the string? Sire, I can assure you that no string like this exists in our world. And I don't think it existed before the Disaster. I can find no reference to it, and unless it is a lost and unknown art. . . ."

"I know what you are trying to tell me," the Wasan broke in. "You want to reopen the theory that other peoples than ours survived the Disaster. But we know it is a futile hope. Ever since the Disaster, at least once in every century, these rumors have started and efforts have been made to find the source. But no other people have ever been found. And if they were found, from this evidence that we have here, you know well enough that they would in all probability be white."

"That is not necessarily so," said Woldi, "and even if it were. . . ."

"It is not something that I want to contemplate," said the Wasan, and he rose from his throne and began to walk up and down in evident excitement and perturbation.

"We may have to contemplate it," Woldi told him, "although I hardly think it likely. If there are other people living on the planet, it is only a slim chance that they are white—at least pure white. A lot can happen in five hundred years, as we ourselves know. But would you rather leave the danger an unknown threat? Consider our history before the Disaster. From what little has come down to us, we know that Afria was isolated for centuries from the rest of the world. And when the white plague finally did spill over and invade our country, many of our peoples were taken as slaves. Do you want to risk its happening again?"

The Wasan made an impatient gesture, as though brushing off an impossible eventuality. But Don Ylma took up where Woldi had left off.

"Would it not be better," she said, "to know the truth and prepare to face it than to live in the shadow of uncertainty?"

The Wasan looked at her with one of his penetrating glances. "I well remember an expedition you persuaded me into some years back, Ylma, and how little came of it that was good."

Ylma smiled. "I do not expect to go on this one myself."

There was a long silence. I had the feeling that Don Woldi and Ylma had said all they intended and were now waiting for the Wasan to make up his mind. At last he sighed. It was clear that the decision was not to his liking.

"We will call the Council," he said. "We will present the problem to the best minds of the Medics, and what they decide we shall do. In the meantime we will send messengers to the mountains and such outlying districts and see what we can learn. That young man will stay under guard till this matter is decided. Only then will I judge his case."

He rose and made the gesture of blessing and I knew

with relief that this nightmare was at an end. I bowed before him with the Dons and followed them out of the hall.

Across the courts I walked at the proper and decorous distance behind Don Ylma and Don Woldi, my face a mask for my boiling emotions. As soon as I reached the sanctuary of Don Ylma's rooms, I fell upon the couch and burst into tears. All the fear, hatred, and protest I had been laboring for hours to hold in check burst forth, and I could not have stopped my tears if I had tried.

Without doubt Don Woldi had planned to come in and discuss the whole session with Ylma, but he took one look at me, muttered something about a later hour, and left, closing the door carefully behind him.

Don Ylma did not try at once to comfort me. Instead she went about putting away the books she had taken with her, and even went into her bedroom and changed from her ritual kente into her everyday skirt. As I observed this through my tears, it struck me as the utmost hypocrisy. I cared not what happened to my ritual kente. Let it be stained with my tears. Let it be torn up and thrown out for the birds to nest in. I never wanted to wear it again or to walk into the presence it was meant to honor.

At last Don Ylma must have judged I was regaining control, for she approached me with a glass of wine.

"Drink this," she said. "And when you can keep quiet, let me speak. You've had a rough introduction to the higher state, and your training paid off. You behaved better than I could have done at your age. But let me suggest from my more advanced position that no man is worth all that emotion . . . even a cousin."

"He's more than a cousin," I sobbed. "In my tribe, cousins are brothers, and he's closer than any brother."

"Then keep him as a brother," she said. "I promise you, you and he will work together for many years here in Har."

"But—but the Wasan said. . . ." I looked up at her through my tears. I thought she could not have understood.

"Leave it to Woldi and me," she said. "You don't trust us even yet. Either of you."

"How can we?" I cried. "And how much less N'Gobi! What must he feel now? Oh, cruel, cruel! And blind! I know N'Gobi. He has the most talent ... the best mind, probably of this generation. And the Wasan would destroy it! That idiot! That monster!"

"Shh!" Ylma cautioned. She looked apprehensively at the door and then closed the window.

"I know it is cruel," she said, coming back to me. "I was afraid of something like this. But we know the Wasan. Give him time to think a bit. Now he is calling the Council. There will be cooler thoughts."

"Cooler thoughts!" I flung out. "But no less blind and cruel. The whole state is founded on it!"

"Perhaps. But consider that our state was born of the cruelest and most blind period in the history of man. It is mere chance that there is a state at all. A little difference in the bombing patterns or in the prevailing winds, and this bit of Afria would be desert, too."

"Better if it had," I cried. "And an end to all of us, for we are all evil."

"That I cannot accept," Ylma said. "And neither do you really believe it. Consider that it is mere chance that any of us is alive, be thankful for what we have, and strive to better it."

"I do strive. I've worked and studied and worked. And only to find everything thrown down, with a blank wall against all progress!"

Don Ylma sighed. "I know that's how it must seem, especially to you who are young. But think what we have done when almost nothing was left to us. What we have built from almost certain defeat. A well-ordered and safe existence. These pleasant and productive fields and mountains, which we are expanding a little year by year, as we learn to push back the desert. The knowledge of the past, which people like you and me can relearn and use to help us. But you must realize that what may be the best wisdom and the best way for one century or even one generation, may not be the best wisdom for the next. That is what it means to rule. That is what it is to be a Medic."

"Then the Wasan doesn't know it," I said. "He's still living in the past."

"The hardest thing for a man to learn is to change," Ylma said. "Do you remember the class you had two years ago when you studied the ants? Through millions of years and hundreds of millions of generations they have survived because they have changed to meet new conditions. Even though they have a specialized, instinct-ridden mode of life, when the climate changed from damp to desert, from hot to cold, they eventually changed to meet it. Individuals may have perished by the thousands, but the organism adapted and persisted and is still with us. I venture to say they may still be found in the poisoned regions today if we could go and look. If the ants can do it, man, with his greater mind, can surely do it. Individuals may perish, but we, the race, will keep our foothold on this planet. I cannot promise or predict the outcome, but we are all working for the same thing—you and I, N'Gobi and the Wasan. In the end, man's survival and the improvement of conditions are important."

"Some people go about it in a peculiar way," I said, but my anger was spent. My tears had dried as I listened to Ylma's soft and reasonable voice. I had been long enough at Har to value the life it stood for. I knew she was right, and also she brought me hope. Surely, I began to think, if she could speak so persuasively to me, her words would be no less compelling when she argued with the Wasan and the Council.

I had then to go back to my studies and my old life, to pretend to my fellow students that nothing had happened, that nothing out of the ordinary was going on. It was more than I could manage. Don Ylma knew this without my telling her, and she quietly arranged for me to move into her rooms and to suspend my regular work and studies until a decision had been reached about N'Gobi. Most of the time she was away, meeting with the Wasan or members of the Council, or just teaching her classes. She left me to my own devices and, without saying anything about it, left the key to her most precious books and ancient manuscripts where I could easily find it. I spent those two uncertain weeks reading—books that might not have come my way till years later in the regular course of study at Har.

I think Ylma had first been drawn to me and had adopted me as her protégé when she saw how I loved and responded to her readings of Shakespeare. She had in her library everything of the master that had survived the Disaster: the two complete plays (*A Midsummer Night's Dream* and *The Tempest*), the quotations and fragments from other works, and the many books of comment and reference that had been written about this author both before and after the Disaster. I could well believe her when she said that while we knew him to have been a prolific writer, many hundreds more volumes had been written about him than by him. She even collected the current articles by young upstarts, claiming his works had been written centuries later than the accepted dates. I agreed with Ylma that this was nonsense. The argument was all the rage at the time, however, and she had a little pile of these writings, which she referred to as "comic relief."

To keep myself from brooding about N'Gobi and the Council's probable decision, I sat in Ylma's garden and read for the third time that masterpiece called *The Tempest*. After five hundred years of his own time, after another five hundred of our peculiar, restricted world, he still spoke to my heart as though he were alive today.

"Oh, brave new world that has such people in it!"

Was there really another world, still alive, beyond the poisoned seas? If we followed the migration route of the little duck, would we be able to find it? What sort of people would there be in it? Would they perhaps possess the lost works of this poet, saved miraculously from the holocaust? Could I find them and return triumphantly to put an end to the silly arguments in the literary salons at Har? I knew such dreams were against all the teachings of the Medics, contrary to all knowledge and established fact for five hundred years. No wonder the Wasan and the Council were worried and looked with suspicion at N'Gobi. With one shot of his arrow he had shaken the beliefs and traditions of our whole civilization. But they

43

dared not ignore it entirely. There were too many stories and legends of the barbarians from the north who had come with their higher technical skills and enslaved our ancestors. Could such things happen again? If the birds had survived, why not man?

My brain could run in circles after that tantalizing problem, and I determined to leave the solution to the Council. I went back to Shakespeare and reread that wonderful fragment from the lost play called *Hamlet*. "To be or not to be? That is the question." Had the white race asked itself that question and answered in the negative? I fervently hoped they had been successful. I had visions of myself exploring some cave in a distant land or digging among the ruins of a great city to discover what was left of an ancient library that might preserve the cultural relics of a vanished world. But as for the people of that world, I sincerely hoped the mysteriously knotted string on the bird's leg had been a chance occurrence. I did not want to meet any white monsters while exploring. The more I thought, the more I realized the advantages of our compact, united, peaceful nation. I did not forget N'Gobi, but I felt less disturbed about him as time passed. Surely, he must realize the necessity of conforming to preserve that peace.

Then, one day, Don Ylma returned early and brought with her a man I had never met before. True, I had seen him at a distance in Har and knew him to be both a leader of the Medics and a celebrated teacher of the sciences, but I never expected to meet him in Don Ylma's garden.

"This is Ras Menasi, Amhara," Ylma said. "My favorite pupil, Ras. She must know who you are, but you will hardly have picked her out among all our youngsters."

Menasi bowed over his raised hand in the customary salute. "If I don't know her, I've certainly heard enough about her in the last few days."

I looked up to meet the most intelligent eyes I had ever seen, set in a face remarkably like a monkey's. It was the kind of face that does not age, but will seem as homely at fifty as it did at twenty-five—and no more so—when many of the handsome faces of its contemporaries will be falling into decay. Above the monkey face and understanding eyes was a ledge of the most expressive eyebrows in Har.

I looked away quickly, for what came to mind at first glance were the many student jokes I had heard about Menasi's looks, as well as the scathing replies that had been launched at anyone unwary enough to voice them in his presence. For this man was also famous for his wit and learning. One quirk of those brows was enough to throw confusion into any adversary, for shattering argument was sure to follow. Several times I had seen opponents on the debating platform prematurely routed by Menasi's formidable raised eyebrows, to the great amusement of the listening students.

Now his smile was warm and his eyes so quickly observant that I felt embarrassed and tried to hide the taboo book I had been reading. No one noticed in this place where all books had ceased to be taboo.

"Take your nose out of Shakespeare," Ylma ordered, "and start the girl making tea. Then come back and hear the news. A decision has been reached."

I ran off to the kitchen and shouted orders, then raced back again, filled with excitement. Things were going to happen. The period of waiting was over.

Menasi was talking. "If I can't have you, I guess I'll have to settle for her. Especially if you vouch for her."

"I wish I could go," Ylma said. "But it's going to be a hard trip all around—something for the young. I'd only be a hindrance. You won't be sorry you took her. I've trained her myself."

Menasi looked at me. "How about it, Amhara?" he asked. "Will you go with us to look for the nesting place of that mysterious bird?"

Now that the possibility had become a certainty, now that the chance was being offered me, I hesitated.

"Are they really going to send an expedition?" I asked Don Ylma. "How will we go? When? Where?"

Ylma bowed her head. "It has been decided. Ras Menasi will lead it. I think you are qualified, and you are being offered the chance. But there are many risks involved. The decision is yours."

"And N'Gobi?" I found I could hardly pronounce his name. Since our interview with the Wasan and my one talk with Ylma, we had not mentioned him.

There was an uncomfortable silence. Don Ylma busied herself with pouring the tea, which had just been brought.

"N'Gobi is being difficult," she said at last.

Menasi raised his brows as he regarded her. "I'm sure I could manage the boy."

"The person who can manage him will be Amhara," said Ylma. "N'Gobi has every reason to be uncooperative. I can easily understand his feelings. But Don Woldi and I have always had the highest regard for his mechanical abilities and talents. As you know, we have done everything to foster them through this girl. We also feel that he has great understanding for nature and wildlife. And this is really his discovery. We feel he belongs on the expedition. If he knows that you are going, Amhara, perhaps he will consent."

"You mean he doesn't want to go?" I asked in amazement.

"Unfortunately. He wants only to go home and see none of us again. In fact, he has been refusing to eat until the last few days when they promised to send him home soon."

I looked at her in horror. All this time I had been enjoying myself in Don Ylma's garden, while N'Gobi. . . .

"If you'd only let me go to him!" I cried.

"You're to talk with him at once," she replied. "I'm sure you can persuade him that we're not all as bad as he imagines. But drink your tea first, my dear. Time for that. We don't want any more hunger strikes."

I gulped it down, refusing to sit while I did so. Ras Menasi languidly poured himself more tea and reached for the book I had thrown down.

"So you're a Shakespeare fanatic," he said. "Let's see what there is about this man to make you risk life and limb—for you know, it's going to be a risk!"

He looked up at me as though daring me to back out. I was about to ask if he could read the ancient tongue, when I thought better of it. Anyone with his position and influence would know practically all the learning available to us. Instead, I put down my cup and indicated that I was ready to follow Ylma. Menasi stretched out with the book and took another fig from the dish on the table.

"Don't forget to send for me," he said, "if you get bogged down with that boy."

"What does he mean?" I asked Ylma when we were crossing the outer courtyard. "Does he know N'Gobi?"

"Not yet. But he prides himself on his ability to handle people. He certainly handled the Council and the Wasan in this case!"

We said no more till we were at the gates of the stronghold, where I knew N'Gobi was confined. Ylma spoke briefly to the guards and we were conducted inside. We stopped before a narrow door in the stone façade where an armed guard of the Wasan stood motionless at either side.

"Let her go in alone," Ylma said. Then to me she said, "Tell him he is free, of course, that you want him to go with you; that he'll have much honor from the expedition, whatever role he chooses. You'll know best how to say it."

She pushed me inside before I had time to think, and I heard the door close. I would have run to N'Gobi, but the room was so small I was almost upon him before I could think. The light was dim, coming from one small window high up in a perpendicular wall. N'Gobi rose from the straw mattress on which he had been lying and I was shocked at his appearance. He had lost much weight, and he seemed even lighter skinned than usual, because of his two weeks away from sun and air. What struck me most forcibly was his expression of stubborn distrust and hatred. Then he saw it was I and smiled; and I felt that we were back in the forest by the lake, watching the darting fish in the clear water.

"Amhara!" he cried. "I thought I'd never see you again!"

"Well, here I am," I said. "And you're to be set free and everything will be all right."

"A strange way to be free," he said. "The door's shut as

tight as ever and I haven't heard anything about when I'm going home."

"Oh, but you don't want to go home!" I said. "The Council has met. It took a long time to bring some of them from the outlying districts. But they decided you were right about the bird and the snare. There's to be an expedition to find out about it, and you and I can both go."

A shade seemed to pass over N'Gobi's face, like a blind being pulled or a door closing. "Not me," he said. "You can go if you want to. But they'll never get me. Not of my own will."

"But why, N'Gobi? It's a chance in a thousand. Who knows what we'll discover! They say your talents are just fitted. . . ."

"They say!" he interrupted. "Who can believe what they say! You were there. I saw you. You heard what the Wasan said. I am a thing that should not be alive! Completely taboo! I should never have been born! And now that that mistake has been made, I can never be allowed to have children!"

"No, no!" I cried. "They're going to set you free. They let me come to tell you."

"And how about the expedition? There's that catch, isn't there?"

"I don't understand you," I protested. "There isn't any catch. They want you to go on the expedition, of course. . . ."

"Of course, of course."

"Well, I thought you wanted to go. We often talked of the idea. I want to go. I am going."

"You can do what you like," he said. "I'm going home. In one piece, I hope. But I'm going home anyhow."

"But why?" I insisted, feeling blocked by that closed door in his mind. "Why won't you go with me?"

"I should think you'd see it," he said with great bitterness. "But in words of one syllable, I don't like the Wasan. I don't like Har. I don't like the Medics. And I won't risk my neck for them. Do you know why they're so anxious for me to go on this expedition—aside from some

48

slight skills I may possess? It's because we're sure to go into poisoned territory. And you know what's liable to happen. It will save them the trouble of negating my dangerous posterity. The same holds true for you, too, though perhaps not as much so. That's your lookout. I understand it's less dangerous for a woman."

I stared at him in horror, shaking my head. "I don't believe it!"

"You think about it, Amhara. We've read the same books. The world wasn't destroyed entirely by the bombs. It was the radiation that wiped out the populations. Deformity and sterility for man and bird and flower. Above all sterility. No life. That's what the poisoned deserts mean."

I found myself repeating, "I don't believe it!" But at the same time I remembered things I had heard Don Ylma say. She had put her work and excavations first—and she had never had children. Perhaps if she had not visited these regions, her life would have been different. Perhaps she would have thought it expedient to marry. A woman like her must have had many offers.

"Believe it or not," N'Gobi said, "it's what I think. As for all your fine people at Har, they're no better than the white men who destroyed the world. We'd do the same in their place. Perhaps not you or I. Though how do you know what you'd do until you meet the situation? But the Wasan would. And he'd have some fine, idealistic reason for doing it, like racial purity or saving the nation."

He spoke with such conviction that I could not gainsay it, but at the same time I felt sick. There was the blank wall again, and we were arguing in circles. I knew everything he said was right, but at the same time I felt that Don Ylma and Woldi were right—yes, even the Wasan was right in his way. It was all so jumbled up in my mind I could hardly make head or tail of it. It was all hopeless. The expedition seemed hopeless, and life itself. I sat down on the straw and was very close to tears, hearing N'Gobi go on and on about what criminals we all were. Then the door suddenly opened and Menasi came in.

He understood the situation at once.

"Well, Amhara," he said, "hard going? And this is the

young genius, I take it. Getting packed to go home, my boy?"

N'Gobi obviously had nothing to pack unless he should carry the straw matting home with him. But Menasi walked up to him and pulled out a sheaf of papers from his belt.

"Before you leave us," he said, "I'd appreciate your interpretation of these designs. Just handle carefully; as you can see they're old and valuable. Let me know if you think we'll break our necks in the machine. You can send your opinion by Amhara. There'll be an expedition meeting in Ylma's court in two hours, my dear." He thrust the papers into N'Gobi's hands and went out the door.

My cousin made a gesture as though to throw the papers on the floor.

"Who is that idiot?" he demanded. "What right does he think. . . ."

He glanced at the drawings, and in that moment I could see that he was lost, at least as far as going home. He made a funny noise in his throat and moved nearer the window, not that it made much difference in the light he got. In two seconds he had forgotten me and the room and the fact that there were probably guards outside. He leafed rapidly through the sheaf of papers.

"Incredible!" he muttered. "Who could imagine . . . ?"

"What is it?" I asked, vainly trying to see over his shoulder to make some sense out of it all. N'Gobi did not hear. He was in another world—a world that began with the internal-combustion engine and led who knows where? Finally, he came to the end and looked up.

"Who was that man?" he demanded. "Where did he get this?"

"He's only the leader of the expedition, that's all!" I told him.

"Well, I've got to see him again if the guards will let me out of here."

"I've been telling you that all along, but you wouldn't listen. If you'll just agree to go on the expedition. . . ."

"Of course I'm going," N'Gobi said. "What are we waiting for?"

50

We pushed the door open, still half expecting to be stopped. But there was no one there except Don Ylma, patiently waiting.

"At last!" she cried. "I thought you were never coming out. But Ras said he could hurry you up, and I guess he knows what he's talking about."

"Just tell me one thing," I said to N'Gobi, as we headed toward Ylma's rooms. "What's in those papers Menasi gave you?"

"Couldn't you see, silly? I'll show you when we get there. It's a flying machine, and I'd sell my soul to have a chance at one of these!"

People were beginning to gather for the meeting when we reached Don Ylma's rooms, but Menasi steered us into a quiet corner while Don Ylma went to get N'Gobi something to eat. I saw that Menasi was studying N'Gobi with evident satisfaction.

"Better give me back those designs, young man," he said, "before you spill the wine on them. I don't believe you more than glanced at them."

N'Gobi reluctantly withdrew the papers from his belt and handed them over.

"I looked at them all," he babbled through a mouthful of chicken. "I'd like to discuss them with you. When do we start building. And what's the fuel?"

Menasi looked quickly through the papers, as though to be sure they were all there. Then he folded them carefully and tucked them into the pouch at his belt.

"There's nothing to build," he said. "We have the finished article."

I thought N'Gobi was going to choke. To cover his confusion, I spoke up.

"How can we have made one so fast?" I asked. "I thought all such things were taboo."

"Oh, very," said Menasi. "This one in particular. It's the Wasan's secret. Taboo for five hundred years. N'Gobi and I are going to fly it. I think I could figure it out myself, but this sort of thing needs young muscles and young nerves. What the ancients called reflexes. Something I see you have plenty of. So eat up. No more hunger

51

strikes. You're going to need every bit of that chicken. And when you're done, you and I and the Wasan are going to the secret place and get the flying machine. Any objections, N'Gobi?"

At the mention of the Wasan, I saw N'Gobi stop eating as though he had suddenly struck a bitter mouthful. Then he swallowed twice and looked up at Menasi with decision.

"No," he said. "No objections. If the Wasan can stand me, I guess I can stand him."

The Wasan and Menasi left Har the next day, taking N'Gobi with them. I had scarcely had time to speak three words with N'Gobi since our meeting, but now everything was moving fast and I had little time to think. I knew only that as long as N'Gobi was cooperating, I had to do likewise. A feeling of general excitement and expectancy, the glowing eyes of Don Ylma, and the concentrated frown of Don Woldi carried me along.

"Hurry, hurry!" said Don Ylma.

"No time to lose!" echoed Don Woldi.

The two of them had given up all thought of teaching and delegated their classes to colleagues. Between them they took over the job of organizing the expedition. Word came from Menasi, who was working on the ancient flying machine in the secret place in the mountains, that no more than five people could go. We'd be lucky if we could crowd that many into the machine, but we had also to take enough provisions for those five. We could not be sure where or when we would find unpoisoned, edible food outside the borders of Afria. We had also to take tools for excavation and exploratory work, weapons for defense and possible hunting, and laboratory supplies for testing the land and water over which we would fly and on which we might land.

Our personal belongings had to be cut to a minimum, but Ylma spent a lot of time worrying over clothes.

"Clothes may seem unimportant to you," she said. "Here where it's warm and likely to rain for the next few months. But you're going to the north—the far north. If the Wasan's flying machine turns out to be all he promised, you may find yourself in a very different climate sooner than you expect. Of course, it will be their summer, but by the time you take off, that summer will be half over. That's why we're in such a hurry. We don't want to wait another year, but we don't want you to be caught up there in the cold weather. Nothing about this undertaking is certain. Everyone must take at least one long, heavy cloak, and we must be sure to have enough blankets among the stores."

She went on making lists of things to do or get or consider. She had meetings with our dietary specialists to determine what dried meats and vegetables were best, and sessions with the Wasan's guards on the subject of defensive weapons. Those officers were loath to give up their exclusive prerogatives even for this most important enterprise; and at first they demanded that a special member of the guards go along in the defense capacity. When the Council quietly vetoed this proposal on the grounds that a maximum of five places were available, it was finally agreed that Ras Menasi, the leader of the expedition, who had been trained to use the weapons of lightning at one point in his career, would be suitably armed with these ancient and terrifying weapons. The rest of us must be satisfied with spears and arrows, which after all had a certain advantage. As there was a limit to everything we could take, there would be a limit to the amount of ammunition for the firearms, whereas spears and arrows could be retrieved or replaced from materials at hand.

"I'm giving you a nice selection of rock hammers and chisels," said Don Ylma, counting over my things. "Let the others worry about bows and arrows. These are far more useful for what you'll want to do, and they can double as weapons in a pinch."

I tried to imagine defending myself with a rock hammer against some unimaginable monster or native, and gave up. It was too fantastic. Probably we would find nothing but bare rocks, in which case Ylma's idea about rock hammers was right.

I went away to look for Don Woldi and to see if there was news of N'Gobi or if the other members of the expedition had been selected. He looked up momentarily from the table, where he was checking an assortment of maps.

"It's difficult to know," he mused. "These are all pre-Disaster maps, but we don't know how reliable they now are. You see, we know the Disaster caused a general rise in world temperature. No doubt there has been considerable melting of the polar caps, which would cause some change in the coast lines. But how much? You must take careful note and correct the maps as you go along. I hope that airship really works. Seems inconceivable after all this time. But the Wasan was positive. These secrets that are handed down with the office! Not that he ever tried it out. He's hardly the type! He probably would still have it hidden away if we hadn't threatened him with another invasion from the north in the next few hundred years!"

He looked up at me with his sidelong glance, as though wondering whether he had said too much, and I saw he decided to change the subject.

"By the way," he said, "the fourth member of the team has been chosen. The medical profession. Oh yes, you have to be protected from all ills, real and imaginary. A relative of yours. You'll find him in my yard."

Don Woldi never alluded to the ground outside his back door as a garden. He left such embellishments to Ylma, and his garden received only the cursory care of his unimaginative servant. The grass was always in need of cutting, the flowers were often weeds, and at this time of the year the whole place was apt to be a mud puddle. The garden did boast one spreading shade tree. When I stepped out it was between showers, and I saw there was a man reclining in the reed chair beneath the tree. His head was bent over a book, but as I approached he looked up. We could have been back in his rooms two years ago.

"Hello, sister," said Tadessa. "Going by the library today?"

I could see he relished my obvious astonishment, and while I tried at first to hide it, I soon gave it up as useless and decided I might as well let him have his little moment of triumph. Probably because of that we were soon on the friendliest footing, with me asking and getting news of all our family and friends at home.

"What do they think of it all? Do they know about the expedition and that I'm going? And N'Gobi?" I was curious to see how he felt about that, but he gave no sign of surprise or disapproval.

"It's the sensation of the century!" he said. "Holy Congo! they all know and talk of nothing else! Pretty smart of N'Gobi, I must say, finding that bird. And keeping it quiet like that! How'd you manage it? And why didn't you come to me? But of course, if he'd taken it to the forester or the headman, he never would have gotten up here himself! Pretty smart. And I won't say he doesn't deserve it."

"He's learning to fly the machine, you know," I said.

"And he'll be good," Tadessa replied. "Always was good at anything like that. Should have been up here at Har long ago. Just a matter of his color."

His voice trailed off and he stared reflectively at Don Woldi's stone wall where a lizard was chasing flies, and I imagine he was thinking of other things that could chain man to the village for life when his whole soul cried out for change and excitement. Perhaps, after all, he could understand what it meant.

"But how does it happen that you're going?" I asked. "Three members from the same clan! Weren't there objections? Or are those in the village afraid? Everyone here would like to go despite the dangers."

"It's not that. Of course, at home they don't begin to realize the implications. Members of the expedition must be specialists. It's natural that they should come mostly from Har. As for me, I saw my chance and applied at once. A few years back I did a paper on radiation and its effects. No one paid much attention. It's a forgotten subject nowadays. But it helped. And then, to tell the truth, I think I had just the right amount of learning. Not too little and not too much. You understand. They've got to have a good doctor go along, and one with my special interests fitted right in. But not their best. They don't want to risk the best. You know, there's a very good chance that none of us will come back."

It was a possibility to which I had carefully closed my mind. Was Tadessa trying to frighten me? Or test me?

"Don Ylma went on the last one," I protested. "And Don Woldi, too. That was thirty years ago and they both got back and have been doing fine ever since." I refrained from mentioning the fact that they'd never had any children, and Tadessa seemed unaware of it.

"That was close to home," he persisted. "They just walked out into the desert and walked back, with a few mules or something to carry their supplies. This is a long-range project. We'll be covering thousands of miles—we hope. And suppose the machine breaks down or blows up? Who will know? And who can help us?"

"Are you trying to scare me?" I demanded. "And if it's that bad, what makes you give up your new thoroughbred and racing stable, not to mention your many patients!"

"I'm not trying to scare you," he said softly. "I just wanted to be sure you knew what you were getting into. Sure, I hope to come back to race my black again, but not to the patients of one village. This is my big chance to get out of my little niche. If we do come back—no matter what we find—we'll be at the top. The best places will be open to us. Of course, it doesn't matter for you. You were going to the top anyhow. I could see that. You don't really need this expedition, sis. Are you sure you know what it means?"

"Of course, I know!" I cried hotly, annoyed that he thought he knew more than I did about it. But for the first time I let myself consider the possibility of not coming back. I pictured us all stranded in some poisoned desert, probably dying of some insidious radiation disease, with the air machine hopelessly broken down and the food and water low. In that moment I knew that even if this were to be the end, I would still have to go. I could not stay behind and see N'Gobi and Ras Menasi fly off to the lands of ancient civilization and culture, perhaps to unravel the mystery of Shakespeare without me.

"You don't understand," I said to Tadessa. "I've got to go. N'Gobi and I found that duck. At least, he found it and I brought it here. We first thought about what it might

56

mean. It's the most exciting thing that's happened in my whole life. I'd die if I couldn't go along!"

Tadessa laughed, and suddenly I thought I must sound like a silly little girl.

He said only, "Don't do that yet. Time enough later. If that's the way you feel, I guess you'd better go. Don't listen to me. I've gotten to be a pessimist stranded down there in the village."

We talked a little more and I asked him who he thought would be the fifth member of the expedition. He knew no more than I, but he hazarded a shrewd guess.

"I've no idea who he'll be," he said, "but I'll tell you two things about him. He'll be young—old enough to know a lot, but not too much—and he'll be someone close to the Wasan. Well, look at the rest of us," he went on, when he saw my questioning look. "We're three of us from the same village. I'm in the lowest category of the Medics. You're only a candidate, and N'Gobi's nothing at all. None of us has ever been near the Wasan. Menasi, of course, is top category. They couldn't have picked a better leader. He must have browsed in pretty near every line of learning, taboo and nontaboo. God help us if anything happens to him. But he's not of the Wasan's household. He's a top Medic and of course he answers to the Wasan, but at his own discretion. No, my guess is that the Wasan will try to put his own representative in place number five."

About this time Don Woldi called Tadessa, asking him to give the exact weight of his medical kit and the amount of room needed for his laboratory supplies. Tadessa would have to make tests and measurements of air, water, soil, and food, and if necessary try to purify them. At the same time, his requirements would have to be kept to a minimum. As I left, I heard them arguing about what could go and what could not.

Three days later the flying machine arrived with N'Gobi at the controls and Menasi and the Wasan sitting behind him in the cabin. We had been told to make a place ready for it to land, and for days groups of workmen and teams of students had been laboring on the plain before the city to prepare a suitable landing field. Don Ylma had translated descriptions from the ancient manuscripts, and every day she came out and criticized the results of the previous day's work. It was too short for the speed of the aircraft, which would surely run into something before it could stop. It was too rough, and the aircraft would break up and be destroyed before we could ever use it—not to mention what would happen to the Wasan and others riding in it. It was not laid out according to the direction of the winds and would be utterly useless. The workers marveled that anything could go as fast as Don Ylma seemed to expect, or that it could be affected by such small sticks and rocks. When the subject of the winds came up, they began to wonder if she knew what she was talking about.

At last word came from the Wasan's guards that the air machine had started out from the secret place and could be expected to arrive at Har at noon, and we were to prepare to receive it. The whole town and university were in a turmoil of excitement, and classes were suspended so that all the people could gather to welcome the Wasan and his remarkable machine. Just how the guards could know when to expect him was something of a mystery, for wherever the secret hiding place might be, it was obvious that no messenger could leave there at the same time as, and arrive here before, the aircraft. However, the Wasan was the greatest and most learned of the Medics, and it was presumed that he had means of communication at his disposal unknown to the average man.

That afternoon, Don Woldi was directing students in raking and leveling the last rough places when a humming sound was heard from the mountains to the west. The sound increased from a humming to a rumble to a roar. We were all craning our necks and shielding our eyes to peer against the sun, when suddenly Tadessa cried, "There, there! Above the trees!"

Then we saw it. It was not high in the sky as we had expected. It was not swooping in at unheard of speeds. It did not look like any of the pictures I had seen of pre-

Disaster air machines. In fact, it was the most peculiar looking vehicle I could possibly imagine. There were no long, graceful wings for soaring upon the air currents. This outlandish mechanism had a long, snakelike body with what appeared to be windows in the sides. It had a flat roof, which I later learned was used to catch the rays of the sun. The undercarriage was equipped with springs and wheels for landing. Over it all and dwarfing it were the tremendous propeller blades. These were revolving so fast as to be almost invisible. The machine did not glide and swoop and soar in the manner we had been led to expect. It advanced steadily over the forest trees, clearing them by a safe margin, and finally came directly above our heads. There it hovered for a few moments, as though to demonstrate its complete defiance of the laws of gravity, and then settled slowly down upon the ground.

Don Ylma's field could have been one tenth the size and constructed with one day's labor. She must have realized something of the sort, for I heard her mutter to herself, "A helicopter!"

However, the watching populace did not stop to consider any of these matters. It was enough that the proclamation of the Medics had proved to be true and not just the wildest of rumors. With a great shout, they rushed upon the aircraft. Fortunately, the Wasan's guards were there first, standing in an iron ring around the machine and holding off the enthusiastic crowd. A door opened in the side and steps folded out. The Wasan appeared and descended, followed by Menasi and finally N'Gobi. The shouts and yells from citizens and students were deafening, but when the Wasan drew himself up and made the sign of office and the guards stood at attention, the crowd fell upon their knees in obedience, and many touched their foreheads to the ground.

The Wasan spoke. "I am come from the sacred places of our ancestors and I bring you a gift from the past. From the ancient people before the great Disaster. In the days when the world was destroyed with all the people and their creations, this machine was hidden away in a secret place until it should be needed. The secret has been handed down from Wasan to Wasan, and only now has it seemed that the time has come. I was not sure we could still find the skill to use it, to make it rise again and to control its flight. But this young man has succeeded—with Ras Menasi's help, and a word now and then from me—in making it soar again into the skies. He has successfully brought us home, as you can see. I therefore commission him to be the chief pilot of the expedition of exploration that Ras Menasi will presently lead. In the meantime, let there be a permanent guard over the machine. Let no one approach it without orders or permission, and let there be a shelter built over it as soon as possible, for there will be rain before night. Now we travelers need rest and refreshment, and in the evening the Council will meet and we will see what you have accomplished at this end. For as soon as the weather clears, they must be off on their journey to the north."

The Wasan mounted his horse that was held ready and rode off with a detachment of his guards, followed by most of the people. I hung about, hoping to see N'Gobi. I noticed that Don Ylma and Don Woldi were talking to Menasi, and Tadessa was also standing quietly by. Just then N'Gobi came through the guards and saw me. He ran up, his eyes shining.

"Isn't it wonderful, Amhara!" he cried. "What do you think of our little craft?"

"It's not so little when you see it up close," I said. "But I guess it will seem little when we start packing all our gear into it."

Don Ylma came over and laid a hand on his arm. "Were you surprised?" she asked. "Was it difficult?"

"I was so surprised you could have knocked me down. I'd been worrying all the way there. I was sure I couldn't manage it. I'd read about how hard it was . . . all the training required. But this is easy. A baby could do it. Once we got her in working order, she just took off. We pointed her head in this direction and Menasi and the Wasan picked out the landmarks. It was easy."

"We rather overdid things with the landing field," said Don Woldi. "We imagined some sort of high-speed machine that would take hundreds of yards to stop. Don Ylma had us working our heads off."

We all laughed and Menasi said, "It is a little overwhelming, your landing field, Ylma."

Then they showed us the inside of the craft. We climbed the ladder and walked through the aisle and sat in the seats. They were bare metal. If they had once been cushioned, the cushions had long since fallen to dust. N'Gobi had already done a good cleaning job, and he told me that the cave where it had been hidden was so dry and protected from the elements that there was hardly any rust.

"I couldn't believe it would be this easy," he told me. "Ras Menasi and I studied the instructions. You should have been along, Amhara. They were all in ancient Anglic, of course. But he can read it, too. Not as well as you, though. We had to puzzle some of it out."

From the other end of the cabin Menasi made a sound between a laugh and a cough. "That's why she has a place on the expedition. She's a genius with the ancient tongue. I don't claim to be able to speak it, but I dare say she's fluent."

I looked at the floor and poked N'Gobi with my toe. Why did he have to embarrass me in front of them all!

"I suppose you just got right in and flew it," I said sarcastically.

He seemed unaware of my annoyance. "After we'd figured out all the controls, we pushed it into the open and I took her up first alone. If anyone got killed, it would be me. Didn't want to endanger the Wasan." There was an edge to his voice, but he went on quickly. "Of course, we had to wait for clear skies before we could fuel her up."

"That's something that's been worrying me," said Don Ylma. "What kind of fuel does it use. From everything I've read. . . ."

"Simplest thing in the world," cut in Menasi. "It's fueled by the sun. There are solar batteries on that flat roof surface. It was the latest thing; developed just before the disaster. Our ancestors showed great discrimination, if they were going to preserve a machine, to pick this one.

61

No fuel industry required. No large landing field. She goes straight up and sits down on a coin. And with the forward propellers, she can do up to two hundred miles an hour. The only thing that can stop her is a cloudy day. This rainy season is what slowed us up."

We inspected the ship in detail, and I could see Don Ylma mentally figuring where all the provisions and supplies could be stored. As we left the machine to the vigilance of the Wasan's guards and made our way back to our respective quarters, I could hear her arguing with Don Woldi and Menasi about space and weight and what could or should be curtailed.

N'Gobi went off with Don Woldi for rest and refreshment, and I did not see him again until the evening meeting with the Council. There we were to meet the fifth member of the expedition and receive our final orders and instructions. After that N'Gobi would sleep in the ship. In fact, he literally lived in it. It had become the center of his existence, and nothing could pry him away. He was forever oiling, polishing, and testing. He exhausted the guards with orders to drag it into the shelter or out, depending on the sun and the clouds. Every possible minute of sunlight was needed, he claimed, to recharge her batteries and store up fuel for our trip. But at the first sign of one of our recurring storms, she must be dragged back to shelter and safety.

I wondered what would happen when we were once embarked upon our journey. It was evident that we would have to endure both fair weather and foul, and there would be no shelters waiting for us at the other end. But I forbore to ask questions when N'Gobi insisted upon treating the machine like a baby, and indeed it is doubtful that I would have received any answer. His entire time was taken up with screwing screws, adjusting wires, reading dials, and hastily rechecking the faded instruction sheets. The only attention I received during the few days remaining before our departure was when he wanted me to translate some doubtful and obscure passage in the ancient tongue.

However, he did attend the meeting of the Council on

that first night of his return. All members of the expedition were ordered to be present, and we gathered in the long hall where I had first met the Wasan. His throne was moved forward, and he sat surrounded by his guards. Behind him in a semicircle were the members of the Council. Facing them were as many Medics, students, and citizens of Har as could crowd into the hall.

The Wasan began with a speech that seemed to go on forever. He outlined the horrors of the Disaster and the crimes of the white madmen who had brought it upon the world. He described the ruined deserts that surround us and extolled the wisdom and courage of the Medics who had led us out of this confusion and saved us from destruction. Finally, he got down to the business at hand. He told about the duck with the snare on its leg and expounded the various theories advanced to explain it. Now it had been decided, he said, to send an expedition to explore the lands to the north and try to find a solution to the mystery.

"You all know that after the Disaster, the first Medics determined that such crimes should never be repeated. They destroyed the few remaining machines and declared those techniques and sciences to be taboo. But they still thought there might come a time when some of these machines would be helpful—yes, even necessary for the survival of their people. They selected a very few and hid them away in secret places. The knowledge of these secrets has been handed down from Wasan to Wasan until it came to me. Only now did I feel it was right and necessary to bring out the flying machine that was shut away for us by our ancestors five hundred years ago. You all saw it arrive today. You saw me come through the air like a bird from the distant mountains. Remember that before the Disaster the air was full of machines like this— even more remarkable ones that flew faster and higher and farther. It was these machines that made the Disaster possible. In bringing this one forth for our use, I say that it is still taboo! It is forbidden for anything but the most necessary and extraordinary uses, such as the expedition we are now planning. It will be used only at the discretion and on the orders of the Wasan and the Council of Medics."

He paused here for the approval of the Council, and it was given at once in a series of yeas and ayes and a wave of murmurs and nodding heads that swept from one end of the seated dignitaries to the other.

The Wasan then called for Ras Menasi, who came from our little group and stood before him.

"Ras Menasi," he said, "do you undertake to lead this expedition as agreed upon with me and the Council, to advise and protect the members to the best of your ability, and to bring them safely home again if so the gods decree?"

Menasi knelt before the Wasan and promised to do as he was asked. Then it was Tadessa's turn, and he was likewise sworn as the medical doctor, to safeguard the health of all the members of the expedition. Finally, it was my turn and N'Gobi's, and we both knelt before the Wasan and swore, he to be the pilot and to fly the aircraft and bring it back safely; and I to study the lands and the ruins and the people if there were any, and to bring back all findings for the greater glory of our people.

When I stepped back to my place beside N'Gobi, I was surprised to hear the captain of the guards call yet another name.

"Zulli of Gondal!" he announced, and a small, slim woman stepped out from a group at one side and knelt before the Wasan.

I could feel the eyes of all my companions, including Menasi, whom I would have expected to know of this, riveted upon the small figure.

"Zulli, do you undertake to go with this expedition, to follow the leadership of Ras Menasi, and to keep your Wasan in communication with all that happens to the best of your ability with all the forces at your command?"

Her yes was a musical whisper, so soft I could hardly catch it. Then she rose and stood back with the four of us and I could see that she bore the fine tattoo on her face that marked her as a member of the Wasan's personal staff. Tadessa had been right when he guessed that the fifth member would be someone close to our ruler. We all watched her from the corners of our eyes, but no one moved or said a word.

The Wasan was continuing with his speech to us. He was detailing the probable dangers from many sources and the great care to be used before landing anywhere. He did not fail to mention the fact that no rescue expedition could be expected. He told us that besides all the obvious dangers, there was the insidious one of poisoning and disease that might be picked up from the tainted lands. Long after we had returned, we might develop some incurable illness, or find ourselves unable to produce children, or our offspring might be deformed infants that would have to be killed at birth. After a long catalogue of possible perils that made it seem unlikely that we would ever return, the Wasan put the final question to us five.

"Knowing all these things, do you still determine, of your own free will, to go on this expedition? Choose now, for hereafter there will be no further choice."

No one spoke. No one moved. After a full minute, the Wasan declared that this was how it should be, and that we should bend every effort to make ready, so that when the weather watchers said the time was right, we could depart at once. The Council rose and stood behind him, signifying complete agreement, and the session was at an end.

N'Gobi went back to the ship and continued his practice of recharging the batteries and testing and inspecting the motor. The rest of us were busily engaged in loading and packing our supplies and belongings. No one mentioned Zulli, for the Wasan has ears everywhere and none of us wished to be displaced at the last minute. Unattractive and dangerous as the expedition had been painted, there were many Medics and students who would willingly have stepped into our places.

Zulli took no part in the loading of the ship. She came often and stood at one side, watching but making no comment. Once Ras Menasi asked her how much room she would need for her gear, but she replied she would take no more than she could carry or stow under her seat.

After that we left her strictly alone, although each of us wondered privately how she was going to maintain communication with the Wasan over the many thousands of miles that we would travel.

At last, the day came when the weather watchers prophesied clear skies for at least a few days. The Wasan sent a messenger to ask whether we were ready to leave and whether N'Gobi thought the aircraft sufficiently fueled. As we all agreed that we were ready, he declared that the expedition should take off early the next morning.

A great crowd assembled to see us start. My own parents and many members of our family had come from the village to say farewell to me, Tadessa, and N'Gobi. The same was true for Ras Menasi, who belonged to a powerful clan from the north. Whether anyone came to say good-by to Zulli, I never learned. She was one of the first to board the ship, and went at once to the rear bench, where she stowed her luggage under the seat—all except a strange square box that she placed on the bench beside her and guarded with utmost care.

Tadessa and I entered next and occupied the two middle seats. Finally Menasi and N'Gobi climbed in. N'Gobi of course, took the pilot's chair, and Menasi sat beside him as what the ancients had called the copilot. He had with him the roll of maps and charts that Don Woldi and his students had laboriously copied for us. In addition to following and correcting these as we went along, he would help N'Gobi with the reading of dials and instruments and, if necessary, take over the controls to give him a rest.

At length everything was ready. All the supplies had been stowed and the good-bys said. Menasi, the last to enter the ship, stood near the ladder and saluted the Wasan and the members of the Council. The crowd held its breath as he climbed aboard and pulled the ladder up after him. Then, as the Wasan raised his arm in farewell, the chorus of the Medics burst forth in the inspiring strains of our people's anthem, a beautiful choral, one of the few pieces of music that has come down to us from before the Disaster, and credited to the forgotten genius Schweitzer-Bach. Hearing it swell out upon the morning air, the women's voices rising to new heights, the men's filling in with their solemn and powerful cadence, my heart was filled with hope. Surely, this was the beginning of a new and greater period for man. Surely, we would find new valleys of prosperity to develop and would bring back fresh knowledge and culture that had been lost with the ancient world. I felt inspired and elated that I could take part in this great enterprise and vowed to dedicate myself wholeheartedly to its success.

Then N'Gobi started the motors, and the whirring of the great blades above us drowned out the music. The ship quivered and rose slowly, and before I was aware of it I could look down and see the cheering crowds, the singing chorus, the Wasan, and my family, all standing below us with upturned faces.

Higher and higher we rose till we were well above the tallest trees, and then N'Gobi cut in the forward propellers and set our course for the north. The buildings of Har, the fields of our homeland, and the waving people grew smaller and smaller and vanished from our sight.

PART
TWO

Chapter One

I think the dominant feeling we all shared during that first day's flight was of wonder and amazement that we were flying at all. Perhaps it was not as strong in Menasi and N'Gobi, who had already experienced the flight from the mountains. However, even they showed a tendency to hang on when the ship hit what Menasi called an "air pocket" or when they rose to make their way about the cabin. As for the rest of us, we literally clung to our seats. The whole thing was alien to our culture and our experience. True, we were educated people who knew that flying had been common in the ancient days before the Disaster; but not only was flying unheard of for us, it was also taboo. If anyone had told us three weeks earlier that we would ourselves be flying in an airship, we would have dismissed the idea as pure fantasy.

The one most obviously frightened by the trip was Zulli. I reminded myself that she could hardly have known she was going until a few days ago. The rest of us had had a longer period of anticipation, and of course Menasi and N'Gobi had one day's flying to their credit. Moreover, I doubt that Zulli had studied much about the ancient days. History she must have had, but not the hours I had spent steeping myself in the old ways and customs so that in spite of my fears I had a feeling of elation to be reliving a little bit of that vanished glory.

I reflected that she was the only other woman in our company, and so in spite of her coldness, I made every effort to be friendly and to take her mind off our perilous mode of travel. I pointed out the farms and villages below and the mountains and rivers that served as landmarks. Yet, to all my efforts she replied in monosyllables or not at all, and so I finally gave it up. If she wanted to keep to herself, that was her privilege. However close she had been to the Wasan, she could hardly talk to him now. Or could she? The mysterious square box that she hugged protectively in her lap could be no other than a radio such as I had read about in my studies. I longed to see her use it. Then, I wondered if perhaps she was using it, unknown to us. Perhaps when she stared right past me and ignored my remarks she was in conversation with the Wasan, telling him all about our trip. But I heard no words from her nor sounds from the box, and she wore nothing in the manner of earpieces. Unless there were far more to it than I had found in the ancient manuscripts, Zulli was not talking to the Wasan.

Tadessa watched my efforts with interest and at last he touched me on the arm and suggested that I let her alone. A little later he asked Menasi if he thought we could land somewhere while we ate lunch.

Menasi and N'Gobi had paid scant attention to us in the back seats. They had been entirely taken up with the problems of the aircraft and following the landmarks on the map. Tadessa's recommendation recalled them to their passengers, and they began to scan the land beneath us for a possible landing place.

"This is pretty wild country," Menasi said, "and I doubt that anyone lives here. But I don't think it's outside the safety border. Perhaps it would be a good idea to set down for our first meal. After this we'll have to be more careful."

He continued to peer out the window and direct N'Gobi in lowering the machine. The forward propellers had been turned off, and we were skimming over the treetops. Presently, Menasi located a clearing on a high plateau and N'Gobi made a safe and gentle landing.

We were scarcely down and Menasi was anchoring the machine with rocks around the wheels while I opened a locker to bring out the first day's lunch, when Zulli pushed roughly past me, still clutching her box, and stumbled down the steps. We all stared and Menasi let out a shout as she ran off into a thicket. The idea crossed my mind that she was seeking solitude for her message to the Wasan, but Tadessa thought otherwise. He reached under his seat, brought out his medicine bag, and rushed down the steps after her, exclaiming, "Great Congo, the first one!" When I followed with the basket of lunch, I heard her being sick in the bushes. Tadessa was saying soothingly, "It's all right. You'll feel better in a minute."

By the time I had the lunch spread out on the ground, they returned, Tadessa supporting her and Zulli looking very shamefaced.

"I really don't know how it happened," she apologized. "I tried and tried, but I couldn't seem to stop." She looked at our ship and shuddered.

"Just a little airsickness," said Tadessa. "It'll wear off. Quite common in the old days, wasn't it, Amhara?"

Zulli looked at me wide-eyed. "You mean to say the ancients did this, too? I thought I was being so ... so...."

"So unprofessional?" finished Tadessa. "Not at all. Sit right down and eat your lunch," he urged, holding out a sandwich to her.

Zulli shook her head in distaste.

"Oh, I couldn't. Not now. And we have to get back in that thing, I suppose."

"Just as soon as we're through eating," Menasi said, "I want to get farther than this the first day."

"Oh!" cried Zulli in alarm, and you could see a thought had just struck her. "What time is it?"

N'Gobi looked at the sun. "About two o'clock, I should say. Well after noon in any case."

"Oh, no!" She glared at him as though it were his fault. "It can't be that late! It can't! Oh, whatever shall I do?" She clutched the box, which in all the excitement she had not let out of her hands.

"What's the matter?" asked Menasi. "What's the time got to do with it? We go as far as we can in the time we have each day. That's all there is to it."

"It's the Wasan," she whispered. "I was supposed to contact him by eleven, but I felt so sick, I forgot."

"Well, get busy and contact him now. There's nothing special to report anyhow except that you got airsick, and I imagine you can leave that out. I'll give him our exact position. That ought to help."

He dusted the crumbs from his hands and picked up the map, but Zulli was backing away from us.

"Oh no, you don't understand," she protested. "I'm to do it alone. You're not supposed to know. And I've missed the very first contact. He'll be sitting there waiting, just ready to kill me!"

Menasi raised his eyebrows, and the rest of us stared at her in amazement.

"How's he going to kill you when he's five hundred miles away and doesn't know where you are?" our leader demanded. "Of all the ridiculous setups! He expects me to lead a successful expedition with a divided personnel!"

As Zulli continued to retreat in obvious alarm, he quickly changed his tone. "Don't worry about it," he said. "Go on up in the cabin and get your contact alone. No one will bother you, and I'll be right there to tell you what to say. When he hears how far we've gotten he won't give a thought to the time. You'll see. You can tell him we were outrunning a storm and you didn't have a chance to call till now."

Zulli and Menasi climbed into the airship, and the rest of us finished the lunch and packed up the scraps. We could see them through the windows. Zulli working mysteriously with her box and Menasi reading from the map. After what seemed a long time he motioned us to come aboard, and N'Gobi took the ship up into the sky.

Nothing more was said among us about Zulli's behavior and the Wasan's strange orders. I could see Tadessa glance sidewise at her now and then, but Menasi and N'Gobi kept their attention on their instruments and the map. Zulli was as silent and withdrawn as before, and I could not be sure whether she was again airsick or pondering her discussion with the Wasan.

We covered another four hundred miles by Menasi's calculations before darkness made us look for a place to land. We had been flying northwest, taking our direction from the sun and the ship's instruments. Early in the afternoon we saw below us the Abba river, and Menasi suggested that the easiest thing would be to follow it as it left our country and made its way to the sea.

"We know that it continues north and before long joins one of the great rivers of the world, known to the ancients as the Nile," Menasi said. "I expect Amhara can tell you all about it."

"Of course," I cried in excited anticipation. "Are we really going to the Nile? Its history goes back thousands of years before the Disaster, back to the beginnings of man. It is mentioned in the histories of all periods. It had great cities on its banks and strange animals in its waters." I peered out the window for the first sight of that fabled river.

"You've neglected to mention the most important fact," said Menasi, "which is that it flows into the great sea to the north. The name slips my mind for the moment."

"The Mediterranean," supplied Tadessa before I could speak.

"Right. You're not so bad on the ancient world yourself," Menasi said. "The point is, if we can get to this Mediterranean we'll be a good halfway along. According to Don Ylma's calculations, the bird must have come from one of the lands to the north of that sea."

Lands north of the northern sea! The words sobered us with the thought of how far north we must go. Without our airship it would have been unthinkable. The land slid smoothly by below us as we followed the river. We soon left behind all country familiar to us—and by that we meant all land known to be safe and healthy. Still it gave us a feeling of familiarity and safety to be following this river that had its birth in our country and whose waters we knew to be clear and pure at their point of origin.

By the time the sun was approaching the western horizon, Menasi judged that we could not be many miles from the junction of our river with the famous Nile. However, he thought it best to find a campsite before dark in order to make the necessary tests while we could still see. N'Gobi accordingly set us down on some high cliffs above the river, with the first trees some hundred yards back.

At Menasi's orders, no one left the ship until Tadessa

had first climbed gingerly down the ladder with his testing instruments and sampled the earth, air and vegetation. "It seems healthy enough here," he said at last. "But I'd have to do a lot more tests before I could guarantee the forest."

"Well, it's interesting to know that the land along the river is clean," said Menasi. "You might put that in your report, Zulli. But no one is to go near the forest. I think we can eat and sleep outside the ship tonight. We'll divide the night into thirds and the men can take turns at guard duty."

I wanted to protest that women could do that, too, but he cut me short. That time would come, he said, but the girls should get a good rest the first night. When I looked at Zulli, I guessed his reasons. I said no more, and she and I hastened to carry out the food and arrange it upon the ground.

My feelings for Zulli were continually shifting. At the moment I felt sorry for her because of her airsickness and her fear of the Wasan. I reminded myself that we were all strangers to her, whereas there was the warmest friendship between the rest of us. With this in mind I spread her place beside me and prepared to make the meal pleasant for her. No sooner had she sat down on one side of me than N'Gobi came and sat on the other. Zulli looked at him with distaste, and gathering up her plate of food, she moved around the circle until she was as far from us as possible and sat down upon a stone near Tadessa.

I felt as though I had been slapped in the face and can only surmise what N'Gobi felt. Menasi pretended not to notice. He went on eating his food with one hand and crumbling the soil with the other, as though reckoning its value to possible future colonists. I saw Tadessa look around speculatively and then hand the tray of dried fruit to Zulli in an obvious effort to gloss things over.

But I knew N'Gobi. Without looking at him, I guessed his face was a thundercloud. My appetite seemed to have vanished, and I had to remind myself that eating was necessary on this trip. At last I muttered in a whisper only he could catch, "Give her time. She'll learn. She won't be able to flit about when we take to living in the ship."

"She needn't fear!" he whispered back. "I'll keep to the pilot's section. She won't be contaminated."

"Don't talk like that!" I hissed, "because of a foolish girl who has much to learn!"

As usual it was impossible to tell N'Gobi anything.

"She's already learned her piece, and well!" he muttered.

Soon afterward he took himself off to the airship, where he stayed in the pilot's compartment, checking the instruments and controls until it was time for him to take the first watch.

I saw that Menasi was worried, but he said nothing at the time. I recalled his remarks about leading a "divided personnel." Then I remembered how well he had handled N'Gobi, and I thought he should easily do as well with Zulli. When we had finished eating he sat with her while she contacted the Wasan, and read her our position on the map, our course in following the river, and the data Tadessa had recorded about the favorable condition of the land thereabouts.

I thought they both looked more cheerful and reconciled when they came back from this task, but then I saw that Menasi had other more pressing problems on his mind. He spent some time deciding on the safest spot to spread our blankets and arranging with N'Gobi for a light from the ship to fall between us and the forest as a defense against any prowlers from that direction.

That first night in the unknown wild we all slept little. Yet we heard no sounds and found no signs of any animals such as those that lived in our forests at home. Only the chirps of insects rising from the river broke the silence, and the forest loomed menacingly just beyond our lights. I know that I was glad to see the first brightness that heralded the sun, and I lost no time in picking up my blanket and beginning preparations for breakfast.

My this time we had eaten most of the prepared food and drink that we had brought with us, and I longed for a fire to make tea. I had collected a few twigs near the cliff's edge and was wondering if I dared approach the forest for a larger piece, when N'Gobi stopped me.

77

"Where are you going? You know that's out of bounds."

"Yes, but can't we have a fire the whole trip? We might as well have left the tea at home!" I complained.

"We've something better than a fire," he said. "Come and I'll show you."

He led me into the ship, to the back part where customarily Zulli sat. At his touch a panel slid back, showing an arrangement of metal shelves and wires. N'Gobi turned a switch and the wires glowed red.

"I believe they called this the galley," he said. "Get out your pots and pans and water." He showed me how the other controls and switches worked.

With that he left the job of cooking to me. In a few minutes I had breakfast prepared, and shortly thereafter we were ready to take to the sky.

The discovery of the cooking facilities caused a flurry of excitement. Even Menasi had not known about it, for N'Gobi had learned of the panel and its uses after he had brought the ship to Har. Tadessa greeted the new mechanism with enthusiasm, saying that now he could quickly sterilize his instruments and laboratory utensils for any emergency or tests. Everyone stood around and watched the water boil, and I marveled at the convenience that would make hot meals possible while in flight and thought of how Don Ylma would envy me, cooking with the methods of the ancients.

Zulli was most impressed of all. She kept asking how it worked and seemed unsatisfied when I told her it was powered with the same fuel that flew the ship.

"Where does it come from?" she asked.

I realized with surprise that while she controlled a still greater wonder in her communication box, she knew nothing of the forces that made it possible and would probably be quite unable to repair it, should it break down.

Later I asked N'Gobi about the fuel for the ship and the cooking stove, and he said that as long as the sun shone we would be all right.

"But if we run into some cloudy weather," he warned, "we may have to go slow on such things as lights at night and hot meals. Still, it can't rain forever. At the worst we might have to wait around a bit."

I had little idea at that moment of how bad that "worst" might be.

We continued to follow our river, and long before noon we reached the spot where it joined a mightier flood. The ancient Nile, I told myself. We were still over a thousand miles from the sea, and this river could be expected to grow wider and swifter as it went along. I stared down at it, straining to see signs of the cities or the strange animals that I had read about, but from our height the whole country seemed devoid of any life save vegetation.

Perhaps the monotony of our journey was responsible for the discord and division among us. But the seeds were already there when we first climbed into the ship and set out upon this venture. Now, we tended more and more to separate into two groups. Whenever there was pause or a halt for eating or sleeping, Zulli and Tadessa would sit close together, and I would go to sit with N'Gobi in the pilot's cubby. Menasi obviously did not like this state of affairs, but he said nothing at first, probably hoping that things would work themselves out and our relations would improve.

The situation came to a head on the afternoon when we first saw the northern sea extending across the horizon. There was a general feeling of exultation and relief that the sea should appear at the time and place predicted. We knew now that much of the distance lay behind us, and everyone was smiling and friendly as Menasi gave the order to set the ship down on the beach.

This must be the turning point, I thought. Everything will go better now and we'll stop fighting over silly things. The beach was hard and smooth and the landing was perfect. We sat in silence and gazed at that great expanse of water with the waves curling up on the shore. None of us had ever seen anything like it before, but it reminded us of the lakes of our homeland. I imagine there was not one of us who would not have liked to bathe in those cool waters.

However, extensive tests would first have to be made by Tadessa, and immediately an argument arose as to whether we should spend the time and effort required. N'Gobi wanted to continue right across the sea. He argued that according to the map we should be able to sight some land before sundown. Menasi was against the idea and insisted that we fly westward along the coast, saying that eventually we would find a much narrower and easier place to cross. While the ship had performed remarkably well so far, it was not built to land on water; and if anything should go wrong over the sea, we would never survive it.

N'Gobi, with the overconfidence of youth, put great trust in his machine and insisted that this was the more direct route and would save a great deal of time. I was amazed to hear him argue so vehemently with Menasi, who was much older and the leader of our expedition besides. When I saw how seriously Menasi listened to his words and weighed his arguments, I was proud.

At last our leader cocked an eyebrow. "Well, there's always one other opinion to call in. We'll contact the Wasan."

At that N'Gobi tossed his head and turned away, as though he considered this irrelevant.

"Come, come, my boy," Menasi said, "don't discount the counsel of your elders. The Wasan may not be here in person or know all you do about the machine. But he has had many more years' experience, and don't you forget it."

With that he came back to the rear of the ship and told Zulli to bring out her box and try to get in touch with home. There was a distinct look of triumph on Zulli's face as she prepared to do so. N'Gobi went back into his cubby and slouched in his seat, but I knew his ears were tuned to the rear, where the rest of us sat in expectation and watched Zulli turn the knobs on he box. Some of her snobbishness had worn off, in spite of the friction among us, and she now allowed us to watch while she established contact.

This time nothing happened as she turned the knobs. Time passed—much longer than usual. A strained and worried look began to grow on Zulli's face. "Something's the matter!" she whispered, appealing to Menasi.

"Give them time," he replied. "You can't expect them to be sitting around waiting for you to call."

"There's always someone on watch to return the signal," she said. "And besides it doesn't sound right. There isn't that little buzz. Oh, Simba! It couldn't break, could it?" She sounded as though she were close to tears.

Menasi bent over and pressed his ear to the box. "It does sound awfully dead," he said. "But I don't know anything about it. What did they tell you might happen?"

"They didn't tell me anything," Zulli wailed. "The Wasan just showed me how to work it. He didn't say anything about it's *not* working."

Menasi looked at her and his eyebrows quivered. "The old hope of perpetual motion," he muttered.

Tadessa put his arm around her comfortingly. "Don't get excited," he said. "There must be some explanation. Perhaps we're too far away."

"He said it would reach to the ends of the earth," she wept. "And besides it doesn't sound right."

We all regarded the box, and I thought Menasi actually seemed pleased. Perhaps I should have left things as they were, but something impelled me to speak.

"If you're sure it's broken," I said, and they all turned to look at me, "the sensible thing is to let N'Gobi fix it."

"No!" cried Zulli, and she grabbed the box to her.

"A very good idea," Menasi said. "He's the mechanic. If he can understand the working of this ship, he should be able to fathom that box."

"No, no!" Zulli cried again. "It's taboo. And he's taboo. He can't touch it!"

Menasi stood up and his eyebrows came together like a menacing cloud. "I want it understood from now on," he said, "nobody is taboo on this ship. Nobody and nothing. Is that clear? Logically, everything we're doing would be taboo. So if we're to continue and expect any kind of success, we must throw out all such ideas. All of them! Understood, Zulli? Then give me the box."

There was a prolonged silence. Zulli looked as though she thought the Wasan should materialize in our midst and strike Menasi dead. Since nothing of the sort happened and the Wasan was clearly beyond reach unless the faculties of the box were revived, she reluctantly handed it to Menasi.

Our leader looked the box over curiously. Then he took it up to the pilot's cubby and proffered it to N'Gobi.

"Take a look at this, son," he said in a matter-of-fact tone. "Is there something wrong with it other than our distance from home?"

N'Gobi took the box, and if he was feeling triumphant it did not show in his face. He turned it over and fiddled with the knobs.

"The machine's dead; that's obvious," he said. "But why?"

He got out his tools and unscrewed the back of the box. A maze of wires and unbelievable parts were revealed, but N'Gobi did not seem to be baffled. He did more screwing and unscrewing. Finally, from somewhere in the interior he brought out a long wire end, with an exclamation of satisfaction, strode to the rear of the ship, slid back the galley panel, and pushed the end of the wire into a small hole at one side. Immediately the box began to hum. We all stared unbelievingly.

"It was out of power," said N'Gobi. "Now it's getting power from the ship."

"Which one of those books Amhara got for you did you learn that from?" asked Tadessa.

N'Gobi gathered up his tools. "None of them. I've read the instructions about this ship and I guessed."

"You're a good guesser," Menasi said. "It's a valuable talent to have on an expedition like this. Now get busy, Zulli, and contact the Wasan. Be sure you report everything just as it happened."

Once more Zulli began the process of turning knobs and dials, the tapping and listening that should alert some watcher in our far-off homeland. I thought she seemed a trifle subdued as she worked, but perhaps I was only imagining how I would have felt in her place.

At last she took her hand from the box and a whole series of clicks and chatterings came from it—the secret language in which Zulli conversed with the Wasan. After several minutes, she looked up at Menasi.

"I told him that we are here at the northern sea, and he is amazed that we have really come this far and that our signals come in so clearly."

"Have you told him why that is possible?" asked Menasi. When Zulli only stared at him, he persisted, "Go ahead. Tell him that the box was broken and that N'Gobi fixed it. Tell him we are now using the power of the ship and that it is N'Gobi's work."

Zulli bowed her head. After a moment her fingers began to play over the keys, and a little later the mysterious clickings and chirpings came from the box, fantastically propelled in one instant over the thousands of miles that we had traveled.

At last the clickings ceased.

"Well, what does he say?" demanded Menasi. "Did you tell him everything as I said? And about N'Gobi? And what does he say?"

"I told him as well as I could," Zulli replied. "Yes, about N'Gobi. And he says that it's no more than he expected!"

A sigh went around our circle as the tension broke. Menasi began to laugh. Then Tadessa joined in and N'Gobi came out of the pilot's cubby, a big grin on his face. We were all laughing except Zulli, who looked puzzled. Finally Menasi got himself under control.

"I wonder what else his expectations predict," he said. "Well, back to the job. Don't lose contact, Zulli. Explain the difference of opinion here. N'Gobi wants to go the direct route, straight north across the sea, regardless of possible danger. I prefer to take a little longer and go westward across the land. Get his opinions and expectations on that if you can. Perhaps with N'Gobi in such good favor, he'll endorse his plan."

When Zulli had again communicated with the Wasan and explained our problems, the orders came back to follow Menasi's counsel and take the more cautious route.

"Good enough," Menasi grunted. "Now tell the Wasan one more thing. Tell him that since we will be needing all our power, we cannot spare enough to talk with him several times a day—or even every day. Tell him we will call him when and if we need advice or have something important to report. Otherwise only every three days."

Zulli looked insulted. "That is outside my orders. I cannot tell the Wasan that."

"Tell him from me. Your box will not work without the ship. I am the captain of this ship, and I cannot spare the fuel for unlimited contact. Not now when we will soon leave the lands of sunshine. Tell him."

Reluctantly, Zulli moved to obey. Her fingers touched the keys in an erratic burst of speed and then stopped. In a few moments came the answering clicks and then silence. Zulli turned the dial and the box ceased to hum.

"And what did he say?" asked Menasi.

"He said he expected it," Zulli whispered. "He said to go on with his blessing."

For three days we flew on, following the sea and the coastline ever to the west. Below us stretched a vast expanse of desert. We were sure this must indeed be poisoned country, and no more was said about stopping to test the water and refresh ourselves with swimming in the sea. There were no signs of life or even ruins, and I noticed that N'Gobi tended to fly at a higher altitude, as though to put a good distance between us and these desert wastes.

At last, on the third day, we came to high mountains and as we increased altitude to rise above them, we clearly saw the land beyond the sea. Menasi gave the order to turn north and N'Gobi smiled as he pointed the aircraft in that direction. We all felt relieved, I think, as we crossed the narrow band of sea and left that terrible desert country behind us. I know there was more talk and laughter among us, and Menasi began to tell how the huge rocky promontory we saw below had once been a mighty fortress, with armaments and living quarters built into the rock and defended for many centuries by the white men.

All this made me wish I could stop here for a few days and explore and excavate that ancient rock. Surely, there would be interesting artifacts to find and secrets to discover. But I knew we must go on to our goal in the north, and so I only suggested that perhaps we could find water and a better camping place for the night now that we had crossed the sea.

This was an idea that appealed to everyone, and Menasi agreed that we should put down a few hours earlier if we saw a likely place, in order that Tadessa could make the necessary tests of water and surroundings. Not long after passing the straits, N'Gobi saw a lake and guided us to a cleared place beside it. The landing was made with some difficulty, for as soon as we came close enough it was evident that the edges of the lake were marshy. N'Gobi hovered over several places, while Menasi leaned out the open hatch and tried to gauge the character of the land. At last they found a spot that they thought could support the weight of the ship, and they gingerly let her settle to the ground.

We followed the procedure we had developed during our trip down the Nile. Tadessa was the first and only one to alight. He took with him his scientific instruments and radiation detectors and tested first the ground immediately around the ship. Satisfied with that, he circled a wider area, and at last made his way to the shores of the lake. He was still testing samples of the water when the rest of us crawled out of the plane. We were all stiff from three days of sitting with scarcely enough room to stretch properly, let alone exercise. We walked and jumped and ran. Zulli and I retired to a spot behind the airship, that had been designated as a private corner for the women. We were enjoying our unusual space and freedom and wondering how soon we could safely bring a bucket of water from the lake, when we heard Tadessa bellowing at N'Gobi.

"Come back here! Son of the Zebra! You know I haven't been out that way! I can't be everywhere at once. Don't touch the vegetation till I give the word!"

Reluctantly, N'Gobi came back toward the lake. "I was just going to look for tracks. With all this stuff growing, there must be some kind of animals."

"Not necessarily," said Menasi. "Life must come from life. And if everything was poisoned as in so much of Afria. . . ."

"Well, at least give us your verdict on the water," said N'Gobi. "You've been puttering around there long enough."

"Water seems all right," Tadessa admitted, as though hating to give his final seal of approval. "At least as far as radiation. No harm in bathing in it. I'd better run some microscopic tests before we drink it."

N'Gobi waited to hear no more. He was striding out through the reeds and soon was swimming in deep water. Tadessa looked after him, frowning.

"He should not go too far," Menasi muttered. "Not beyond sight and hearing, or help if needed. We know so little here." He stood at the water's edge, washing the day's sweat from his body and staring after N'Gobi, who seemed to be swimming directly across the lake.

Tadessa continued methodically with his testing. A little later he came to Zulli and me, when we had finished our toilet, and said that the water was safe for drinking but that he advised boiling it to be sure. We promptly filled our kettles and began to prepare the evening meal.

A short time later N'Gobi came back and astonished us all by bringing a white bird he had caught.

"Meat for the table!" he announced, "if Tadessa will sanction it. Around the bend in the lake there's a whole colony of these birds. Nesting. We can have fresh eggs for breakfast. But I'll tell you one thing, there are probably no animals here, at least of any size. Or snakes either. The birds are not afraid. I was able to get as close as I am to you, and I knocked this one over with a stone."

We all examined the bird. It was obviously not the duck we were seeking but some kind of long-legged water bird. N'Gobi gave it to Tadessa who tested it and then passed it to Zulli and me. There was not much on it, but we would each have a taste of fresh meat. Tadessa allowed us to collect firewood here and we roasted the bird on a spit.

That night there was bright moonlight and since N'Gobi insisted there could be no large predators in this country, we dispensed with the guardian light. We stretched out on the ground in greater comfort than we had enjoyed for many nights and divided the hours into five short watches. Now at last Zulli and I were permitted to take our turns in equal responsibility.

Zulli was given the first watch, when the moon was still bright, and then allowed an undisturbed sleep. Since I liked to rise early and begin preparations for the morning meal, I was given the last watch. Menasi woke me an hour before dawn, and I sat on a rock by the lakeside and watched the first faint streaks lighten the eastern sky. The insect chorus of night was beginning to die down. It had seemed unusually loud. In fact, Menasi had commented to me upon it just before he rolled up in his blanket for a couple more hours of sleep. He said he had not seen anything all watch, but what he heard made him expect almost anything to come out of the forest. However, I attributed it to the contrast with the desert silence we had so recently experienced. As dawn came and the sounds died out, I was sure this was the explanation. There were no strange animals in this forgotten land. As Menasi said, life must come from life, and nothing had survived here but a few birds, which could migrate away from danger and return when the environment was safe again. Birds and insects. There were still insects for the birds to feed on.

I was sitting thus on my rock, watching the early dawn and thinking I must soon start the fire with the faggots N'Gobi had collected the night before. Then a sound went by my ear that made me sit bolt upright and peer frantically behind me. It was like an arrow in flight, except that I heard no twang of the bow. Like a bird, but faster and louder. Would a bird fly that close? Another whiz—whiz! I was turning in circles, trying to catch sight of the swift flyers. Then my eye fell upon the lake, and I stopped and stared, unbelieving.

In the ancient literature I had read references to the insects of the remote geologic past, the evidence dug up and compiled by those scientists of the pre-Disaster period. No pictures or specimens have come down to us since the holocaust, but if we were to believe the writings of the ancients, our world was once home to dragonflies with a wing-spread up to two feet. This, of course, was long, long before man appeared upon our planet. If I could believe my eyes, I was now looking at something very like those primitive, giant dragonflies. For they certainly were dragonflies. They swooped and darted across the surface of the water, feeding no doubt on the clouds of midges rising from the lake. These insects, compared to the dragonflies I used to watch on our lake in Afria, were like the ancient elephant if compared to N'Gobi's dog.

The thought of N'Gobi made me run to wake him. As I touched his shoulder, he sprang up, rubbing the sleep from his eyes, and followed my pointing finger. I heard him draw in his breath as he looked. Then he made his way to the lake. Together we stared in wonder and incredulity. Our caution was unnecessary. The insects were oblivious of our presence. More and more arrived, weaving a fantastic and incongruous dance across the water.

Presently, our talk and excitement awoke the others, who came and joined us, to gape incredulously at the giant dragonflies. Tadessa was the first to collect himself, and he suggested that perhaps we should catch one as a specimen to take back and astound our scientists and prove that we weren't all liars. Then a problem arose as to how to do it. They were much too big for Menasi's insect net. N'Gobi set about making a giant net with some wire and his extra shirt, but by the time it was ready, the dragonflies had begun to disappear. Where they went was a mystery. They were too big to settle on a blade of grass. Tadessa suggested that they might make their home in the trees, and come to the lake to feed when the smaller insects were thickest. We could not spare the time to search the forest. N'Gobi waded out among the reeds with his improvised net and tried unsuccessfully to catch the giants. Unlike the birds, they seemed wary of his approach, from which he deduced that the birds might feed on them.

At last Menasi called a halt to our efforts. The sun was already well up the sky and few dragonflies remained for N'Gobi to chase.

"We can't delay our whole operation for one specimen and an insect at that," he declared. "Get on with breakfast and let's get off the ground."

Zulli and I went back to our fire. Soon we had cooked the eggs collected the night before, and we served the best breakfast any of us had enjoyed since leaving home. The dragonfly hunt had delayed us, and that day our flight covered only half our usual distance.

That night we camped in the shadow of high mountains. They towered above us to the north, their snowy crests reaching into the cold of high altitudes. N'Gobi was afraid to fly over them in the late afternoon lest darkness overtake us or our power give out before we should reach the other side and find a suitable landing place. We put down in a valley in the foothills. We found fresh water in a rushing stream, and plenty of firewood, but no signs of animals or birds or even the giant dragonflies. With the coming of darkness, the insect chorus from the surrounding forest grew louder and more menacing than ever.

In the morning Menasi told us we had our choice of two paths, each with its dangers: the sea or the mountains. The peaks towered above us to the northeast, their summits glittering in the early sun. N'Gobi could hardly take his eyes off them. They represented a challenge to him and his machine. He scarcely listened to Menasi's description of the many accidents to the ancient fliers in such mountainous country.

"Those were the jets or the straight-flying airplanes," N'Gobi insisted. "This kind of craft was used regularly for rescues in any kind of terrain. I have no doubt she'll make it, and if not, she can put down on any small space."

"You can't be sure she'll make the altitude," Menasi said, "and if we have to put down in those mountains we'll never get out."

"We'll never get out if she puts down in the sea, that's sure."

"According to the map," Menasi persisted, "it should be only an hour's flying. If we cross like this to the northeast, we'll hit the coast of what the ancients called France."

"Suppose the map is wrong?" N'Gobi turned impatiently away to stare at the mountains.

"It can't be that wrong. There does seem to be a certain raising of the ocean level, but not enough to matter."

At this point Tadessa voiced the deciding opinion.

"After all, we came to look for a duck. Where are we more apt to find this duck, by the sea or in the mountains?"

There was not much answer to that, for although the duck in question wintered on our lakes and rivers, we had all read the treatise on its habits, prepared by Don Ylma.

That specifically mentioned the migration flyway along the seacoast, and the probability that it nested in rocks or marshes near the shore. In fact, we were prepared, if necessary, to follow it to the northernmost lands where there is no night in summer. In the meantime, if we now flew over this seacoast, we could rule it out as a possible nesting site.

I think we all sighed with relief that we would not have to dare the high mountains—all except N'Gobi, who took his breakfast and went to eat in his cubby where he could check his instruments at the same time.

When we had finished the meal and reloaded our few possessions, we took off and flew north until we saw the sea below us. Menasi ordered that we continue thus until we lost sight of the coast, with only the high mountains receding behind us. Then only did he give the word to turn our course slightly to the east, lest we lose all contact with the land.

When after more than an hour we again saw land low on the horizon, we were all happy. I for one was glad of this evidence that the white man's Disaster had not destroyed his land as well as himself nor caused it to sink beneath the sea.

For the rest of the day we followed the coast, sometimes rocky, sometimes low and marshy. We went slowly, searching the land for birds or other life. The few times we sighted a rookery we flew low and circled the spot until all inhabitants had been identified. There would be a great rush of air and flapping of wings, as the astonished birds left their nests in alarm. Nowhere did we find the particular duck that was the cause of so much toil and speculation.

After one such futile search, when it seemed our hopes had been dashed for the hundredth time, Tadessa was heard to mutter, "What a lot to hang on a piece of string!"

Menasi contradicted him sharply. "This is only the beginning," he said. "We'll go on as long as we can or the season permits. But I expect no results till we reach the Arctic. So don't get discouraged now."

"Who's discouraged?" asked N'Gobi. "We're flying, aren't we?"

Tadessa and Zulli exchanged glances, but no more was said.

The land beneath us had once been one of the most populous regions of the ancient world. Here had stood great cities and smoking factories: well-husbanded fields and storied castles, all the wealth and beauty for which that world was famous. As we gazed at it, it might have been the jungles of our southern continent. There were no signs of animals. Only vegetation had survived and come back in fantastic forms after what man had wrought. Only a few birds, the descendants of those that had fled to some place of safety and now returned with apparent impunity, were enjoying this lush wilderness. A few birds—and, of course, the insects. We could not see them from our elevation, but remembering the dragonflies of the lakeside camp, we could not doubt that they were there.

Now I tasted the real meaning of what Don Woldi had taught. Man had traveled in a circle and was back at the springs of his existence in ancient Afria, whence he had once spread out in remote ages to conquer the world. In one fit of madness he had lost it all and slipped back to the beginning—a handful of beings struggling against nature in a corner of a continent. But surely not as helpless and indigent this time. Now we had knowledge and learning and science. Much had been salvaged and much might come from this expedition—a firm foundation to build on, a chance to expand and develop.

As I looked at the wasted country below us a profound depression filled me and I could not argue it away. I felt this mood reflected in my companions. Toward evening Tadessa expressed it.

"It seems that man has given over these latitudes to the insects," he said.

Menasi looked at him, and I knew he had similar grim thoughts.

"That is what we are here to find out," he said. Shortly afterwards, he gave the word to put down for the night on a beach along the coast once called Normandy.

This was the last night we would spend on the continent of Europe. Tomorrow we would fly to England, and my heart lifted as I thought of that country of Shake-

speare whence so much of the ancient culture had come
Menasi showed me the map and explained that we woul
search here as much as we could and then go on to th
arctic lands. I extracted a promise from him that w
would camp a few days in those British Islands and tha
while he made search flights of exploration I could try m
hand at digging in the earth—always presuming Tadess
found the terrain to be safe and free from poison.

"You owe that much to Don Ylma," I insisted, remem
bering her words: "Don't be discouraged if you don'
see anything. Get to work and *dig* for it!"

A sense of excitement and expectation boiled up in m
as I realized that soon I would be able to do just that—
excavate in Shakespeare's England! There was no limit t
what I might find. I hurried through my tasks of th
evening, preparing supper and helping to set up the tem
porary camp, in the hope that this might make time g
faster.

In the morning the sun was shining, seeming to beli
the stories we had read of the foggy, sunless countries t
the north. We repacked our gear and took off in hig
spirits. Soon we were flying over the English Channel—
that famous waterway, once the path of a thousand ships.

"This part of the world got a great deal of radiation,
said Menasi. "It may still be hot. You can see not man
birds have come back."

"Better give it a quick check and go farther north,
agreed Tadessa.

I felt my opportunity slipping away. "You promised!"
cried in protest. "You promised a few days digging i
England!"

"We can't promise anything in these circumstances,
Menasi replied. "When we find a likely spot, Tadessa wi
check. If it's safe, of course you can dig."

"But it's got to be safe," said Zulli. "No use in takin
chances."

I saw her glance at Tadessa, and it suddenly struck m
that these two had reached an understanding. I remem
bered little things of the last few days, when Zulli ha
smoothed out his blankets and Tadessa had inquire
about her airsickness. A glance. A tone. I saw at onc

92

where it was leading and that neither of them wanted to jeopardize a happy marriage when they should return home.

"There may be different ideas of what's safe," I said. "I'm not afraid to do what I came for and I know N'Gobi isn't either."

"After all, it doesn't matter for N'Gobi," Zulli said, "and if you want to be a fool, that's your business."

She spoke softly, but I knew N'Gobi had sharp ears. I was collecting myself for a really cutting retort when Menasi broke in.

"There's no question of safety or of being foolish," he said. "You all swore obedience and dedication. Have you forgotten already? Until the hour we return, your lives belong to the state, and it is for me to decide what is safe and what is foolish. Now stop this argument and get back to your watch. I have enough to do checking and correcting the maps."

There was silence for a long period after that, but I was more than ever aware of the meaning of glances between Tadessa and Zulli. I reflected that she might soon be my sister, but with small feeling of sisterly affection.

Then N'Gobi spoke. "There's your England, Amhara. Straight ahead."

We all stared at the barren land rising out of the sea. The rocks, the cliffs, and behind them, mist-shrouded hills. We flew on across the water and presently N'Gobi increased our altitude so that we crossed the shore a few thousand feet up and could take a good look at the land we had come to.

We knew the old descriptions of this famous countryside. The crowded cities; the plots of suburbs; the checkerboard of cultivated lands; and the graceful woods. All this had been blotted out, as when a painter sweeps his brush across the canvas before beginning a different scene. Now there were shapes of rocks and mountains, and over all the vegetation gone wild. Huge fernlike trees towered here and there above the impenetrable mass. The word that came first to my mind was "bracken." But this was bracken on a fantastic scale. I said as much to Tadessa and he agreed with me.

"It bears out the ancient documents I studied in my research on radiation—some work with pre-Disaster vegetation. Seems the tendency is to break down the genes. The plant reverts to its primitive ancestors. Since this was a badly burned area. . . ."

"A revival of the carboniferous forest?" Menasi mused. "Complete with giant dragonflies? I wonder what other giants there may be. Those dragonflies would have had no trouble moving south to where we saw them. But what about the wingless insects?"

"This ought to be interesting," said Tadessa, becoming enthusiastic in spite of the dangers and Zulli's frowns. "Probably no animals at all unless they've been able to move back like the birds. And that would suppose they could get away in the first place."

"What I don't understand," broke in Zulli, evidently hoping to get Tadessa's mind off the interesting prospect of unusual biology and back on the track of possible dangers, "is if they had made all those tests, and if they knew what was going to happen—why did they do it?"

N'Gobi spoke for the first time in this discussion. "People do a lot of things that don't make sense. Otherwise they wouldn't be people."

"If you mean that remark for me," cried Zulli, "remember it includes the Wasan, too. And that's treason!"

Menasi sighed. "How many times do I have to break this up? The next exchange of this sort will be entered in the report, and the Wasan will consider it when we get back. There's no point in arguing the why of the Disaster. Our best minds have discussed it for the last five hundred years and found no answer."

Suddenly our airship turned and dropped; and before we could protest the unexpected maneuver that nearly threw us from our seats, N'Gobi was calling out in excitement. "Over there, Amhara! By that pile of rocks to the right. Among the reeds. Do you see it?"

He had slowed the ship considerably, and we circled downward. I pushed back the window and leaned out. "It's the duck!" I cried. "You're right, N'Gobi! Our little duck! At least a dozen of them, and they're nesting!"

N'Gobi did not need the word from Menasi to continue the circling descent. Instead, it was to the rest of us that Menasi shouted. "Keep your seats! You'll be able to see well from both sides."

For there was a tendency among us to crowd to the windows on the side nearest the ducks.

N'Gobi had switched on the top propellers for landing, and we hovered over the nesting site. The frightened birds took to the air, and we all had a good view of them. There was no doubt that we had come to the right place.

"I guess we need go no farther," Menasi said. "We're in luck." He ordered N'Gobi to survey the immediate vicinity for the best spot on which to build our camp.

The ship climbed again, high enough for a view of the surrounding country. The ducks were nesting on an island not far from the mainland, which extended in a long, mountainous peninsula. Menasi was pleased with this arrangement. The fern forests did not grow high on the island, and most of the land was rocky and fairly clear of the wild, junglelike vegetation. He hoped that any dangers inherent in that wilderness would be kept from us by the surrounding water. We circled the island and at last put down on a sandy beach tucked among rocks in a protected cove.

Following our usual procedure, we all stayed in our seats while Tadessa ventured out with his instruments and made tests. Zulli watched him go with a troubled frown, but after the lecture Menasi had given us, she kept her feelings to herself.

At last, to take her mind off her worries, I imagined, she suggested to Menasi that she might report our success to the Wasan. He readily agreed, and N'Gobi came back and connected her box to the ship's power.

Menasi joined us, too, and sat down beside Zulli in order to read off our exact position and his major corrections to the maps. I saw N'Gobi glance to the west where the sun was going down behind a bank of clouds.

"Try to keep it down to fifteen minutes," he cautioned.

"Oh, stop worrying," said Zulli, as she tuned the instrument. "We're here, aren't we? We won't be going any place for a while and then only home. You'll have lots of time to fuel up."

N'Gobi did not deign to reply. He only looked at Menasi.

"I'll watch the time," our leader reassured him. "But I think we should give them a full report now. Let me know what Tadessa is finding if you can get something from him before we sign off."

Then the reply signals began to come in from Afria. N'Gobi turned away and went to the door of the cabin, where he leaned out to watch Tadessa moving about the little cove.

I went up forward, too, leaving Menasi and Zulli to their task. I gazed out the wide pilot's window at this land where we hoped to camp for some time. Over by those rocks would be a good place for the cook fire. They were far enough from high tide, as well as I could judge, and protected from the sea wind. Back beyond the ship's wing was a likely spot for sleeping quarters. Although the bracken here was not high as on the mainland, there was plenty of it, and it could easily be made into some sort of shelter.

I had the plan for our camp well in mind by the time Tadessa came back. I heard him talking to N'Gobi near the hatch, and then my cousin went back and told Menasi the place seemed safe enough according to Tadessa's first tests. I heard Zulli translating this into the clicking language of her box, and then N'Gobi said impatiently, "One hour of power you've taken so far and if we don't make camp soon, you'll be wanting lights for cooking!"

Menasi laughed and told Zulli to sign off. He came forward, stretched as much as the ship would allow, and looked out the window curiously.

"So this is to be our home for a bit. I can't say I'll mind. Much more inviting than I'd imagined, and the sea keeps outsiders at a distance. Come on, Zulli, get busy. We want all the work done by dark so we don't need to call on N'Gobi's precious lights."

Zulli looked at the sinking sun and the gathering clouds. "That's impossible," she said.

"A minimum," he told us. "Nothing but the essentials. We'll plan the camp tomorrow."

We hastened to do our work according to established procedure. Menasi and N'Gobi first secured the ship against all possible wind or storm. Zulli and I set up an outdoor kitchen and prepared a simple supper. Tadessa extended his investigations to a search for water; and by the time we were ready to eat, he came back with news of a spring of pure water back in the bracken, near enough for easy use.

We ate in the dusk and arranged our watches for the night. The evening was balmy and we all spread blankets on the beach. For a while we watched the stars and Menasi pointed out the different constellations seen from these northern latitudes. At last I slept, with a feeling that now we had reached our destination. In this camp we would be at home and there would be time for exploring and excavations and pleasant work. As I fell asleep, without my being aware of it, the chorus of insect noises began and grew in volume to a weird and alien tapestry of sound.

Chapter Two

The next day was still sunny, and we spent it building our camp. Tadessa's tests had been negative. Because of the hopeful sign of the nesting ducks, Menasi decided we could make this the center of our operations. Thus he was willing to devote a little time to building an adequate headquarters. The bracken proved to be excellent material for constructing huts in the manner of our country people. They were arranged strategically around the spot where our airship was secured, leaving a wide, smooth path where the ship could be wheeled out into the open before taking off.

We built four huts. Two for sleeping—one for the men and one for Zulli and me. Another housed the provisions as we moved them out of our storage lockers in the ship. Here we built our kitchen, with fireplace and cooking arrangements. N'Gobi even contrived an oven so that we could bake bread. Finally, there was the main hut, larger than the others and open at the front. There was a long table where Menasi spread his maps and Tadessa later dissected specimens. This was our common room, where we gathered when not otherwise occupied, to discuss our plans and discoveries. We had a place for an open fire near the entrance, and we sat there in the evenings watching the sun go down beyond the sea, warmed and lighted by the fire in the night. N'Gobi would not let us use the ship's power for light or cooking unless absolutely necessary.

We had scarcely finished our camp when we began to

see the wisdom of this frugality. The next morning we woke to a steady rain. We had completed our shelter just in time. Our stores were safe and we kept dry under our thatch. The sea was blanked out with a fog that to us was unbelievable. Clouds hung low over our island and all plans of exploring by air had to be postponed. N'Gobi hung lovingly about his machine, checking the dials and reading the gauges. He confided to Menasi that fuel was very low and that we could not take to the air again till we had had one full day of sunlight to replenish the batteries.

He also worried about the effects of rain and damp, and we spent the day constructing a thatch shelter for the ship. I heard Tadessa complaining about this, which he thought unnecessary labor, as the sun would soon return and dry everything off. But N'Gobi worried about rust and deterioration, saying that we had few, if any, spare parts. Menasi backed him up and made us all work until a passable shelter had been constructed.

Tadessa was impatient to begin searching for and cataloging the animal and plant life of the island. Already, he had samples of the several kinds of bracken that had served to build our shelters, and he begrudged the time taken from his researches for the physical labor of shelter-building. As though to reinforce his objections, that night the stars came out and we all looked forward to a sunny morning when we could get on with our work.

"You see," Tadessa said, "tomorrow there'll be sun in plenty. The ship will be dry before you've rolled out of bed, and all that fuss was for nothing."

"Always good to be on the safe side," Menasi told him. "Tomorrow you can go back to your work and no time lost in the long run."

"Tomorrow, if the sun's out," said N'Gobi, staring straight-faced at the fire, "there will be no work done by anyone until we've removed the ship's shelter and dragged her to a nice sunny spot."

There was a short choking sound from Menasi, but Tadessa paid no attention. "We've helped you build that cover when we might have been better employed," he said. "Taking it off and on is now the job of the pilot, or so it seems to me."

"You know perfectly well that it takes at least three of us, and the men in that case, to move that shelter, unless we take it all apart."

"You and your precious machine," cried Zulli. "You'd think it was a baby! Has to be washed and dried and fed!"

"That's just about it," N'Gobi told her. "That is—if you want to get home in it." He stared coldly at her. "I don't imagine you two want to spend the rest of your lives here."

At that Zulli subsided, and Tadessa dropped the argument with the remark, "If we must, we must."

He was saved from the hateful labor on the morrow. When dawn came, fog had once again closed in. Rain held off, but the bracken dripped from every frond. Not to be further put off, Tadessa ventured out into the mists and returned at noon, drenched, with a collection of plant specimens. He reported no signs of animal life, and it was too misty to detect birds. He and Menasi spent the afternoon arranging and inspecting the plants. Menasi also prowled among the sea pools near camp, where he was more successful in finding small specimens of living things. Soon he and Tadessa were deep in discussions of scientific questions well outside my field.

I spent this period of enforced idleness checking over our stores, while Zulli took upon herself the task of cooking our meals. N'Gobi spent most of his time in the ship's shelter; and since I was there also to check the stores, he soon had me help him wipe and polish and check the shelter for leaks.

After three days of this, even N'Gobi grew tired of wet-nursing the ship. It was obvious that nothing could be done until the sun came out. This country was beginning to live up to its reputation for fog and rain.

"Sometimes I wonder if we'll ever get away from here," he confided to me. "Let alone make any scouting flights."

"It's only a matter of time," I said. "The sun has got to shine eventually."

"But for how long and how strongly. We didn't believe the stories, and now we're liable to pay for it."

I looked at him curiously. I could not imagine it was at

serious as he seemed to think. My check of the stores had revealed them all in good condition and lasting as well as planned. If things went according to schedule, we should get by even without supplementary food if we were careful. There must be something to eat in this land. We had only to look for it.

"Don't worry," I told N'Gobi. "You take things too hard. In any case, it's not your fault. No one could have done better."

"I could have made us wait over a day in the southern country, where there was plenty of sun. Our batteries would not be depleted now."

"I doubt that Menasi would have agreed. Fly while the sun shines was the plan."

"I know. It seemed best to me, too. But every day we sit here in the fog a little more drains off. If this keeps up, we may not be able to take off in an emergency."

"Who wants to take off?" I asked. "We only just got here and made camp. Don't worry. There's plenty of exploring for Tadessa and Menasi right here around us. I only wish there were something I could be doing. But if we can't fly there's small chance of finding a ruin for me to dig into."

N'Gobi looked at me, and for the first time in many days I felt the sympathetic rapport of our childhood.

"You must be having a frustrating time," he said. "So near and yet so far! Tadessa has his plants and Menasi his sea creatures. Even Zulli, while she can't talk to the Wasan every day, can cook for Tadessa. You and I are chained down by this fog, shut off from our specialties. What do you say? If it keeps up tomorrow, we'll take a little hike around the island. We can't very well get lost. If we keep going we'll come back where we started from. We may get a look at those ducks if we're careful. Not that I expect to learn anything from their nests, but it would make me feel good just to see them again. Shall we go?"

Of course, I jumped at the suggestion, and when N'Gobi broached the subject to Menasi, our leader agreed. I guess he thought our morale needed bolstering at this point. He flatly refused to let anyone else go, saying a force must always stay at camp with the ship.

It was understood that if the weather cleared the plan would be abandoned. N'Gobi would then be kept busy recharging the plane's batteries. For once, I welcomed the foggy morning. I put on my short, rain-resistant kente, and N'Gobi wore shorts. The wet would not bother us, and the temperature continued warm. I took small digging tools, just in case, and dried rations in my pouch for us both.

N'Gobi was armed with knife and arrows, and at Menasi's insistence he carried a small communication drum to summon aid if needed. He extracted promises from both Menasi and Tadessa that at the first sign of sunlight they would remove the shelter from the airship. Only then could he set out with an untroubled mind.

We left soon after breakfast, climbing around the rocks at the foot of the cove, and presently the camp was lost to sight in the mists. We followed the shoreline to the north. The sky was overcast all morning, and often we could not see more than a few yards ahead. We scrambled over rocks and dipped into pools, and what with the sea and the mist we were both wet before we had gone far.

N'Gobi had hung a small collecting bag at his waist, and whenever he spied a snail or a crab or some vegetation that he thought might be new and interesting to the two scientists back at camp, he would put it in the bag.

Toward noon we rounded the northern end of the island and continued east. Then N'Gobi made me be quiet and walk behind him, for he remembered that the ducks nested in this vicinity, and he wanted to surprise them if he could. Suddenly he cautioned me to complete stillness and disappeared into the mists ahead. I heard the rush of wings and then the protesting squawk of startled birds as they flew past overhead. In a minute N'Gobi reappeared and told me to come along.

"They flew before I was near them," he said. "These birds are not as trusting as those we saw in the south. They are used to being hunted, it seems."

"But what could be hunting them?" I asked. "Surely not men, do you think? Perhaps some animal."

"That I couldn't say. There are no signs to read in this mist."

He led the way over the rocks and up onto a gravel each and showed me a duck's nest in the reeds. We xamined the eggs and N'Gobi said they were probably ue to hatch soon and we'd best get away and let the duck ake over.

"Unless you want to take a chance on duck eggs for reakfast, but I think you'd be more likely to get duck-ings."

Since there was small chance that the eggs were fresh, nd neither of us wanted to carry them for the rest of the lay, we turned to leave, and at that moment the sun came ut of the clouds.

It was so sudden and dramatic that we both stopped nd exclaimed at our good fortune. I think N'Gobi would ave liked to take the shortest way back, but I argued that ur three fellows were quite capable of sunning the air-hip. He had left adequate instructions, and we all knew y now how important it was. Since we had come this far ve might as well continue around the island. As though to einforce my argument, a shaft of sunlight broke through he mists, which were rapidly evaporating, and glinted lown an opening in the bracken that seemed to extend in oward the center of the island.

"Look!" I cried. "It's almost a pathway. Let's explore n there. I'm tired of the seashore and there may be omething different that way."

It was certainly an inviting prospect after all the clam-ering we had done over rocks. Already the sun was varming and drying us off, and N'Gobi, like me, was eized with the spirit of adventure.

"All right, let's go," he said. "This is something differ-nt. And it may be a short way home."

We walked through the little glen, and a wealth of alien lowers and foliage came to sight as the mists cleared and he colors came out. I ran about picking the prettiest for Menasi, and N'Gobi chased strange scuttling forms in the grass, but without much success. By the time we were well way from the sea, surrounded by the low, luxuriant racken, we realized that we were both hot and hungry.

"Where are those rations you brought along," he said. 'Time for a rest. It must be well past noon."

We sat down on a rock and while I spread out the food, he unhooked his water bottle.

N'Gobi took a big bite of his sandwich and then an idea struck him. He sprinkled a few crumbs of our food among the rocks and grasses and we waited to see what animal might come to eat it. We bent over with our heads close together, much as we had done as children in Afria, and watched with satisfaction as an unusually large ant appeared and took hold of a crumb of food.

"That's certainly the biggest ant I ever saw," N'Gobi said, "and I thought we were supposed to grow the biggest at home in Afria."

He reached into his pouch for a small collecting jar and was about to pop it over the unusual insect when a sound reached us that made us freeze into silence. A kind of wail, it rose and fell in the noonday silence. It was not so much a song as an unutterably sorrowful lament.

N'Gobi and I stared at each other. Was it animal or human? Was it something that belonged to neither? We could not be sure. A shiver went up my spine, and if I had been alone I might well have traveled in the opposite direction. But when N'Gobi rose quietly to his feet, thrusting the jar back into his pouch, the ant forgotten, I was ready to go where he led.

We followed the sound toward the center of the island, where the ground rose steadily and outcroppings of rock appeared. The place was wild and desolate and yet there was the hint of a path about the open way we followed. Occasionally the sounds stopped, and we waited to be sure we should not miss the way. Soon they began again, and we knew that the path we followed was leading us nearer. Once N'Gobi pointed to some broken fronds along the way.

"Someone or something has been here," he whispered. But the ground was too rocky to make out a footprint. N'Gobi loosened his knife and set an arrow in his bow and we continued our stealthy approach.

In a moment we came past a bluff in a kind of clearing dotted with large rocks and boulders. We were at the highest point of the island, with nothing but stones, wind, the sound of the sea below, and that unearthly keening.

Then we stepped around a boulder and saw that the sounds were made by a man who was leaning against the largest of the rocks. We both stopped to stare unbelievingly, and I reached out to touch N'Gobi's arm.

We had approached from behind and the man did not see us. Even as I wondered why he stood there so close to the huge boulder, making those unearthly sounds, I realized that here was someone many shades lighter than N'Gobi. Still, it would be difficult to say just how many shades lighter or to fit him into the Wasan's exact classification of skin coloring. He was obviously tanned by the summer sun and the harsh hand of weather, and in addition he was very dirty. His clothes—short pants and an open jerkin—were torn and stained and there was an untidy growth of beard upon his face. What halted both N'Gobi and me was the yellow color of his beard and of his unkempt hair. I knew no human hair like that—even among our own "discarded" children—had been seen since the Disaster.

Just then I stepped on a twig, and at the cracking sound he raised his head and saw us. With that movement, a shaft of sunlight fell upon him, seeming to turn his hair to gold. As he looked at us, we saw the long nose and jutting chin and especially the very blue eyes ... all features that had seemed repulsive to me in Don Ylma's picture books. Yet now, seen in the flesh, they did not strike me so.

N'Gobi went forward cautiously, but the man made no move, either to come or to run away, and so my cousin threw down his bow and ran forward. I called to him not to take chances, but he only laughed.

"Can't you see he's tied up?" he called. "I don't know what it's all about, but we might as well get him loose."

I followed behind, scarcely knowing what to think.

"But he's a white man!" I insisted, still thinking we should be cautious.

"Obviously," said N'Gobi, "but if you think I'm one to trouble about the color of a man's skin. . . ." Then he interrupted himself to call excitedly, "Amhara! Come here! Look at the ropes! The same as on the bird's leg, but many times thicker."

At that I forgot all caution in my excitement. We had

indeed come to the right place! Perhaps from this same island our duck has escaped to fly south to Afria and N'Gobi's arrow, and to initiate this fantastic adventure. I looked at the ropes while N'Gobi sawed at them with his knife.

"They're the very devil to cut through," he grunted. "And they have just that same sticky feeling."

With a final thrust he released the man and stood brushing off his hands as the strange bonds fell to the ground. All this while the white man stared at us with a confused, unbelieving expression, making no effort of his own either to escape or to help with his release. When he was finally free he fell at our feet, chattering incomprehensibly, and tried to grab hold of N'Gobi's knees.

"Take it easy!" cried N'Gobi, moving backwards away from him. "Glad to help you. Here, you must be thirsty!" He unhooked the water bottle and held it out to the man, who after a moment's hesitation, took it and drank greedily.

"Any idea what he's saying, Amhara?"

"No, it's all gibberish," I said, for so it sounded at first.

After his thirst was assuaged, the man spoke again, and I realized that I could understand at least some of it.

"Be you gods?" he said. "Bringing the gift of life?"

"N'Gobi," I cried, "I *can* understand it. He's speaking ancient Anglic, but with a strange accent. Or perhaps we never knew the right way to speak it."

"What's he saying then? You've got to translate it!"

"He thinks we're gods, as nearly as I can make out."

"No wonder," said N'Gobi. "Well, get busy and tell him who we are. That'll be quite a mouthful. Maybe you can find out why he was tied up out here and where the rest of his people are."

I paused a moment, casting about in my mind for the right Anglic words and hoping I could pronounce them so that he would understand.

"Friends," I said. "We are friends from a country many days to the south. We search for people like you. Many days we travel—through the air—like the birds."

He looked at me, at first hopefully, as he realized he

could understand my words, and then in doubt as I spoke of flying like the birds.

"Like the bees," he interjected. "Gods of the bees come through the air."

"Not gods," I told him. "People like yourself. But black. We are all black. All the people left are black except you. Now we find you, with yellow hair. Are there many like you?"

He remained silent a moment, trying to comprehend my words. I was not sure how much of my accent got through to him or whether he saw anything strange in our being of a different color. At length he answered the last question I had asked.

"In the hive. There are many people like me in the hive. Many women, many workers." He stopped again as though thinking it all over and I saw him cock his head to listen and to look up toward the sun.

"What's he saying? Have you found out anything?" asked N'Gobi.

"He says there are lots of his people in what he calls the 'hive.' Must be their word for village. He insists we're gods if we come through the air."

"Natural enough," said N'Gobi. "Well, maybe he's hungry as well as thirsty. Have we got any of our lunch left?"

I unwrapped what was still in my pouch and offered it to the man. He examined it closely and then wolfed it down, and N'Gobi gave him another drink from the water bottle.

"How long do you suppose he's been here like this?" he asked. "From the way he gulped what must be strange food, he didn't eat yesterday."

The man had begun talking impatiently as he handed the bottle back to N'Gobi. The words came out in a rush of excitement, and he grabbed my arm and pointed to the east and then to the south.

"What's he saying now?" asked N'Gobi.

"It's hard to follow," I said, "but he seems to want us to fly away with him, down south where we came from. He keeps saying something like 'the executioners' will soon be here."

"If that's so, maybe we'd better get back to camp and

ask questions later." N'Gobi picked up a piece of the rope that had bound the white man. "I'll take some of this for Menasi to mull over. Now let's get out of here if there's anything dangerous coming."

"Should we take him with us to camp?" I asked, for the whole thing seemed so fantastic and unlikely that I could scarcely reconcile myself to the facts.

"Of course. We came to find the white men. Now we've got one specimen to examine. What more could you want? Just tell him we can't fly out of here. We've got to walk for the time being."

N'Gobi started down the path, back the way we had come, and when he saw I was going, too, the white man came after us. Before we had rounded the boulder, he gave a strange, high-pitched cry.

"Nay, nay!" he called, when he saw that I turned to look at him. "That way lies death. They come from the east."

"Who is coming?" I asked, while N'Gobi stopped and looked questioningly at us.

I could get no satisfactory answer from my white-skinned savage. Now, after his first hesitation, he seemed anxious to get away from there, and he beckoned us frantically to follow him to the south, away from what he kept calling the "path of the executioners."

I finally gave up questioning him and explained what I could to N'Gobi. My cousin stared at him in perplexity.

"Well, let's follow him," he said at last. "There must be some explanation for his being tied up here. If there's any danger, he should know of it. Though how he's going to get down through that tangle of bracken, I couldn't guess. Still, it's the right direction for the camp, and if he knows a short cut, let him show us."

"Perhaps if there's any danger we should warn the camp," I suggested, though the whole business seemed most unlikely and peculiar, with the sun now shining in an azure sky and the peace of a summer day spreading around us.

"It's hard to know what to tell them," N'Gobi said. But he got out the communication drum and sounded a few alerts. "After all, I can't begin to explain *him* to them with this." He contented himself with saying that we were coming back and to be on guard.

The white man watched these proceedings with a puzzled expression, all the while dodging about among the rocks and glancing at the sky. When a few muffled drum-beats came from the southern end of the island, he seemed to understand what we were about, for he nodded his head and motioned us to follow him.

"Lead on, MacDuff!" I cried. For here, on his native heath, even a misquoted fragment from the Bard seemed appropriate.

The white man paused at the edge of the thicket and looked doubtfully at me. Pointing at himself, he uttered the one word, "Evan!" Then he plunged confidently into the tangle of bracken, finding a footpath where none seemed to exist. We had to hurry to keep up with him.

"What do you think he meant by that?" panted N'Gobi, as we struggled down the incline in the wake of our guide.

"I think it's his name," I answered. "If we ever get back to camp we can find out."

"We'll get there if he keeps on this way. It's a short cut all right, and I believe there once was a path here. I'd like to know what the terrific hurry is."

"We'll find that out in time, too," I muttered, hoping I wouldn't sprain an ankle first.

At last our precipitous descent brought us to the shore, and we came out upon a pebble beach. Only then did the man stop running and lean, panting, against a rock, staring at the sea as at an unexpected obstacle in his way.

N'Gobi and I broke through the jungle and came to stand beside him.

"Now what?" I asked, for in our struggle through the bracken I had lost all sense of direction.

N'Gobi looked at the sun and was quickly oriented. "I imagine the camp is down there to the right," he said. "It can't be far. He's certainly brought us home much quicker than I thought possible."

We started along the shore to the right, and our companion followed without urging. In a short time we rounded a point and our camp came into view. We heard

Tadessa give a shout. They were on guard all right. Soon the three of them came down the strand to meet us, and when they caught sight of our white man, they all stopped. The variety of surprised expressions on their faces was quite ludicrous.

"We've brought you the best specimen of the local fauna that you could hope for," N'Gobi shouted.

"A white man!" cried Tadessa. "Where'd you find him?"

"What's the meaning of your alert?" interposed Menasi. "Are we about to be attacked?"

"Not that I know of," said N'Gobi. "But he insisted there was danger, so we thought we ought to warn you. However, the most dangerous things I've encountered so far are the briars in the bracken."

"Are you sure?" Menasi insisted. "If there's one, there must be more. We can't afford to be careless."

"I assure you I haven't seen or heard a thing, and my eyes are open for signs. He seems to be the only one on the island. We found him on the top of the high point up there. He was tied to the rocks, suffering from thirst and hunger. And here's a bit of the rope."

He flung down the alien cord at Menasi's feet.

Cries and exclamations of surprise went up as it passed from hand to hand. At last Menasi looked up.

"This is quite a haul," he said. "We should be able to get answers to a lot of questions. Well, bring him along to camp. He looks tired, and we'll be more protected there."

Evan—as I had begun to think of him—made no objection to following us to camp. Having accepted N'Gobi and me, he showed no further surprise at meeting the rest of our party or at anything about our camp, but followed us to the main hut, where he sat down on a rock near the cook fire.

Menasi put Zulli and N'Gobi on guard at either end of the camp, and he and Tadessa set about an examination of our captive. They soon discovered that I was essential to that project. Menasi had read the ancient manuscripts in his youth and had therefore studied Anglic. But he had never tried to speak it, as had I in the study of Shakespeare; thus his accent was not as good as mine and he found it harder to understand when Evan spoke. Tadessa was even rustier, having done most of his reading in translation.

Menasi had a long list of questions that he wanted Evan to answer. Where were his people? Was he alone on the island? How many people in his tribe—or clan or nation? Did they know of any other tribes, clans, or nations in these islands or on the European mainland? How long had they lived here? Generations? Centuries? Did they know about the ancient Disaster? Was all this country clean or poisoned? He went on and on, receiving only grunts in reply or a blank stare. At last he gave up but demanded that I take over the questioning.

I had little more success. Now that he was sitting by our fire, Evan appeared to have lost his previous feeling of urgency and fear. He seemed to go into a kind of stupor, gazing at the flames and looking at me as though he could not expect to understand a word I said. Still I went on, turning the questions about, framing them in different words and phrases, and trying a variety of accents in the hope of finding a medium familiar to him.

Finally Tadessa intervened. "If you want to know, I think you're going about it the wrong way."

"All right," said Menasi. "What would you do?"

"I think the man's suffering from shock of some kind. Look at him. He's exhausted, dirty, famished. Give him some good food and let him sleep. In the morning we'll clean him up and take a second look at him. I wouldn't even make a guess at his age in this condition."

Menasi was obviously loath to be put off, but he saw the logic of Tadessa's arguments.

"All right," he agreed. "Call in Zulli and let the women take care of him. But we'll have double watches tonight. We've got to be careful till we know where we stand."

Tadessa grumbled at the double watches. "He's probably been tied up there for several days and nothing dreadful has happened to us down here. However, have it your way." He squatted down a few feet away from Evan and stared at him reflectively, trying to diagnose his condition.

Meanwhile, Zulli began preparing some food, though she insisted that I must serve it to our captive.

"He has a dreadful odor," she said, wrinkling up her nose, "but I suppose that's the dirt. Do you think they're all like that, or is it just him and all that dirt?"

"How should I know?" I replied. "We're trying to find out about him. Just remember that his people have not had a clean, unpoisoned land to live in as we have. It may have done all sorts of things to them."

"And whose fault was it?" she demanded, as she ladled the hot soup into a bowl.

"Certainly not Evan's," I told her. "You don't blame the child for the parents, and certainly not for the great-great-great-grandparents!"

I took the bowl of soup to Evan while Zulli went about preparing supper for the rest of us. At first he paid no attention to the food but continued to stare at the fire. I sat down beside him and dipped the spoon in the broth, murmuring softly in what I hoped was intelligible Anglic.

"Good soup," I urged. "Come on, have a taste. You'll like it."

As the aroma struck his nostrils, he suddenly raised his head and looked at the spoon and bowl. Then he opened his mouth and let me give him the first spoonful.

"Nectar," he whispered, or so it sounded to me. "Nectar from the gods!"

Then he reached out for the bowl and drank it down in several swift gulps.

I took the empty bowl back to Zulli. She had baked while I was away that day and was setting the crisp bread for our meal.

"Fill it up again," I told her. "And a big hunk of that bread."

She paused in her work to serve me, but she still voiced her objections.

"So he can eat if he can't talk," she said. "If he keeps this up for many days, we'll end on short rations. Can he help us to make it up?"

"First things first," I replied. "We can't expect information from him till we get him back to a normal condition."

"I wonder just what is normal for him?" she asked.

I took the food to Evan and left her muttering to

herself. This time he had no reluctance about eating. He knew what the soup was for. Although he turned the bread all over and sniffed at it, it quickly went the way of the soup. Then he stretched and yawned and I could see he was ready to rest. I took an extra blanket to the back corner of the main hut and spread it on the ground and there Evan curled up and was soon fast asleep.

By the time I joined the others at our meal, night was coming on and they were nearly through eating. I took my plate and sat down to eat my share. I could see that Zulli was right about our stores, however unfriendly she might sound, and I began to re-estimate them in my mind, figuring in the extra mouth. There was always the chance that he might lead us to food, but we could not be sure it would be safe or palatable. As I thought, I listened to the conversation. Menasi had been questioning my cousin about our trip and the place where we had found Evan. He went over every detail, till I should have thought N'Gobi would be ready to scream. He only answered calmly and with an amazing amount of detail that I had somehow missed.

Thus, he insisted that while the rope was remarkably strong and well tied, and certainly a restriction to the man's movements, still Evan was not completely bound, and N'Gobi felt that in a similar situation he, himself, would have been able to get away. He had also noticed some broken pottery shards about the place, and he produced one for us to look at.

"It may have no bearing at all," he said, "and yet I feel that it was only recently broken. Evan himself may have thrown it down to break. Smell it."

Menasi passed it around and we all sniffed. It certainly had a pungent odor. The pottery had a design on it, as with vessels of ritualistic purpose, but the shard was too small to tell us much.

"Wine?" suggested Menasi.

"Or drugs?" added Tadessa.

We all looked at him inquiringly.

"Have you considered," he asked, "the idea of human sacrifice? It was practiced by many primitive tribes when they felt their existence to be threatened. And it sometimes was carried down into later generations and made into a ritual. These people, whoever they are, have gone primitive, and they've certainly been up against it for more time than I care to think. In fact, it's a miracle that they're here at all."

"But he hasn't been sacrificed," protested Menasi. "The Aztecs, halfway around the world, did it. But when they got ready for the sacrifice, they threw the man down on a rock and cut his heart out. They didn't tie him up in the wilds, away from any temple, as far as we can see. . . ."

"How did the top of that hill look to you, Amhara? Could it suggest a primitive outdoor temple?"

"It might at that," N'Gobi put in before I could answer. "And it would fit in with a lot that he said. Something was coming, he kept saying. How did he put it, Amhara?"

I thought back to Evan's first excited words. "Executioners. That's what he said. The executioners were coming."

"There you are!" said Tadessa. "What more do you want. I predict you'll find this unfortunate man is the victim of some ritualistic murder."

"How brutal!" cried Zulli, with what I thought was growing sympathy, and she glanced toward the dark corner where Evan slept.

"Only a theory," Menasi said. "Not yet proven. And they hadn't cut his heart out, I notice."

"Don't talk about it. It's dreadful!" Zulli said.

Tadessa looked at her and grinned teasingly. "Perhaps they left him there to think about it and are coming back tomorrow. Much more terrifying and impressive."

Zulli shuddered and stuck out her tongue at him.

"But then why didn't he run away?" N'Gobi objected. "I certainly would."

"Drugged," said Tadessa. "Some sinister herb in your pottery bowl. That's why he's so dazed. As a matter of fact, I was watching him and I thought his eyes looked peculiar."

"Eyes that color would look peculiar to anyone," said Zulli, and nobody contradicted her.

114

Menasi broke up the discussion by telling us to hurry and prepare for the night. "And I hope nobody objects to double watches."

Nobody did.

Chapter Three

Whether or not there was anything to Tadessa's theory about "human sacrifice," it was evident that the idea had its effect upon us all, for the next morning there was a concerted effort to "be nice to Evan." Even Zulli had overcome her original feeling of repulsion and looked upon him as another human who had suffered the last word in unspeakable cruelties. Menasi easily fell in with the proposal that there should be no more questioning until Evan was entirely restored.

The first thing to be done, he told us after Zulli and I had served breakfast, was to get Evan cleaned up. N'Gobi volunteered for this task, and it was agreed that he was the best one for it. Whether it was because N'Gobi had personally released him or because he was more similar in color and appearance, we could not tell. It was obvious that Evan had developed an attachment for N'Gobi and followed his every move with his remarkable blue eyes. For this reason we believed N'Gobi would stand a better chance of persuading him to do what we asked.

Before starting on his task, N'Gobi had me repeat several times the Anglic words for "wash," "water," "soap," "clean," and several others. He pronounced them after me, and then, armed with soap and towels and a clean kente that Menasi had donated, he led Evan down into the sea. The rest of us watched from a distance, not wanting to do anything to alarm our white man. When it was evident, after much argument and gesturing, that N'Gobi was getting him to disrobe, Tadessa went to join them and brought back the pitiful, ragged garments, which he gave to Zulli and me to wash. Zulli wanted to turn up her nose at this, as the clothes were obviously infested with parasites. But at my suggestion she hastened to kindle a fire under a pot of water and we first boiled the clothes and then scrubbed and pounded them clean on the rocks and spread them to dry in the early sun.

By that time N'Gobi had finished with the washing and they had Evan back near the huts, wrapped in the kente like an Afrian, and Tadessa was cutting his hair and endeavoring to show him how to use our razors for shaving. N'Gobi later told me he had no trouble getting Evan to wash. As soon as Evan understood what was wanted, he took the soap and waded well out into the water, handing over his clothes without objection. All the time, to N'Gobi's amazement, he kept laughing and crying, throwing the water about, jumping up and down, and shouting what sounded like "new life!" "clean life!" Since none of the men who witnessed this performance was adept at Anglic, they were not very sure just what he said or meant. Tadessa suggested that since many of the ancient religions had washing as an important ritual, perhaps he was making a religious rite out of it. This worried Menasi, as he did not want to encourage the idea that we were gods. He decided we would spend two or three days getting acquainted before we undertook any serious questioning of Evan. With this in mind, he decreed that strenuous efforts must be made by all of us to learn Anglic and at the same time to teach Evan a few words of Afrian.

Needless to say, I was brought into this at once. They were already at it when I joined them to watch the haircutting and shaving. Tadessa would hold up the razor and say "razor," and then wait for me to say it in Anglic. Here we hit a snag almost at once, for the word "razor" did not register with Evan. The same was true of the word "mirror," which came up shortly. Either I was unable to pronounce them correctly, or they had disappeared from the language. In place of them, Evan persisted in using "knife" and "glass."

In spite of these and similar hurdles, there was a gener-

al feeling of friendship and cooperation. By dint of seriou
effort we all learned a great deal of Anglic, with Evan'
pronunciation, and he picked up a smattering of Afriar
In a remarkably short time we were able to communicate
at least in everyday matters.

Evan never tired of wandering among our huts an
looking at our belongings and equipment, much of whic
seemed completely strange to him. He was especially fas
cinated by the ship. In fact, early that morning we had t
take a break in the language lessons while the coverin
was removed from the ship, which was wheeled out t
soak up the sun. N'Gobi directed this work, and Eva
followed him about all the while and put a strong an
willing shoulder to the task.

Later in the day, when he had followed N'Gobi for a
interminable period and peered over his shoulder a
screws were screwed, levers adjusted, metal polished, h
approached me with a puzzled look on his face.

"What," he asked, "does it do?"

"That's our ship," I told him, surprised that he had no
understood. "That's what we came here in. That's how w
fly."

He looked completely unbelieving.

"That flies? I don't understand. Where are you
wings?"

I led him back to the ship and touched the blades t
show him.

"These are the wings. We don't fly. We get in the shi
and it flies. But it takes more than wings. It takes power
The motor. The blades help it to glide, but it takes th
motor to run the propellers. That's what N'Gobi is work
ing on. I don't really understand it. It's a taboo science."

N'Gobi left his work and came over to us.

"I've been telling him and telling him," he said, "but h
doesn't seem to understand."

"I wouldn't understand either," I said. "Explainin
won't do. You've got to show him. Can't you give
demonstration?"

It was getting late in the afternoon, and the ship ha
had the benefit of sun for the entire day. Menasi, who ha

heard our conversation, came up and seconded my proposal.

"You've had sun for two days now," he said. "You must have some fuel stored up. Suppose you take us up for a look around. Now that we know there's something to look for, perhaps we can spot his village."

N'Gobi was reluctant. Where the ship was concerned, he was the soul of caution. He finally allowed himself to be persuaded and he climbed into the cabin with Menasi. The rest of us cleared the necessary space and stood back to watch the vertical take-off.

At first Evan did not know what we were going to do, but when he understood, he ran toward the ship for a better view. It took the combined efforts of Tadessa and myself to drag him back to safety. As I held tightly to his arm and the motors began to whirl and the wind from the propellers reached us, I could feel the excitement mounting in him. It was all we could do to hold him back.

"Stay here!" I cried. "It's dangerous! You can be knocked down . . . killed!"

Tadessa yelled, "Idiot! Get back and do as you're told!"

Nevertheless, as the ship rose in the air and gained headway, passing low over the highest bracken, Evan slipped from our grasp and ran to the spot where it had recently stood. He stared after it with fascinated eyes. Then I was aware that he had seized hold of me and was shouting in terrific excitement. "It flew!" he cried. "It went right up! It has the strength of unnumbered storms to fly like the wind! It flew! It flew!"

What with his excitement and his unfamiliar accent, I could scarcely understand him. I sensed the abyss of ignorance and misunderstanding that must lie between him and us. I was overwhelmed by the problem of making him understand, and yet I felt impelled to attempt at least a little of the education I knew he must have.

"Come here," I said, "and sit down and I will try to tell you a little about it."

He looked at me gravely, as he felt the import of my words, and followed me to a seat among the rocks. All the time he kept looking into the sky for a sight of the airship.

"The ship is a wonderful machine," I told him, "but it is not really ours. Do you know who made it?" As he shook his head, I continued, "Your people made it."

Evan looked at me as though he thought our translation system had broken down and continued to shake his head.

"Yes. It is your heritage. Your fathers' fathers made it more than five hundred years ago. But you have forgotten and for us it is taboo. This is the first time in five hundred years that men have been masters of the air. As far as I know, this is the only ship left, though once there were many thousands."

Then I realized from his look that he did not comprehend the meaning of thousands. In all probability he could not read, nor count much higher than his fingers. I must try to get it across some other way.

"Don't you have any stories of how things used to be?" I asked him. "Tales of the long ago that you tell around the camp fire. Legends of the heroes in your past?"

He brightened immediately. "Stories they tell the children!"

"That's right! Aren't any of them about men who tried to fly?"

"There's the story about the Rights," he suggested. "That's a funny one."

"Go on," I urged him, feeling I was on the track of something very interesting. "What's funny about it?"

"You see, they weren't right . . . they were wrong. Only the bees can fly. And of course the birds. For men to fly is against the gods, and when these two brothers flew, it brought death and destruction from the gods until they were all dead."

So that's the story, I thought. I was about to tell him that the gods had nothing to do with it, but I changed my mind.

"So what do you think of our flying?" I asked him. "Will the gods be angry this time?"

Evan gazed somberly at the aircraft. "I don't know. It's a story to frighten the children. I'd forgotten it till now. But I want to fly. . . . I must! Please, Amhara! Are there really no more than this one?"

"This is the only one. It brought us here and we must guard it carefully so that it can take us home."

He seemed to understand this last well enough, for from then onwards he was always offering to help mount guard over the ship.

N'Gobi did not return with Menasi until almost an hour later, and by then the sun was on the horizon and they felt it inadvisable to take her up again. They saw Evan's disappointed looks.

"You'll go next time. No fooling," N'Gobi told him. "We'll want you to guide us. We couldn't spot a sign of your people. They must be well covered."

"The jungle is very dense on the main island," Menasi said. "Well, tomorrow you'll come along and show us where your people live. We should have thought to take you this time. At least the motors seem to be working well."

"Does that mean I can use the box tonight?" Zulli demanded.

N'Gobi frowned, but Menasi hastened to overrule his refusal.

"You're well fueled now and a lot has happened that we should report."

Zulli had her way, and the people at home learned of our discovery of a race of white men still inhabiting these islands. However, as it turned out N'Gobi's fears were justified. The next morning we woke to a dense fog blowing in from the sea, and later in the day it settled down to constant rain. There was no hope of taking Evan for his promised first flight, and once again communications were broken off in the interest of conserving fuel. I could imagine the impatient questions that were piling up at home, the excitement and speculation. But they would have to wait for better weather, just as we in the camp were waiting.

For four days we were held prisoners by the weather. It did not rain all that time, but the clouds were heavy and the fog always with us, and flying was out of the question. Menasi tried to get from Evan some idea of the kind of weather we could expect, but Evan merely stated that it would be as the gods wished. We schooled our impatience

121

as best we could and continued to study the problem of communicating with our native.

N'Gobi took him through the ship and showed him the points of interest, including our seating arrangements and the galley. These things held his interest only momentarily. What he wanted to know was how it flew. I could see that N'Gobi understood and sympathized with this drive for knowledge, but satisfying it was another thing. Many of the words and ideas seemed untranslatable. First we had the problem of getting it all clear in Afrian, and then I had to find the proper Anglic words. When I was at my wit's end, we would refer to Menasi's instruction booklet. Then, when we proudly pronounced the Anglic words to Evan, he had never heard of them. Moreover, while N'Gobi could explain which levers and controls produced which effect, and what dials indicated what condition, he often could not explain why. The theories behind this feat of engineering were not included in the instructions. No doubt such books could be found at home, locked up in some very, very taboo hiding place. In the meantime, N'Gobi operated in ignorance. He confided to me that as soon as he returned he was going to demand complete access to such books as his reward for his part in the expedition. And now when Evan asked "Why?"—as he was doing more and more often—N'Gobi was left scratching his head.

While the two of them spent happy hours bent over the motors and tracing the complicated network of wires, Zulli and I checked our supplies and came up with the expected answer. Unless something was done soon, rationing would have to begin. Menasi frowned when we explained the situation to him.

"If N'Gobi can discuss mechanics with him, we should be able to discuss the food supply. Perhaps we can go on from there to some of the other things that have been puzzling us. See if you can get those two away from the hangar and over by the big hut for a conference."

The boys did not like being interrupted, but when N'Gobi came, Evan followed. We all crowded into the hut out of the drizzle, and Zulli provided hot tea.

"It comes down to this," said Menasi. "Our supplies are

being used up faster than we expected. We don't begrudge the food to you, Evan. In fact, since you seem to be able to eat our food without ill effect, I imagine we should be able to eat yours. Now if you can show us what edible food your land provides, we'll be able to replenish our larder."

"You know," I simplified it for him, "plants . . . animals . . . what do you eat here?"

Evan looked at us in surprise. "You have not enough to eat?"

Plainly, he thought that "gods" like us must have a never-ending supply of good things. He considered for a few moments, and it was hard to tell whether his trouble was what to say or how to say it.

"This island," he said at last, "is the land of the drones. No good grows here. Not much to eat. But I'll find something."

With that he got up and went out into the fog, leaving us all in some perplexity.

"What do you suppose he means by 'land of the drones?'" asked Tadessa.

"That's a question," Menasi said. "Have you noticed that many of his allusions are to insects? And from what we have observed on our way up here, it seems likely that few, if any, animals survived the Disaster. In fact, I would guess that Evan's people survived in some distant and isolated spot and trickled back in only when the land became safer. At such time they probably found only insects, and these must have assumed unusual importance for them."

"What a horrible idea," said Tadessa. "No animals would mean no horses."

"Worse yet," said N'Gobi. "No dogs."

We all contemplated the idea of a world without animals, particularly horses and dogs.

"How dreadful!" exclaimed Zulli. It was becoming her stock phrase.

Menasi cocked an eyebrow at us. "It's only a suggestion. But we might ask him when he comes back. About cattle and chickens and wildlife, too."

"Of course, there are the birds," put in N'Gobi. "We know they hunt them, and probably eat their eggs."

We sat there, thinking up questions about animals ... enough to keep Evan busy answering for the next three hours. Then he returned and put all the questions out of our heads.

As he came in from the fog it was evident that he brought something in his hands. I don't know what we expected—a bird, or perhaps a rabbit. He held it out to Zulli and said, "Here. You can cook it."

It was a spider, and the biggest spider any of us had ever seen, fully as big as Tadessa's fist, and Tadessa had big hands.

Zulli screamed and knocked over her stool in her haste to get behind Tadessa. The men leaned forward with interest, and I could see "specimen" written all over their faces. Evan did not think of the spider as an interesting example of the local fauna. "Very good uncooked, too," he said. And before us all he began to pull off the legs and to take big bites of the still squirming body of the spider.

I felt my stomach rise up into my throat and determinedly pushed it back down. The men drew back and averted their gaze, and N'Gobi stepped hastily out into the fog. I presumed he had not been as successful as I in putting down his stomach's revolt.

Evan seemed unaware of the sensation he had created. He tossed the creature's legs into the fire and dusted off his fingers.

"Very good. I'll get some more for you," he said, and before we could protest he had disappeared.

"Did you see what he did?" cried Zulli. "He . . . he ate it!"

Fortunately for Zulli, she had been behind Tadessa and so had missed the full force of the demonstration. Otherwise, she would surely have joined N'Gobi outside if she could have gotten there in time.

"Like an animal!" she stuttered. "A savage beast!"

"Let's be calm about it," Menasi said. "Plenty of our people eat the flying ants at their swarming time. But I imagine our questions have been answered. No man would eat those things if there were animals available."

124

"If he brings another in here and eats it, I'm really going to be sick!" said Zulli.

N'Gobi, who had returned and was wiping his face, glanced at her with amusement.

"He's going to make you eat the next one," he said. At Zulli's cry of outrage he added, "Don't worry, we'll head him off. I take it Tadessa would like it for his collection."

"I must say I never saw anything like it," said Tadessa. "But perhaps he should be allowed to eat them and save our rations."

It was the only time I ever saw Zulli look disgusted with my brother.

"I'll go on short rations if necessary," she said. "But only make him stop, N'Gobi!"

"It's an interesting problem," Menasi mused. "I imagine they must grow something. Insects and spiders seem very little to build a hunting society upon. But we saw no signs of fields from our survey."

"Big country, few people," said Tadessa. "Take Evan next time you look. I think you'll have no trouble with him now. Have you noticed how his attitude has changed in a few days? He's happy, interested, cooperative."

"Almost another person," Menasi said. "Has he just gotten used to us, do you think?"

"It's my opinion he was suffering from shock that first day. Either that or he'd been drugged. I haven't made up my mind."

"He's really very nice when he isn't eating spiders," Zulli said. "But what changed him was the bath and shave. He's quite good looking now."

Tadessa appeared almost shocked. "You surely don't mean that! No white man. . . ."

Menasi put an end to the discussion with a critical quirk of his brows.

"There's something in what Zulli says. The change stems from the moment we cleaned him up. He seemed to take great pleasure in washing."

"I should think he would," said Zulli. "The way he smelled before!"

"Remember what N'Gobi heard him say," I put in, feeling that we were on the track of something important.

125

"He said that washing brought the gift of life, or something like that. You thought it had a religious significance."

"It must be more than that if it accounts for a complete change of character," Tadessa said.

"Well, whatever it is, there's another consideration." Menasi obviously thought this discussion had gone far enough. "What are we going to do with him when we go home?"

"Who said anything about going home?" demanded Tadessa.

"We may have to—and sooner than planned. For one thing, this weather poses a serious fuel problem. And for another, we're going to run out of food unless you can resign yourselves to eating spiders."

"Well, I suppose when you come right down to it, we've about covered our objectives. We have a small collection of specimens. And with a little more questioning of Evan and a couple of flights over his home camp or village, we ought to be able to leave here in a few days."

I saw the trend of their conversation and came to life in lively protest.

"But we can't go yet!" I cried. "You may have accomplished your objectives, but I haven't even begun. I haven't dug up a single site. I haven't even found one to dig! I didn't come all this way just to look at some overgrown spiders!"

"You've had a fine opportunity to practice your ancient Anglic," Menasi told me. "You'll be able to write a book on the proper pronunciation."

"But I haven't dug! I haven't found a single clue or artifact, and I'm not going till I do!"

"You'll do what I say. When I decide to go, we'll go. You and your diggings! You're as bad as Don Ylma."

"But you promised I could dig!" I cried, close to tears. "You promised on the way up here!"

"Well, get busy and dig! You don't need sun for that! Get Evan to show you where. But get on with it, for when I decide it's time to go, we're going!"

At this point N'Gobi came back with Evan—and without a spider. He looked at us in surprise, for it was unheard of to argue with Menasi.

"Amhara is feeling frustrated," Menasi told him. "She's afraid she'll go home without having dug up a site. Do you suppose Evan could show her a good place to dig? As long as we're tied down with this cursed weather, perhaps something could be done on the ground."

We all looked at Evan expectantly. It took a little while to explain just what I wanted. A ruin. An ancient city. Where people had lived in the long-ago. At last understanding came.

"I know one," he said. "I'll show you. Tomorrow I'll take you where the Old Ones lived."

Chapter Four

That is how I found myself, early the next morning, following Evan as he walked at a rapid clip around the south end of the island, back toward the spot where he had first led us down from the heights. I was armed with all my digging utensils, from pickax and shovel to the stone chisels recommended by Don Ylma. We had so much of this nature to carry that our other equipment was down to a minimum, and I brought only a light lunch in my pouch.

N'Gobi came along to see just where Evan was taking me. I had pooh-poohed the notion that there might be any danger that Evan could not cope with. N'Gobi did not want to leave the ship again, in case of clearing skies; and as Menasi and Tadessa both had scientific work to complete, they finally agreed that we two should go alone.

Evan's long legs covered the beach and climbed over the rocks at so swift a pace that even N'Gobi found it hard to keep up. I was soon trailing and out of breath. I could not understand what the hurry was, but as Evan had been urging haste since first light and I was only too anxious to get started at my long-awaited excavations, I did not protest but saved my breath to scramble after them as best I could.

At last we rounded the southeastern tip of the island and started north, and soon it was evident why Evan was urging speed. The tide was out, and extending into the sea toward the east was a long line of low rocks with the water breaking over them. At low tide they made a perfect bridge to a neighboring island, perhaps a quarter mile away, but as soon as the tide was turned the link with our island would be cut for another twelve hours.

Evan pointed. "Over there are dwellings of the Old Ones. But we must hurry before the sea locks the door. When the sun is low, the door will be open again and we can return."

N'Gobi looked at the water doubtfully. Menasi had explained to us about the tides, but it still seemed like black magic, and my cousin did not trust these wild waters.

"Are you sure?" he asked.

"As sure as the stars rise and set."

"And it's safe over there? No danger of any sort?"

"Oh, very safe. Nobody there. Just we two," said Evan, and as though he could read N'Gobi's thoughts, he added, "My people are far away, far beyond those shores." He pointed toward the rocky cliffs of the main islands that showed vaguely through the early mist.

N'Gobi threw off his obvious reluctance.

"Well, you'd better go while you can," he said to me in Afrian, speaking quickly so that Evan might not understand. "This is Evan's country so he should know what to expect. But keep your eyes open. Remember, after all he is a savage, without understanding of civilized ways."

I laughed. "Evan? Really, N'Gobi, are you losing your mind? You know he's all gentleness. And after what we've done for him, he literally worships us! I'd as soon be afraid of my dog at home."

"Dogs have been known to turn," muttered N'Gobi, but I could see he was ashamed, for he had come to like Evan. "It's Tadessa and Menasi who've been worrying me with objections. But if we're to accomplish anything, we can't all stay in one place. Well, hurry up, and don't fall in the sea while you're about it!"

He helped me out along the rocks for a few feet and then with a friendly pat let me go on alone.

Evan was already halfway across, and I gave my attention to the footing among the stones, balancing myself with the tools I carried. Soon I joined him on the other side and, turning, saw N'Gobi disappearing along the way we had come. Already the tide had turned and the sea was beginning to rise. I could see that it would not be long before the rocks were again covered.

Evan waited till I was safely across, and then picked up his burden and began to walk along the shore. I was glad we could now proceed at a more leisurely pace and I could once again get my breath and my bearings. The island seemed much like the one where we were camped, and although the beach was rocky, still walking there was easier than pushing through the bracken. We went around by the shore until we were once again opposite the mainland. The sun was beginning to break through the mists, and I congratulated myself that we had gotten off on this trek just in time. If we were now to have fair weather, it would be only a matter of days before Menasi finished his observation flights and ordered the whole expedition to start home. I had best take every advantage of this one day of opportunity.

When we approached the point of the island nearest the mainland, I noted some posts standing in the sea that struck me immediately as the work of man. They recalled the poles set up in our lakes by fishermen to support their nets. Even at ebb tide they stood low in the water, covered with the weeds and barnacles of centuries. Then it occurred to me that perhaps this land had been higher in the old days, as Menasi had observed during our flight up the western edge of the continent. In that case, the island where we now stood was once a part of the mainland, and the poles must have been near the shore, much higher, and perhaps used as a breakwater or to moor boats.

I asked Evan if this were so, but it took a deal of explaining to get the idea across to him, and then it seemed to be one that he had never considered. All I got out of him was that the island had always been thus and the sea thus as far back as his people could remember.

I recalled old pictures and descriptions of English fishing villages, and I felt that if the sea were to recede a few hundred yards, such a site might be revealed. In fact, the more interesting ruins might now lie beneath the waves, protected there from the erosion of weather and the creeping cover of the bracken above.

I walked slowly around the little bay with my eyes scanning the ground, and it seemed to me presently that the stones lay packed together more closely and regularly than could be expected in nature. Yes, there was a definite length and breadth and direction to it. A cobbled street! I was so intent on following this discovery that I failed to note that Evan had seated himself on some stones a little ahead of me and was waiting for me to catch up. When my "cobbled street" led me to his perch his voice woke me from my reflections.

"Look, Amhara!" he called. "The homes of the Old Ones!"

I looked and saw that he was sitting on the ruins of an ancient wall of stone and plaster. The sand had drifted into the interior and the bracken had grown over it, and little was left of the original house. Nevertheless, by careful scraping I could trace the outlines of rooms and walls. Evan soon caught on to what I was doing. His quick eye followed the lines of the buildings where they disappeared among the underbrush, and his skillful hands helped to clear the areas I indicated. At last, I had a respectable sketch of the probable outline and arrangement of the little village, or as much of it as still remained above the waves.

This work occupied the whole of the morning, and by noon we found we were tired and hungry and not a little hot. I called a halt, for Evan could apparently go on working indefinitely. He gladly followed me to a bit of shade and sat down with me to share our lunch.

"We'll eat now," I told him, "and then I must pick out the best spot and get to digging. I don't really expect to find anything startling here. This was only a little village, quite simple probably, and no great works of art or culture would likely be kept here. Still we may find interesting artifacts. What I should really like is to dig in a big city, but I suppose it's impossible the first trip. And those places may still be unhealthy for us."

I spoke in Anglic, as much as I could, so that he could understand, although he already followed a certain amount of Afrian. He seemed to find the idea of a city hard to understand.

"Old," he said, pointing at the ruins. "Very old. Always

131

like this . . . in pieces." He picked up a stick of driftwood that he had collected for our fire and tried to break it across his knee.

I watched with interest, surprised to note how tough it was. And then it came to me that it was not only driftwood. It had the definite shape of an oar and undoubtedly was just such an artifact as I was seeking. With a shout of "Don't burn that!" I jumped up and took it away from him.

Evan watched, astonished, as I examined it and pointed out its uses.

"Don't you see," I explained. "It's an oar, used to row a boat. It may have been in the sea and only lately washed up on the beach. But you can see the shape of it. Here's where it fitted into the oarlocks. And see how smooth it is, from much handling and use."

He listened closely but seemed to have little understanding, and I received the impression that his people did not follow the sea. This theory had been propounded by Menasi when explaining why they had not penetrated to our part of the world. But I was puzzled that they should not go to the sea for food. If they did not eat fish, and there were only insects on the land, what did they eat? Of course, there was the possibility that the fish were unhealthy from poisoned ocean waters, or had been so in the past, and that this had kept his people from developing that food source.

I was considering these things as I laid the oar down at my feet. My first artifact. I could see it displayed in the museum at home, and I fervently hoped I would have something more interesting to hang beside it. I went back to eating my lunch and let my eyes stray about the place in the hope that I might locate some other prize above ground.

It was then that I saw the pretty flowers. In fact, I had noticed them before, but had paid scant attention in my enthusiasm for mapping the ruins. Now it occurred to me that Tadessa did not have this kind in his collection and that I might as well take some back with me. The plants grew low to the ground but had remarkably large flowers and the colors were bright and pleasing. I rose and dusted off the remains of the meal. Picking up my oar, I walked over to decide which would make the best specimens.

Only then did I see the bee. It must have just come to the flowers, for no insect that large could easily escape notice. Perhaps I should have been prepared by the dragonflies and the spider, but a bee as large as a sparrow made me stop in my tracks. My next thought was that here was a far more interesting specimen than any flower.

I had not come prepared for such collecting and had nothing in which to carry a live bee. It would have to be a dead one; and without hesitation I raised the oar and brought it down on the unfortunate insect where it buzzed among the flowers. I had no idea how much force it would take to kill such a monster bee, but I did not want to tangle with an angry live one, and I hoped my blow would not crush it.

The next moment there was a startled yell from Evan, who came tearing up to me, grabbed the oar out of my hands, and began to shout.

"You killed it! You killed it!"

"Well, naturally," I grunted, stooping to examine the bee, which was indeed dead. "I'm not prepared to cope with a live one, but Tadessa would never forgive me if I let this specimen escape."

I was so intent on examining my trophy and stowing it away in the almost-empty lunch bag, that I did not notice the continued protests from Evan. Finally, it reached me that he was putting up strenuous objections to the slaying of one little—well, not so little—bee.

"I'm sorry if it distresses you, Evan," I said. "There must be lots more where this came from. Or don't you have lots of them here? Where I come from the bees are counted in the thousands and tens of thousands. But of course, they're only a fraction the size of this one. Surely, you can spare us just one to take home as an example of the remarkable insects in this land!"

My voice and words had a quieting effect, and Evan calmed down. He did not look quite as much as though he wanted to hit me with the ancient oar. But he was still very worried, and he strove, with words from our two languages, to make his feelings clear to me.

"The gods. . . ." he said. "The gods will be angry. You break the laws. A crime against the gods. Very bad things will come!"

"You mean bad luck?" I suggested.

"Bad luck? Bad work! Punishment is strict. I am already screened out. But you . . . you are only beginning. You have a long life ahead."

I was still trying to extract the meaning from this remarkable statement, when I saw him staring at me with a look of great intentness on his face.

"You are young—yes?" he demanded. "So you seem to me, young and have not yet borne children?"

Startled by this sudden shift to the personal, I began to think N'Gobi might have been right. This must stop right here, I told myself, and I stood up with all the dignity I could muster.

"I am not too young for an important expedition like this. I could have married and had children, but I chose to study. When I return will be time enough. Now let's get busy or we'll have wasted our time here to no purpose. I'd like to dig at the foundations of that large house on the knoll."

As I led the way to the site, I pondered his peculiar words. If it was true, as Menasi had theorized, that these people had no animals and that only insects and a few birds had survived in these lands, perhaps they had developed the ancient art of bee-keeping—as old as man himself—as one means of supporting themselves. Certainly, bees this size must produce great quantities of honey and wax. We had already seen how clever these people were at turning the spider's web into a kind of rope. What might they not do with the produce from these bees? If this were the main sustenance of the tribe, it would not be strange if the bees were held sacred.

The more I reflected on these things, the more fascinating they became. I told myself that if I could not now unearth valuable evidence of the ancient civilization, perhaps I could at least learn something of the present culture, and thus prove or disprove Menasi's theory.

As we worked, I tried tactfully to question Evan about his home and people. First I would have him dig for me with the shovel or the pickax. He was much impressed with these tools and delighted in using them, and his powerful arms soon loosened an area of earth and rocks—far more quickly than I could have done. Then I would tell him to rest, and while I carefully sorted through the debris, I threw occasional questions at him.

I began with the animals. Did they have dogs at home, I asked? Or cows? Or horses? To all of these words he returned a blank stare. Is it possible the language has changed that much, I wondered. Or am I mispronouncing again? Or is Menasi correct? I took time to smooth out the dust and draw a rough picture for him of each animal. He continued to stare and shake his head. To clinch the matter, I drew a bird.

"Bird . . . fly?" I said, drawing the wings both up and down.

He caught on at once.

"Yes, yes! Many birds. They fly. All are good to eat. Their eggs are good to eat, too." He seemed so glad to be able to respond positively at last that he babbled on about birds and eggs and where they built their nests, till I thought he would never stop to draw breath.

Well, this proves it, I thought, as I sifted through the rubble for anything made by human hands. Unless something very peculiar has happened to the language, Menasi is right. Evan has never seen an animal outside of his own kind. My mind tried to take in the implications of this, but I found it hard to envisage such a state of nature. What I did discover was that I was feeling extremely sorry for Evan—much as we had all felt when Tadessa suggested the idea of human sacrifice. I spoke kindly to him and thought that while he might not always understand the words, he warmed to the tones of my voice.

At last I noticed that the sun was getting low and there were dark clouds in the west. "I guess we might as well stop," I told him. "There just isn't much here. The oar is the best find after all."

Evan was reluctant to stop. Perhaps he realized without my telling him how disappointed I was.

"Little more digging," he grunted, thrusting the shovel between the rocks and heaving with all his strength.

The stones came up with a sudden spurt and sand flew in all directions. Evan inserted the shovel once more, and when he pushed, it went on through into a deep hole.

"Look, Amhara!" he called. "A cave! I found a cave for you!"

He tore out a couple more stones with his hands, making a sizable opening, and we peered into the darkness below.

"It's not a cave," I told him. "It's a cellar or second basement. Perhaps it's been sealed off for centuries. There may be all sorts of things down there. Oh, do hurry and make a bigger hole!"

I had no need to urge him. Evan was as excited as I, and with the shovel and pickax soon had made an opening big enough for us to climb through. The drop was about eight feet, and Evan easily let himself down and then helped me after him.

While we waited for our eyes to grow accustomed to the dark, Evan felt about with his hands, testing the smoothness of the walls and roof.

"A very good place," he muttered. "Dry . . . protected . . . make a very good hive."

I was going to ask if his people needed a room this size to house their bees when I remembered the size of the one in my pouch and I held my tongue.

Meanwhile, Evan enlarged the hole to give more light and arranged the debris we had knocked down into makeshift steps so that we could easily climb out again.

As soon as I could see a little, I began to explore. I felt my way around the walls and found the place where the stairs had led up to the house above. They had long since crumbled into dust, and the stairway was blocked where the house had fallen down on top of it.

I stumbled around in the darkness, sure that all sorts of treasures were escaping my notice. At last in desperation, I told Evan to light a fire. I knew this would probably result in a lot of smoke, but I decided to chance it, and sent him out to get materials while I continued my exploration of the darkness.

It appeared that the cellar we had discovered must have been looted before the stairway was blocked and its existence concealed. For how else account for the total lack of stores, tools, or such things as are generally kept in cellars. It looked as though I was to be disappointed once again, and the only question now was whether this was the original floor or a layer of debris beneath which I still might hope to locate something. If only Evan would come back with some wood and light that fire! At last, when my patience was exhausted, I fell over something at the back of the room. I felt around and my hand closed on metal rods. They seemed to have fallen from the wall, for they led into the earth against the wall, and by dint of stretching I could feel similar rods extending from the ceiling. Pipes! I had come upon some part of the plumbing system—an art in which the ancients excelled. With my fingers I tried to gauge the size of the bore. If only I could see what I was doing!

Just then Evan returned, but with very little kindling. Instead, he began objecting to building a fire at all, saying that it was later than he thought and we should leave at once in order to catch the low tide and get back to our island.

To be thwarted at this last moment was too much for me.

"Light a torch and bring it here!" I cried. "I've found something interesting. Hurry, so I'll have something besides that old oar!"

While I strained in the dark to loosen the pipes, Evan struggled with his stones and flints to make a fire. In exasperation I threw the firebox at him.

"Use that, and hurry up!" I scolded. "I could do better myself with the flints!" It was the first time I had spoken harshly to him, but at the moment I was taken up with my work and I realized he was right about the time.

Evan had learned the use of our mechanical firemaker at camp, and he quickly had a brand lighted and came over to me. If he felt the sting of my temper, he did not show it. Instead, he stared at the pipes, now clearly revealed along the floor.

"What is it?" he asked. "Do you want that? But for what purpose?" He was clearly puzzled at my interst.

"These were pipes," I explained. "They carried water to

the rooms above. Perhaps there was a well down here or a spring, or more likely they connected with water from another part of town. Everyone had water piped into his home this way. And look, here is a handle, probably used to turn the water off and on. And this looks like a faucet. Yes, so it is. Just help me dig it out."

Still looking doubtful, Evan went for the pickax. With one blow he severed the ancient pipe where I indicated. I soon had several short lengths, together with the faucet and handle. These we quickly carried out of the cellar along with our tools, and having extinguished the almost gutted torch, we set off as fast as we could on our return journey.

This took a bit longer than our trip out in the morning. Now we were tired after a day of exertion, and furthermore, loaded down with the pipes and the oar. The sky was darkening in the west, and I could not be sure whether it was from the lateness of the hour or the approaching storm. In any event, I was conscious of the need for haste; and I ran after Evan through the bracken and scrambled over the rocks till I felt ready to drop. At last we came out upon a little rise from where we could see the causeway of rocks, and Evan, who reached it first, signaled me to stop.

"No need to run farther," he said. "We are too late."

Still, I could not believe it till I climbed up beside him and stood panting and staring at the waves that broke over our rocky bridge, rushing across with such force that I knew neither of us could make it that night.

"Now what do we do?" I asked, sitting down to catch my breath.

"We wait. Tomorrow early the door will open again."

At least there was that assurance.

"I'm sorry," I said. "It's all my fault. If I hadn't stayed to get the pipes!" Still, I knew I'd do it over again if I had to. I stared at the curved faucet I held and wondered how it would look when cleaned up.

But Evan was thinking of more immediate things.

"We must find shelter," he said. "A big storm is coming."

I looked where he pointed and saw that even while we were talking the black clouds had gathered overhead.

"We could go back to the cellar," I suggested.

"Too far. I know a cave nearby. The storm will come quick now. I hear thunder."

I stopped to listen, and mixed in with the thunder was a different beat. Our talking drums! I jumped to my feet and stared at the distant shore. Yes, I could just make out N'Gobi walking back and forth and talking with his drum.

"Amhara!" the drum was calling. "Where are you, Amhara? Answer!"

"That's not all thunder," I cried. "That's N'Gobi talking. He's probably worried sick about us."

I ran down to the strand, with Evan after me, shouting and waving my arms. Unfortunately, the communication drum was one thing I had decided to do without on this little jaunt. We had too much else to carry. Still, if we could not talk to N'Gobi, he saw us when we waved from the shore, and it was evident that he was greatly relieved.

"Don't come now," he signaled. "Impossible. Find shelter and come in morning. Tide will be out again. Is everything all right? Stretch your arms high if you're all right."

I held my arms over my head, longing at the same time to be able to tell N'Gobi all about everything—our trip and the oar and the pipes and the faucet and why we were late, and that Evan knew of a good cave. But the waves and the wind drowned out my voice. All I could do was make the signal, and after N'Gobi had rapped out a quick "Take shelter then ... till morning," he turned and walked away around the point, back to our camp, where they would be busy making the ship safe to withstand the coming storm.

I turned to Evan and found him watching me with the greatest interest.

"He talks to you?" he asked. "Very good. Your men know many fine things. What does he say now?"

"He said we should find shelter and go back in the morning."

"He's right."

Without more delay, Evan picked up the tools and pipes and led the way along the shore until he came to a great rock. He pushed aside the bracken around it and revealed a small entrance to a snug, dry cavern. The first rain was just hitting us as we squeezed through the opening into our shelter for the night.

Evan went out almost at once to gather kindling for a fire; and I stowed our tools and other burdens out of the way at the back of the cave and brought in a few armfuls of fronds to spread upon the rocky floor. By the time Evan was back and we had the fire going near the opening, night had set in and the storm was upon us.

The thunder really roared now, and the lightning turned night into day. The rain came down in angry gusts, but behind the fire our cave took on a warm and cozy feeling. I searched in my pouch and found a few bits of leftover lunch. These I spread out in the firelight and divided evenly with Evan. At first he did not want to take any, and insisted that I should eat it all. I was quite touched.

"Go ahead," I said. "We've both worked hard. You were a tremendous help. Everything is fifty-fifty on a party like this."

"Fifty-fifty?" he repeated after me. "What's that?"

I was confronted again by the gulf between cultures.

"As soon as I get some time," I told him, "I'm going to teach you to read and write and count. Fifty-fifty means half. I'll explain it some other time. Look." I picked up a stick and broke it in two. "Half for you. Half for me. Fifty-fifty. Same with the food. Same with the watch. You think we should keep a watch?"

Evan was stumped again.

"Watch? Watch what?"

"Watch for danger. You sleep; I watch. I sleep; you watch. We did that all the way up here. Everything fifty-fifty. Fair and square."

Evan shook his head as he put the last crumbs of food into his mouth and licked his fingers.

"This is a safe place," he said. "No danger here. We'll both sleep. There's nothing to worry about."

I looked at him unbelievingly. He might feel safe, but I certainly did not. "But Evan—in this wild place?"

Yet I could see that he found nothing strange or threatening about it. After all, this was his home.

"But there must be some dangers," I faltered. "Don't you have enemies? The people who chained you out there? Some animals? Those giant bees I just saw?" I was grasping at straws. I remembered that Evan had intimated that the only animals in this jungle were insects and things like spiders.

Evan only laughed. "The bees! They cannot fly in this storm. They can bring death, yes. But only if you are marked, as I was at the Rock of Sacrifice. Now I am clean. You saw how N'Gobi helped me to wash."

I stared and held my breath. I was getting at something really basic.

"You mean—the executioners you mentioned were bees!"

"What else can fly to a signal and attack with a purpose?" Evan apparently thought it all clear as morning.

My thoughts were running over the bits and pieces that we had observed since that day when we rescued Evan, and a horrible picture built up in my mind. A swarm of angry bees, all the size of the specimen I now had in my pocket, descending upon the unfortunate captive, each ready with a poison sting.

"You mean to say, you were waiting for a swarm of bees? You were marked—with a smell?" He smiled and nodded cheerfully, but I was busy following the implications. I remembered how he had urged us to hurry away. "But they might have attacked all of us! They might have attacked the camp! We didn't make you wash till the next day!"

Evan seemed amused at my agitation.

"Surely not. I have told you that they cannot fly in bad weather. And the keepers would not release them. And they go straight to the Rock of Sacrifice, where the scent is strongest. So many have been marked there for death. As long as my people live in this Hive, they have used that place for the drones."

The drones. The word had a dark and sinister sound. I

recognized it as the word for the male bees, and I realized that I had stumbled upon some symbolism of the culture.

"Drones, Evan?" I asked. "What is a drone?"

He answered quite simply. "I am a drone. All men are drones. Don't you know that, Amhara?"

"Not with us, Evan. Men and women are all equal. But the bee drones—in winter they are thrown out to die." I had to get to the bottom of this. My mind kept asking, why, why?

The answer came without further probing. For Evan it was the natural course of things.

"So are we, Amhara, when we cannot be useful to the Hive. You eat your share of the stores and do not give your share to the future—you are screened."

"The future?" I repeated, still mystified.

"Don't your people have laws about birth and children? Don't you have many born dead or sick or deformed? All men who cannot father strong children are bad for the Hive. They are thrown out."

So that was it. I found myself staring at the fire. I could not look at him and think of what the Disaster had done to his people. What it must still be doing after five hundred years. Perhaps all these lands were still polluted, and we would return to Afria to face childless lives, as Don Ylma and Don Woldi had done before us.

Yet I could not think of myself when I understood the battle for survival that was still being fought by this remnant of the white race. Then another idea struck me.

"But how about the women?" I asked. "It could be as much the woman's fault if the child is wrong."

The answer came almost before I had finished asking.

"Women can work."

So the women were not sacrificed. More docile, perhaps. More ready to work and accept orders. My heart went out to Evan. Had he really fathered a taboo child? Perhaps several? He seemed so young. As I reached out a comforting hand, he looked up at me.

"But you are the bringers of life," he said. "Perhaps this is not so with you, with your people."

"Don't you see, it's the Disaster!" I cried. "You're living on poisoned ground. We have just a little country, but we've kept it clean. No, it's not so with us. And we won't give you back to your Hive. You're safe now with us. You can come home with us, Evan. I promise."

My protective instincts were aroused, and I swore that vow to myself also. Evan looked at me in complete trust.

"You do come from the gods," he said "The gods of life. There can be no danger near you."

Without further talk, he curled up on the fronds beside me and fell asleep. For a long time I lay awake, staring at the glowing embers, and I felt a different fear as I thought of my people. Many were still quick to censure N'Gobi and call him taboo because of his lighter skin. What would they say of Evan if we should be fortunate enough to reach home again, bringing him with us?

Chapter
Five

Evan was right. We slept well that night. Exhausted as I was by the previous day's work, I might easily have slept past the time for low tide. But Evan did not fail, and he woke me with a gentle nudge.

"It is time," he said, "if we are to pass through the door of the sea."

We hurriedly collected our belongings and crept past the dead fire's ashes and out through the narrow opening. As soon as we were in the open the wind whipped about us. It was blowing harder than ever, and while the rain had stopped for the moment, the mists made things almost as wet and it was impossible to see more than a short distance ahead. From out of the grayness came the thunder of surf over the rocks. I did not fancy climbing across that perilous bridge in this storm and fog, but I trusted Evan to find the way.

We went around to where the bridge should be, and once more we were disappointed. Although the time was right, the gale had whipped the waves to such heights that only an occasional rock was above water. It would be folly to try to cross. We sat down on the dripping stones and stared disconsolately at our impassable bridge.

"The gods must be angry," said Evan. "They make big winds and close the door."

I knew why he thought they were angry, but I refused to apologize for killing the bee. Instead I listened to the surf, and presently my ear heard more than the roar of angry waters. Yes, N'Gobi was over there behind the fog talking with the communication drum.

"Listen!" I cried to Evan. "Don't you hear the drum? It's N'Gobi talking to us. Listen, between the waves."

"What does he say?" asked Evan.

"He says not to risk a crossing now. That he'll come back in the afternoon and perhaps the storm will let up by then."

"I don't need N'Gobi to tell me that," Evan said.

"Don't you see, they're worried about us. And this time he can't even see if we're all right. If only there were something I could signal with."

"Why should he worry? I told him I'd take good care of you."

Nevertheless, Evan helped me bang on the rocks with every conceivable stone and stick, including our ancient pipes, although I quickly put a stop to that, as it seemed likely they would not stand up long under his vigorous pounding. Whether any of this got through to N'Gobi, we could not tell, but presently we realized that his drumming had stopped, and we sat in silence on the rocks while I felt deserted and alone. Another twelve hours of this! To make it worse, the rain started again.

Evan gently urged me to return to the cave, which reluctantly I did. We busied ourselves with making a new fire and stacking our tools and pipes once again at the back of the cavern. When these few chores were done, we sat down, and I began to realize that I was extremely hungry. And no chance of eating till evening. I looked at Evan. Perhaps he had been trained to ignore such things. Certainly, he would not mention it first. He sat and stared at the fire and the rain, almost in a trance, as he had done when we first brought him to our camp.

"Evan!" I said softly, and poked him with my elbow. "Evan, I'm hungry."

He came back to life at once.

"Yes, I know. I'm hungry, too. Your food is gone, yes? You should have eaten it all and let me find my own."

"Can you find anything in this godforsaken place?"

"Oh, yes. There's food all around. We just have to

look." He got to his feet. "You wait here. I'll bring something back soon."

A horrid idea struck me.

"Evan!" I called after him. "No spiders, please. No insects. Don't you have anything else? Perhaps a bird's egg. We could cook it in the fire."

"I have only my hands."

"Well, take the spade or anything else we have."

I tried to think what you could catch with a spade and realized acutely our lack of bow and arrow. Or Evan's snares. Still, what could you shoot in this fog? I must leave it up to him.

"Hands are best of all," Evan said, and he disappeared into the mist.

I waited for what seemed a long time but probably was not as long as I thought. To occupy myself, I looked over the pieces of pipe and other objects. Now, in the daylight, I could see them better. I got a stick and poked the dirt out of one so that I could peer all the way through it. I was busy doing this when Evan returned. He had been successful and had forgotten the slight to his gods.

"I bring you the best of all," he cried gaily. "Berries!" He put into my lap a basket of fronds, filled to overflowing with the biggest blackberries I had ever seen.

"Blackberries!" I exclaimed. "And like everything else here, they grow big."

"You know the name?" Evan smiled with pleasure. "Very good berries. You have them, too?"

"They certainly are good," I said, popping one into my mouth. "But now divide them up. Half for you. Fifty-fifty, remember?"

"That's not necessary. I found lots of spiders—where you couldn't see. Very good, too." He began to laugh at the expression on my face. "These are all for you. You eat them."

I was suddenly aware of an impelling need to do just that, and assured that Evan did not need his share, I began to devour the berries hungrily.

"You're sure they're all right now? Safe to eat?" I asked between mouthfuls, reminded that I was eating untested food and that Tadessa would not approve.

"Very good berries. We eat them all the time."

Well, if that was the case, they should be good for me, too, and I lost no time in putting them inside me. While I ate, Evan watched me with satisfaction.

"Good, huh? You like them? Better than spiders?"

He laughed again, teasing me. Then he grew sober and I could see he was thinking as he watched me.

"Amhara," he began, "you know many things. How to read and write and be what you call 'civilized.' Now tell me one thing. Why are you afraid to eat good berries? Why are some things poison? Like those old cities where you want to go and my people say it is very bad? Why?"

"Don't you know?" I asked. "Don't your people know?" Surely, they must at least have a myth or legend to explain it.

But Evan shook his head. No, his people said it was always thus and had been the will of the gods.

Well, I had lots of time at my disposal today.

"Look, Evan," I said, holding out my hands with the fingers spread. "Ten."

He got that right away. They still had the word ten in the language.

"All right. Now ten times ten." I opened and shut my fingers ten times. "That's a hundred. Now think of a hundred years, a hundred summers."

"That's a long, long time," said Evan.

"For us, maybe. But not for your tribe. Three generations, perhaps. How long do your men live?" I figured on the hard life and hazarded a guess. "Fifty years?"

"No man lives fifty years."

"No? Well, how old are you?"

"Twenty-five."

"Well, you're strong and healthy; you should last another twenty-five easily."

"I told you, I've been screened. I am finished." He looked up at me in trusting innocence. "When you and N'Gobi came and cut me loose, I thought you must be sent by the gods. There must be something still for me to do."

In some perplexity, I decided to try another tack. "You

really do not know how all this came about?" I asked. "The poisoned lands?"

"How should it come about?" he asked wonderingly. "It was ever so. It is the will of the gods."

"On the contrary. The gods had nothing to do with it. It is the work of men. You remember how I explained one hundred years—a very long time? Now think of five times that—five hundred years."

"Surely, as many as the stars in the sky!"

"Well, not quite. But a very, very long time. Some five hundred years ago that ruin we dug in yesterday was a village full of people . . . white people like you, not black like me. And the cities where you dare not go were huge dwelling places full of many, many people, and they had all kinds of machines to travel over the land and sea and to fly through the air and to make everything they needed. But they fought among themselves. They had very deadly weapons. They not only killed each other, they destroyed their cities and poisoned all the lands besides, so that nothing could live there and whatever escaped from these lands would never bring forth good offspring. In the whole world, only a very little bit of land remained safe and healthy, and that is where my people live. At first we had much the same trouble you have, but now for many generations our people have bred true again. Now do you understand how it happened?"

Evan only stared at me. "Impossible!" he insisted. "No people would do that. No people. It is the gods who are angry."

How much more pleasant, I thought, to believe the gods did it than to know your fathers destroyed your world! We could always put it off on the white race, whatever the truth of the matter might be. They were no longer around to defend themselves. I was beginning to suspect the truth of that story and to think that all peoples were capable of all things, given a set of circumstances. I looked at Evan, who kept repeating, "It is the gods!" as though to shut any other idea out of his head, and I wondered whether it was right to disillusion him.

"Look," I said, "You may not think it possible that your forefathers could kill off a whole world, but how about what your people are doing right now? They want to kill you and you're still a strong, healthy individual, an asset to any clan, I should think."

"That's different," he said. "It is the law."

I saw that it would take a lot of argument and demonstration to convince him, and I was getting pretty tired of hearing about the "will of the gods." Let him figure it out in his own way, I thought. Then all consideration of the matter came to an end, for just then the pain hit me.

It was a sharp, stabbing pain in the abdomen, and as I stood up to relieve what I thought to be a cramp, I suddenly felt very sick. Without a word to Evan, I ran out of the cave, and I just made it into the bushes beyond the entrance. As I painfully got rid of the blackberries, I reproached myself for having eaten untested food. Tadessa was surely right about that! I leaned weakly against a tree as wave after wave of nausea assailed me, and I fervently wished that I were dead. The rain was coming down harder than ever, and I saw no prospects of being able to return to the cave, for every time I straightened up I felt sick again. Moreover, I was so weak and dizzy that I wondered if I could find my way back. Then, from a long way off, I heard Evan calling me. I wanted to run and hide, to keep this disgraceful sight from him. I remembered with regret how we had all laughed at Zulli when the airplane made her sick. But I had no airship to blame, only a few ridiculous berries. Still I was quite unable to move or to call out, and suddenly Evan was there with his arms about me.

"Amhara, Amhara!" he cried. "How did this happen?"

"Go away," I mumbled. "I'm going to be sick again."

"Then be sick," he said. "But you must not be out here in the rain." And he picked me up and carried me back into the cave.

Well, I thought, there's some advantage to a primitive friend. He isn't disgusted by the rawer aspects of life. Indeed, no one could have been more solicitous. He spared no pains to find the best spot for me to lie on and to bring fresh fronds to lay under my head and water to wash my face.

149

"I can't understand it," he kept saying. "Berries never make me sick."

"Are you sure they're the same berries?"

"All the same. I ate many myself before I brought you those."

"You must be immune to it."

"Im . . . what?"

"You're used to them."

"Still I don't understand." Evan was greatly distressed. "Wait—I'll get special leaves and make you a drink. It cures all sickness. Very fine."

I shook my head. "No. I can't drink it. I don't dare. What's good for you is death for me. Let me alone. I'll get over it."

He saw the sense of this argument and came back to sit by me with a look of anguish on his face. I tried to think of words to reassure him, but I had no idea how potent a poison I had absorbed. I must have thrown up all the berries, I thought. Presently I was sure to get better. But just then the pain returned and so sharply, seeming to rack my whole body, that whereas I had previously thought it would be a relief to die, now I really feared I might. I began to have chills and shook and shivered on the bed of ferns.

Evan ran about, alternately making up the fire, tucking my inadequate kente about me, and offering me water to drink.

"What can I do?" he cried. "There must be something to do! Only tell me!"

What seemed a long time later I found his arms around me and my head on his knees.

"Don't die, Amhara!" he was sobbing. "You're all I have left of life."

"If only Tadessa were here," I whispered. "He's a doctor. He would know what to do. He has drugs and things."

"Tadessa! Yes, Tadessa!"

Evan laid me back and got up to go, with some crazy idea of crossing the narrows before low tide. But I seized hold of him.

150

"Don't go!" I cried. "Don't leave me! I don't want to die alone."

That brought him back and he sat down again, asking how I felt and offering endearments and getting no reply. It seemed to me that the cave was getting colder and the fire dimmer and my last conscious thought was that I had foolishly gambled away all my hopes, the expedition's success, and my life as well, just because I was hungry.

Beyond that I remember no more, for my mind was too dulled for coherent thought. There was only thirst and pain and a grateful darkness that was more than sleep.

Afterwards I was told how Evan, at his wit's end, had gone out to survey the sea and the causeway and had found the storm abated and the waves less violent. Although it lacked several hours of low tide, he had come back for me and carried me, unconscious, down to the shore. Using the ancient oar as a staff to support himself and feel out the rocks, he had somehow waded across, with the waves coming chest high and me across his shoulder.

It was a feat of strength and daring that brought frank admiration from N'Gobi and unstinted praise from the rest of our party. In fact, Tadessa never tired of describing his astonishment when Evan staggered into camp and laid me at his feet with the order, "You cure her quick!"

Since it was much too early for the rocks to be above water, no one had expected us. I can well imagine the consternation when they discovered how sick I was; the scurrying around for a clean bed and medicines and such; the demands that Evan explain the situation and the difficulties with the language.

The first I heard of all this was Tadessa's voice ordering Zulli to "hurry up and get me the sterile syringe, and where in blazes is the alcohol?" I knew I was home at last. I was in camp with my own people and my trust in Tadessa knew no bounds. He had turned out to be a top Medic after all. I lay with my eyes closed and savored the taste of it and I wondered how I had ever mistrusted him or Zulli or any of them. Then I knew that we had become one team that could work together and help each other without question and that whatever happened to us when we returned—if we returned—it would always be so.

Then Zulli said, "She's breathing easier. I think she's going to come out of it."

I opened my eyes and saw them all watching me.

Tadessa said, "Take it easy. Don't say anything unless you feel up to it. But when you do, just tell me what happened. I can't make head or tail of what that native says."

"Blackberries," I whispered. "Just a few little blackberries. I was so hungry I ate them."

A sigh went up from my friends.

"And he gave them to you?" asked Menasi sternly.

"It's not his fault," I cried, trying to sit up. "He meant well. He eats them himself."

"I eat them all the time," said Evan in his odd accent. He was sitting somewhere near my head, out of my line of sight.

"Take it easy!" warned Tadessa, pressing me back onto the blankets. "And the next person that gets her excited can leave the hut!" He actually glared at Menasi. "We've got everything under control. I've shot you full of enough stuff to lick a million blackberries. But who'd have thought it! Now Zulli's mixing you up a nice drink, and you're going to have a good sleep, and when you wake up you'll feel better and can have some soup and we'll get you well in no time."

I had to hand it to my brother. He had the perfect bedside manner. I followed his orders without a murmur and found that I was very tired and happy just to sleep. As I was dozing off I stretched my arm above my head and felt my fingers link into Evan's strong ones. I wondered for a moment if he would now be exiled for exciting the patient, but I was too tired to give it further thought.

It was well on into the following afternoon before I awoke. Zulli was sitting beside me. As soon as I moved she ran to get Tadessa who came, felt my pulse, took my temperature, performed other medical routines, and then told Zulli to bring on the soup.

To my surprise, I found I was ravenous. I ate it all and felt distinctly better, but Tadessa said I must rest for at least twenty-four hours and that it might take several days to get my strength back.

"That was a close call. If Evan almost killed you by mistake, he also saved your life by getting you here when he did, at a big risk to you both." He went on to tell me how Evan had forded the narrows and brought me back.

While he talked I thought over what had happened and I was bursting to tell them all about it. Tadessa said to wait. I should not tire myself.

"At least let me give you the specimen I brought," I said. "It'll knock your eye out!" Then I remembered. "I don't suppose I've got it!" I cried. "All the things I dug up and the pipes and the tools. They must still be in the cave."

Zulli laughed. "That Evan! He understands you all right. He said you'd want all those things. This morning he and N'Gobi went back and got them."

"Everything's safe at the back of the hut. So forget about it till tomorrow," Tadessa advised.

"Just let me give you the insect," I insisted. "It's in my pouch where I carried the lunch. Did they bring that back?"

Zulli was already retrieving it from the pile of my belongings. I turned it upside down and shook, and out fell the bee. I thought their eyes would pop out of their heads.

"What is it?" cried Zulli. "It can't be a. . . ."

"That's what it is," said Tadessa. "A giant bee. The counterpart of those dragonflies that we didn't get. This is something, Amhara!"

He picked it up carefully by the body, avoiding the stinger and trying not to hurt the wings. He whistled softly as he looked at it.

"Alcohol, Zulli, and a good, big bottle."

While he was admiring it, Menasi came in, and the two of them went into a scientific huddle. They couldn't stop thanking me, and said I had presented them with the specimen of specimens, the exhibit of exhibits.

"Even if you don't dig up anything of value for yourself, Amhara, this is terrific," Menasi told me.

"I've got more than that for you," I replied. "I've got

the connection with Evan's people. Look at the stinger on that creature."

"I wouldn't like to be on the receiving end, that's sure," said Tadessa.

"Well, imagine a swarm of those things coming at you. There's the executioner that Evan was waiting for. They couldn't fly as long as the weather was bad. We got there just in time."

"Oh, no!" cried Zulli.

Tadessa and Menasi looked at each other. Then they both sat down beside me and listened to my account of all that Evan had told me. Tadessa's injunction to "take it easy" was forgotten, and, for my part, I was glad to be able to share this story with others.

When I had finished, Menasi sighed. "Remarkable," he said. "Most extraordinary. We really ought to have a look at that village before we leave. What with our short supplies and the apparent toxicity of food sources around here, I was resigned to leaving as soon as you recovered. But now—what do you think, Tadessa? Could we squeeze in a short trip to Evan's village?"

Tadessa was thoughtful, weighing the factors in his mind. "It all depends. If she recovers quickly and we could go right away. . . . But if we have to negotiate with them first . . . and under the circumstances I don't know how good an emissary Evan will make . . . if it takes a lot of dickering to go there peaceably, I'd say not. We'd jeopardize the expedition. And we know quite a lot as it is. If we take Evan home with us and question him further there, when he knows the language better. . . ."

"You surely aren't thinking of leaving him?" Zulli broke in. "To those terrible bees!"

The way she said "terrible bees" made us all laugh and broke the tension.

"I'd like to take him," Menasi assured her, "If N'Gobi thinks the ship will carry the added load. Of course, we have a lot less stores, but then there are the specimens, and we'd have a food problem. And for all you know, he may not want to go."

"I think he'll go," I told them.

They all looked at me.

"You seem to have him hypnotized," Menasi observed. "Well, after all, you saved his life. You and N'Gobi."

"Where is Evan?" I asked suddenly. It occurred to me that it might be tactless if he should walk in and find us discussing him like this. But Menasi reassured me.

"You'll never guess. N'Gobi is teaching him to fly the ship. When he first brought you back, he'd do nothing but crouch in the back of the hut and watch everything that Zulli and Tadessa did. Once he was sure you were getting better, he took to following N'Gobi around. They went back for your tools and things and then they made a couple of scouting flights. I went along once and he pointed out the land below. N'Gobi says he has a natural feeling for the controls and for any kind of machinery. Yes, I think he will go back with us, and not all because of you."

About this time Tadessa remembered his previous order for rest and quiet. He took Menasi away to the main hut to examine the bee in more detail, and left strict orders with Zulli that I should not be disturbed.

It was not till almost twenty-four hours—and two good meals—later that N'Gobi managed to get by Zulli's guard and into the hut for a talk with me. He said that Evan was impatiently waiting, but that Tadessa still insisted on keeping visitors down to one at a time.

On the strength of that order he chased Zulli out.

"Don't tell me anything!" he said to her. "There's absolutely nothing left for you to do. You've fed her so much she'll get sick again if you aren't careful. You've taken her temperature and her pulse and her blood pressure, and Tadessa swears she's on the mend. Now I've got leave to visit her and you can get out. Only one at a time, remember? There must be plenty of chores that you've been neglecting."

Zulli made a face at him and left, urging me to call if I wanted anything and to be sure to let him do all the talking.

When she had gone, N'gobi sat down by me. "Well, that's better," he said. "And you look better, too. I knew if we all went away and let Tadessa do his stuff, you'd get well."

He was trying to be casual, but I could see that he had been worried.

"I want to thank you for getting all my things out of that cave," I said. "Lucky you didn't get marooned over there, too."

"Oh, it was Evan's idea. We rushed over when the tide was low and hurried right back before the door closed, as he puts it." He chuckled at the thought of Evan's quaint expressions. "He's out there now, waiting to see you. But I was sort of glad of the chance to see you first alone. He's got plenty of patience, if nothing else—as long as we assure him you're all right. And he's got native ability or something when it comes to machines. You should see how he caught on about the ship! Learned almost all I know myself. But you have to show him. The drawings mean nothing to him. You must teach him to read, you know. Did you hear Menasi is figuring on taking him back?"

"Will there be room?" I asked, while my whole being cried out that there must be room.

"We'll manage. And he can help with the piloting. He's good at that already. Strange business, though."

"Did Menasi and Tadessa tell you everything I told them?"

"They did indeed. It's hard to believe, except that I know Evan. And I've come to like him, you know. Aside from the fact that he saved your life. You know that? How he managed it, I'll never understand. I'd have been washed away for sure."

He looked at me calculatingly, as though wondering how much he could discuss without breaking Tadessa's orders.

"You really like him?" he asked at last. "You think we should take him back? It will mean close quarters and who knows what they'll say at home."

If he had expected to get a rise, he got one.

"We've got to take him!" I cried. "Menasi agreed! It would be cruel to leave him!"

"Take it easy," said N'Gobi. "Want to get me thrown

out of here? Keep your voice down. I just asked to learn how you feel about it. He's really our responsibility, you know. You and I—we stepped in between him and his tribe."

"It's a senseless and barbarous custom!" I said, trying to keep the emotion out of my voice.

"Granted. One thing we all agree about, and none more than I. I guess I feel it more than any of us, unless. . . ." He stopped, with a careful look at me. "How much does he really mean to you, Amhara? Deep in your heart?"

I nearly jumped from the bed. I was shocked at his suggestion and also that he should try to tell me what to do.

"No more than a human being who sees another mistreated and condemned for no just cause. You should know how I feel about that."

He bowed his head. "I know," he said softly. "But there's much you can never know. Evan will be taboo, even more than I. I hope you need not learn what it's like to put your heart on something—or someone—and have the door closed as taboo."

I wondered then what girl N'Gobi might have loved and lost while I was away at Har, but I refused to ask further.

"We'll have to press the fight against these outworn beliefs," I told him. "Just seeing Evan should help. He's no monster. Even Zulli has changed her thinking!"

"I hope you're right," he said. "But you know so little of how things really are. And then there's Evan himself. Have you thought how he feels?"

"N'Gobi! How can you? You're being ridiculous and you know it!"

"Not so ridiculous when I see how he looks at you—and you sometimes at him. But forgive me if I spoke out of line. I've not had the benefits of education at Har. I only know what I see. Even without taboo, his whole life has been too different from ours! Think about it when you have time."

"I'm not the only one he looks at!" I answered hotly. "I hear he's been following you around like a homeless dog."

"That's because he likes the airplane," said N'Gobi, and

added, "I can't say that I blame him. Now it's his turn with you. I'll send him in."

And as though putting a period to our argument, my cousin went quickly out of the hut.

I tried to put N'Gobi's words out of my mind as I prepared myself to greet Evan. I must thank him for all he had done for me, even saving my life. They all admitted that he'd done that. As I thought about it, I felt my excitement rising. This is no way to behave, I told myself. A serious scientific student on an important expedition! N'Gobi is right after all. Evan's culture—if you can call it that—is too different. And there's no doubt that in Har he'll be taboo. But just that difference posed a fascination, and I saw in my mind's eye Evan's earnest, trusting face and his remarkable blue eyes. Ylma, I thought, you never told me they could be like this!

Just then the curtains parted and Evan came in, ducking in order to get through the hut's low doorway, and sat down where N'Gobi had been. He seemed content just to sit and look at me until I began to feel uncomfortable. I reached out for his hand, and he responded with a warm clasp.

"Feel better? You'll be well soon, and out in the sunshine again."

"Just when I get sick, we have fair weather! But I hear you've been putting it to good use. The airship can fly again."

His face lit up with the most engaging smile, and I realized that I'd had small chance or reason to see him smile till now.

"A great thing, the airship!" he said. "And N'Gobi's a great man. He's teaching me. We go flying all over the sky. You'll come with us soon?"

"As soon as Tadessa will let me. Maybe tomorrow."

He grinned again, but then he grew serious.

"This airship, it is one of those machines you told me about? Made by old, old white men, huh?"

"That's right," I said, and I could see he'd been thinking about the matter and turning it over in his mind. "Five hundred years—remember? Five hundred long years ago your people were flying in such ships. They invented them, were the first to build them and many other wonders."

"But how . . . how could a tribe know all that . . . make such great wonders . . . and also do what you said?"

"Everyone makes mistakes," I told him, and reproached myself for the inanity of my reply.

Evan's eyes glowed. "That's no mistake. That's a crime against the gods. To be paid for with death."

"That's just how they paid, and you're still paying. We must be sure we don't go on making the same foolish and terrible mistakes."

He was staring at me, and I remembered what N'Gobi had said: *"I see how he looks at you!"* Ridiculous! N'Gobi was foolishly worried. I pushed the thought from my mind.

"You tell me many strange things," Evan said. "I don't know which to believe. But I know you want those pipes and other things we dug up on the island."

"That was very thoughtful of you and N'Gobi, to go all the way back to get them."

He shrugged it off. "That was easy. I think maybe they aren't worth so much. I think maybe you are disappointed. And maybe I know where you can find much finer things."

I sat up with a suddenness that almost knocked Evan over. "You do? Where? What sort of things?"

What was I doing, lying around in the hut with only a few days left and a chance of finding incalculable treasures! Evan only grinned as he saw that he had made an impression.

"I know a cave. A sacred cave of my people. It's not easy to get to. But Menasi talks of going to see my people. If we go, perhaps I can show you. It may be difficult, but I'll try."

"But what's in it?" I insisted. "Don't you have any idea?"

"Very old things. Belong to old, old people. But it's taboo for me. Men are not allowed in the cave."

"But you must know something about it!" I was quite tantalized.

"I think some things like yours . . . to read and write . . . books?"

"Well, what do the books say? You must have some idea."

"Nobody reads anymore. Only old, old ancestors read books. I think perhaps they are chants for the gods."

"Religion? Well, tell me how you serve the gods."

Evan seemed to be in deep thought. All at once he began to intone in a strange sing-song voice:

"Where the bee sucks, there suck I."

"Shakespeare!" I literally leaped from my blankets. "Evan, if it's the only thing I do here, I've got to see those books!"

He came alive with a jolt. "If you want it, you shall have it. I'll get you anything you want!"

He spoke with such fiery assurance that once more I felt the jolt of N'Gobi's warning. But my mind was focused on my work and the fantastic possibilities that Evan's words suggested. I could think of nothing but my hope of visiting that cave.

Just then a low whistle sounded from outside the door. I might have thought it some woodland bird, had I not known better. N'Gobi was on guard. I was back in bed by the time Menasi came in, followed by Tadessa, to see what the shouting was about.

"What's going on?" he asked. "A little less excitement around the patient."

"Wait till you hear," I told them. "Evan knows a cave where his people live and it's full of books and other things, and it sounds like Shakespeare!"

Tadessa took hold of my wrist. "Well, aside from the fact that your pulse is unusually high, there doesn't seem to be much more the matter with you. I don't see why we can't move camp tomorrow."

Then they told me that it had been decided to make a short trip to see Evan's people. There was no good landing place for the ship at the village, and N'Gobi did not want to place his precious machine in too close proximity to the primitives. He had picked out suitable camp ground in an easily defended spot near a lake, that was only a short hike from Evan's village. We would move everything to the new site and then a selected group would walk the few miles.

"If you will promise to follow orders and not exert yourself, but let the rest of us do the work, we'll start the move tomorrow. It should take only a few days to set things up, and a couple more to inspect the village. After that we'll head for home. The whole schedule hangs on our not being bogged down by more bad weather."

"How about the cave with the books?" I demanded. "You've got to give me time to look into that!"

Menasi looked at N'Gobi. "What do you think? After all she's been through, it's a pity to bring home only a few pipes."

Our pilot gave me a searching glance. "Well, if you're sure Evan can lead you right to it, and you don't delay the schedule. But don't get into any more trouble or you're liable to wreck the whole plan."

Chapter Six

It took two more days to move the camp. Menasi, N'Gobi, and Evan were the advance party. They took turns, one man flying the machine while the other two unloaded and prepared the new site. At our end, Zulli and Tadessa dismantled the equipment and helped load it into the airship. With all this activity going on, I was forced to sit quietly on a roll of blankets and watch. Tadessa and Zulli made sure I did not so much as lift a finger.

The huts were all pulled down and as much as seemed feasible was flown to the new camp, so that we did not have to waste time cutting material for new ones. We confidently expected that we would need them only for a day or two. The specimens were packed into the back corners of the ship, where they could stay until the day we should return to Har. In fact, the plan was to load the ship as much as possible for departure and set up only a skeleton camp at the new location.

Toward evening of the second day the last of our equipment was packed, and I was invited to enter the ship. So far we had been lucky. The good weather had held. N'Gobi had been able to keep the fuel up in spite of all the flying back and forth. If we had been caught by fog and rain with our camp divided, unable to fly and unable to refuel, we would have been in a difficult position.

It was with feelings of relief and anticipation that we took off from our island for the last time and flew toward the mainland. The western sun lighted the rocks and cliffs of that desolate coast with the waves breaking eternally as they must have done when all this world was alive with ships and sails and human habitations. We passed over the cliffs and the barren land and an expanse of thick jungle and came at last to a sparkling lake among the hills with a clearing where I saw our reconstructed huts (now reduced to two) with the cook fire going and enough space reserved for our safe landing.

The men quickly explained their arrangements to Zulli and me. We two should sleep in the cook hut and the men would occupy the other shelter. We fervently hoped the rain might hold off so that N'Gobi would not bring up the subject of a shelter for the ship. All but the most necessary equipment was left aboard, including our food, which was brought out in meager rations as we needed it.

That night we held a council to decide who should go on the trek to Evan's village. It was obvious that he must go, and I could see that both Tadessa and Menasi wanted to be on the list. But it was equally obvious that sufficient guards must be left with the ship. If anything happened to that, we were lost.

I found that all my companions were looking at me.

"By rights Amhara should not go anywhere," Menasi began, "but I'm wondering about the language problem. Even though we've all improved and seem to be able to communicate somewhat with Evan, still there's no telling what we may run into, and I'd hate to risk a failure just because of that."

"Is that all you're worried about!" I broke in. "How about me? Evan had promised to take me to that treasure cave and if you think I want to miss that. . . !"

"It's not what you want to miss; it's what your health will permit. We can't afford to wait around here until you're stronger. The food situation is acute as it is."

"My health is absolutely fine again," I protested. "I've been resting for the last few days till I'm sick and tired of it. I've done everything just as you said, even when it seemed silly. But now if you don't let me go to that cave. . . ."

"Calm down," said N'Gobi. "You'll get to the cave. The question is how soon. Personally, I think you seem back to normal. But don't try to fool us. We can wait a day or two."

"I'm glad you think so," said Zulli. "Have you counted the stores lately?"

"I'm coming to that. I have a plan. We've all been worrying about what we're going to do if Evan's people offer us food to eat. After your experience nobody dares to eat anything."

"How about it, Evan?" asked Menasi. "Will your people want to feed us?"

Evan looked puzzled. "Never have people like you come before. But, yes. They'll make a feast, most likely."

"It's going to be a problem," said Tadessa with a worried frown.

"Not at all," N'Gobi said, "if you're tactful and skillful. Of course, I don't intend to go. I'll stay with the ship and be ready in case we need a quick take-off. But whoever does go must take enough food in his pouch. When offered a meal at the village, he must pretend to eat, but carefully substitute our own rations. And be sure to collect everything the villagers give you in your pouch and bring it back. We'll take it along and have a couple of days rations for Evan. That way we'll stretch our own food."

Menasi's eyebrows shot up in surprise. "Why didn't I think of that? But we may have to be good actors. How about it, Evan? Will it work?"

"I think it's a wonderful idea!" cried Zulli. "Bring back as much as you can for Evan." She stopped as an idea struck her. "Only suppose . . . suppose Evan. . . ."

The same horrible idea occurred to me. Suppose Evan's people would not let him go. My anger began to rise at the thought. They had cast him out to die! They had no more right to say what he should or should not do! Still, none of us could predict in advance how things would work out. I began to wish Evan could be left at our camp. But that was manifestly impossible. He would be required to show us the way and to introduce us to his people, and, finally, I would never be able to find that cave without him.

Menasi put a stop to Zulli's fears with a quirk of his brows. "Let's hear from Evan about this. Will it work, Evan?"

Evan looked from one to the other, bewildered. The

language barrier kept him from sensing the subtle exchange of doubt and anxiety. It was hard enough for him to keep up with the plans being outlined.

"I think all will go well," he said at last. "My people will be surprised to see me. More surprised to see you. But now you have set me free, they must agree."

"But the food problem, Evan," urged Tadessa.

"The food will work out all right. You'll eat your food. You'll bring food back for me. A very good plan."

"Then that's that," Menasi said, and I could see that the discussion was over and we would now receive our orders. "We'll leave in the morning if you're sure you've recovered, Amhara. Give her a good check-up first thing tomorrow, Tadessa. And you'll come along, of course. Be sure to bring some medicines just in case. Zulli will stay here with N'Gobi. That should be sufficient guard. Now get to bed everyone. You, especially, Amhara. We don't want to postpone this trip unless absolutely necessary."

I spread my blanket near the lake. The cook hut was too stuffy. I was determined that Tadessa should find nothing to balk at in my check-up next morning. But it was a while before I could fall asleep. I heard the soft voices of Zulli and N'Gobi counting the stores and making up our food packs for the morrow. Tadessa was sorting over his medical kit and scientific gear and discussing with Menasi who should carry what. At last the night chorus of insects and the lapping of water from the lake lulled me to sleep; and the next thing I knew Zulli was shaking me and asking if I "really felt like it today," as in that case we must hurry to get an early start.

After that everything went quickly. Zulli seemed to ignore the rationing entirely and made a point of urging food upon me. After breakfast, I went off to Tadessa for my check-up and was relieved when he said he could find nothing wrong with me. When this was announced to the others, there was a great hurrying to get ready. Equipment was checked over and packs donned. Evan insisted that I would not need digging tools in the cave, but I took one rock chisel just to be on the safe side. We all had a day's food rations and took along those items we could spare as presents to Evan's people. At the last moment I agreed to give away the pickax as it seemed that I would have little further use for it. Tadessa, of course, had his medical and scientific kit, and Menasi took a small communication drum. This time we would be able to keep in touch.

When we were all ready to set out, I noted that Menasi also took with him the weapon of lightning that the Wasan's guards had given him. It was the first time he had brought it out . . . a long, spearlike affair that he slung over his shoulder. We were all armed with knives or arrows, but I could guess that Menasi judged this to be the most dangerous undertaking of the entire trip and intended to be prepared.

We knew we had a fair climb and hike ahead of us through hills and jungles. We hoped to reach the village well before noon, spend several hours with Evan's people, and return by nightfall. We would have to set a fast pace, and as we said our good-bys to N'Gobi and Zulli, I wondered if we weren't carrying too much. Still, we would leave the presents with Evan's people, and for all I knew there might be nothing worth bringing back from that cave.

I told myself all this, as we walked at a brisk pace around the lake and headed off into the hills, so as not to be disappointed later. Evan was leading, and I came close behind with Tadessa and Menasi bringing up the rear. After all, I thought, how could Evan know what was important and what was not? What was really ancient and of cultural value? As for his knowing who and what Shakespeare was. . . . Still he had quoted from that most famous fragment of the Bard's. It was all too much for me. When I realized that a lot of our questions were likely to be answered before the sun had set, my excitement rose, and I set myself to scrambling after Evan, pulling myself up the steep path in a frantic effort to keep up. Nobody was going to say that I was not fit!

At last we crossed over the crest of hills and the trail dipped down into a denser jungle. The ground seemed permanently wet, and we were inclined to slide in the steeper places. Suddenly I heard an exclamation from Tadessa behind me, and then he and Menasi stopped to confer. Our trail led along a rushing stream, which splashed over the stones and down so many little falls that it was impossible for me to hear what they were saying.

As soon as I found a firm foothold and could stop without fear of sliding. I turned to see what was attracting them. I had been so engrossed with keeping up with Evan and watching my footing on the hazardous trail that I had not looked farther than the next step ahead. Now I glanced around to see where Menasi was pointing.

The little glade through which we traveled was fragrant with the scent of many flowers, and now I saw them, in every imaginable color, along the stream, up the rocky hillside, hanging on vines from the giant fernlike trees. What excited Menasi and Tadessa was not the flowers but the insects around them. The glade was alive with the giant bees. They were flying from flower to flower, and as I listened I heard their buzzing even above the tumult of the stream.

The two men moved down to join me, and Menasi was saying, "I wouldn't advise collecting here. You might start something we couldn't finish. Besides, this isn't what we came for and you have the specimen Amhara got for you back at camp."

"You're right, of course," Tadessa said, "but it is a temptation. You can't really believe in that specimen until you see the live ones in flight."

By this time Evan had realized that we weren't following, and he came bounding back up the trail. He looked where we pointed, and a smile of extreme pleasure spread over his features.

"The little people are busy," he said. "There will be a good harvest."

I translated for the men, who found it hard to follow the ancient tongue amid the noise from the water and the insects.

"You see," said Menasi, "they're probably sacred, and we'd only make enemies if we caught one."

"Didn't I tell you how Evan reacted when I killed that specimen?" I asked.

In all the excitement, we seemed to have overlooked that point, and I explained it to the two scientists while Evan waited patiently, moving nearer the stream to watch the bees at work. He bent much closer than I would have dared, watching the insects with intense, yet gentle, concentration.

"You see, we mustn't think about collecting," Menasi warned. "That way we're liable to jeopardize our entire relationship. After all, their livelihood may depend pretty much on the bees. Suppose an outsider came to your village and started collecting specimens of your cattle?"

Tadessa laughed. "He'd be thrown in jail quick enough for stealing! Still it's a disappointment."

"We'll have N'Gobi catch us some of those big dragonflies on the way back. That'll compensate. And remember, these people probably don't have jails. They just tie you up on a rock to wait for the bees!"

Tadessa shuddered. "If I were Evan I wouldn't want to see another bee. But look at him now. He's got his face right up to one. How do you suppose he dares do that?"

I wondered myself. I ran down to where Evan waited and grabbed his arm.

"Look out!" I said. "Aren't you afraid it'll sting you?"

He turned and laughed at me.

"She won't sting. She knows me. I don't hurt her; she won't hurt me. She's very hard at work for us. Very busy now."

"But you told me, Evan. You told me they were all coming to sting you. Why is it all right now? Because then you were there and now you're here?"

He looked at me in surprise and I realized he must think me stupid.

"But I have told you," he exclaimed. "Then I was marked for death. Now I am clean."

Menasi raised an eyebrow. "It's as simple as that," he said.

For once Evan caught the sarcasm. He spoke as one who is tired of explaining the obvious.

"When I washed in the sea, I became clean. Now let us hurry for my people wait."

He strode on down the trail, and we put our attention to keeping up with him on the difficult path.

As I jumped and slid down the slippery trail into the valley, I thought about Evan's tone of voice. It not only had an edge of annoyance in it, there was a tone of excitement as well. It occurred to me that Evan was going home. And he was happy. He did not seem to dread the outcome. Whatever lay between him and his people, he did not blame them for it. Perhaps he would not want to go back with us after all. Perhaps even the promise of flight in our airship would not be enough to tempt him. I asked myself if it would be enough to tempt me to spend the rest of my life in an alien environment, and I had to admit it would not. But there was something else that might: The red gleam of his hair as I had seen it by the firelight in the cave; the delight of feeling his strange blue eyes focused upon me. Even as I watched Evan's lithe form disappearing around a bend in the trail, the thought of it overwhelmed me. I could not give him up, but neither could I face living in this wilderness among his terrible and alien people. Once again I felt the gulf that divided us. Frantically, I thought that I must lose no time in persuading him to come with us. Yet I knew it was natural for him to be happy on coming home. If his people took him back, would he be happier to stay? Would he ever adjust to Har?

My mind was running in circles over these problems, and I longed to be alone with Evan, to be able to talk about them quietly and to feel his arms around me. Instead, I had to bend every effort to keep up with him and not break my neck at the same time.

At last I hurried around a corner and almost ran into him. He had paused at the edge of a clearing, sheltered by a thick growth of fern. He held out his arm for us to stop and waited for Tadessa and Menasi to come up.

"Wait here," he said. "I will go alone. When I signal, come also join me."

He left us then and walked out into the clearing, but as he did so, he turned and looked at me. There was something in those remarkable blue eyes and the look he gave me that told me more than words. I saw he felt as I did and the blood rose to my cheeks, for I knew Menasi and Tadessa must have seen that look and could not fail to interpret it.

We watched Evan walk out into the clearing, and only

then I noticed what appeared to be a group of huts, not so different from what our herders build in the outlying districts. They were of bracken, much as we had built our camp; and being surrounded by the jungle, were almost invisible until we were quite close.

As Evan approached the huts, we saw figures spring up from among the bracken here and there along his way. One after another they popped up. These people had evidently been bending over, tending some sort of plants or perhaps what would pass for a garden, and so we had not noticed them until they stood erect. They were not tall even so, and at this distance I could not decide whether they were men or women.

Even paid no attention to them, but walked on toward the huts, and the figures all turned and stood staring after him. Then a door opened in the central hut and a tall figure came out. Evan stopped and it appeared that they were talking, and then he turned with a shout and raised his arm.

"I guess that means us," Menasi said, and we three walked out into the clearing and along the path toward Evan and the village, with the strange "gardeners" staring at us from either side.

As we passed, we saw that they were all women, dressed much alike in drab skirts or over-alls. Undoubtedly they were white women, but so darkened with work and weather and soiled with their labor that there was small comparison with the pale, glamorous creatures I had seen portrayed in Don Ylma's books. None of them made a sound or motion, but stood staring after us as though a a great wonder.

By the time we reached our guide, we saw that he was talking to another woman. This one was nearer to the model I had formed in my mind. She was about my height—a few inches below Evan—and blonde. Her hair was brushed back from her face and fell gloriously to her shoulders. She had an air of authority and command about her—and she was most obviously pregnant. She and Evan were talking together, and I caught the words of Anglic easily as, by now, I had become accustomed to their accent.

"I know not if the queen mother will see you. You have been screened. You have left the hive. This sort of thing never happened before." She kept staring at Evan, seeming to find his presence more extraordinary even than that of three black people from beyond the seas.

Evan saw us approach and turned to introduce us. "These are the gods I told you of from beyond the sea. They came here in the flying ship that flew over the village yesterday. This is Flora," he continued to us. "She is a mother and the daughter of our queen-mother Mona. She has had seven children, all of them healthy. Two sets of twins and one triplets."

He told us this as though it were a great achievement, and Menasi took his clue from him.

"Most remarkable," he said, struggling with the ancient tongue. "A great contribution to your tribe. May I present a fitting gift." He hastily unrolled his pack and offered Flora a mirror.

His action proved to be the turning point for us. Flora accepted the gift with delight. In fact, I wondered if she would ever have done with looking at herself and come back to us and our wishes. Following Evan's lead, we all stood courteously by and waited for her to finish her examination of the gift, which included a minute inspection of her own face.

At last she turned her attention to Menasi.

"Do you have anything else?" she asked.

Menasi glanced at Evan, but it was impossible to guess what he thought.

"I do," he said at last, "but it is for the eyes of your queen."

Flora looked distinctly annoyed. "I don't know what she will think of all this," she said. "Have you brought your air boat with you?"

I explained that we had left it by the lake and walked in to their village. She seemed relieved to hear this.

"It's just as well," she said. "It was a terrifying, noisy thing. I did not care myself, but all the first-time mothers were frightened and ran to hide. If the births turn out evil they will blame it on this. We had a lot of trouble." She glared at Evan. "If Mona had known it was you!"

Nevertheless, the mirror seemed to have won her over, and she told us all to come into the hut. She would send word to the queen mother, who was apparently their ruler.

The dwelling we entered seemed quite spacious, more so than was suggested by the outside. There were fresh rushes on the floor, and a bed at one end indicated a degree of comfort. There was even a rough approximation of chairs and a table. Flora ushered us in and then went away and left us alone.

"Isn't there any way of getting them to hurry?" fumed Menasi. "We haven't got all day, Evan."

"She's gone to get Mona, the queen mother. Be patient and all will be well."

"Won't someone tell me what's going on?" complained Tadessa. "I can't seem to follow the Anglic when everybody talks at once. I gather you won her over with the mirror, and she thinks Evan ought to be dead. But what's all this about evil births?"

"Oh, didn't you get that?" asked Menasi. "Our airship frightened them all out of their wits, and now the prospective mothers are worried about miscarriages. I suppose it was thoughtless of us. But perhaps it will carry some weight in our favor. What do you think, Evan, are they more angry at us for having flown over or impressed that we could do it?"

Evan grinned. "They're impressed. You'll see. Soon they'll make a feast for you."

It turned out as Evan predicted. Before long Flora returned, somewhat chastened, and said that queen-mother Mona had been pleased by her account of us as well as by the mirror, which it seemed Flora had had to relinquish. A feast and entertainment were being prepared for us at which we could present Mona with the rest of our gifts. In the meantime, Flora was to take care of us and show us around.

She asked first if we would like drink or refreshment, but we had already quenched our thirst from our own canteens. Flora was further impressed when we showed these to her, and I promised to give her mine before I left.

Then we began a fantastic tour. The Anglic Village was

spread out through a wide section of jungle and so hidden by the dense foliage that it was no wonder we had been unable to spot it from the air.

We followed Flora and Evan along a maze of paths that crossed and recrossed themselves through the jungle, often making us stoop to pass under a tangle of thick vines and briars or duck to avoid a low branch of a tree. The paths were built to a lower scale, and I noticed that Evan and Flora proceeded most of the time in a stooping posture. Soon we could guess the reason, for we began to pass groups of shorter people, coming and going upon the paths. When they saw Flora and Evan, they pressed aside into the jungle and gave us the right of way. Even in these brief encounters, we noticed they were dressed and looked much alike, and that they appeared to be women who were similar to those we had first seen working in the fields.

"It seems that while the insects got bigger, the people got smaller," Menasi said.

"Not just people," Tadessa replied. "Have you noticed that they're all women? Evan is the only man I've seen around here."

Just then we came upon a group of the little women busily pulling up and cutting down the vines and plants that were encroaching upon the trail. They moved aside for us to pass and then went back to work without a glance in our direction. We paused to watch them for several minutes, until Evan called to us to hurry along.

Immediately thereafter we came out into a clearing upon a scene of great activity. A number of huts and buildings were grouped in a rough circle, and a fire was burning in front of one. The little people were running back and forth, carrying vats and kettles of water and what looked like a mixture of honey—and for all we knew, other less-appetizing forms of insect food. They were running from one hut to the other and back to the fire, or trotting off in groups along other paths into the jungle.

"This is the food center," Evan told us. "You say kitchen. They are very busy making ready for our feast. I told them we must have it soon because you must return to camp before sunset."

Flora beckoned me to the fire.

"You like to cook?" she asked, singling me out as the one woman. "Evan says you don't have our bees in your country. Take a taste."

She stuck her finger into the mixture and put it in her mouth, grinning at me to do the same. I made a quick dab, being careful to miss the contents without letting her see. I put my finger in my mouth and smiled appreciatively.

"Good, huh?" said Flora. "How do you ever get along without the bees?"

"We manage," I told her. "You'd be surprised."

Tadessa and Menasi were following Evan and plying him with questions, and soon they were calling me to come on to the next stop. Once again we were hurrying along a jungle trail. In quick succession we came to huts where the little people were shredding the jungle leaves to make thread and weaving all kinds of cloth and mats; and to more openings that passed for fields, where they were tending their plants. Tadessa asked to see a sample of these plants and said they were a very primitive form of grain.

"They should be able to develop something better than this," he said. "But of course they'd have to clear more jungle. Perhaps the soil is still not right. But we could help them with that, I'm sure."

"We'll bring it up with their queen," said Menasi. "That is, if it seems like a good time to do so."

We continued on our survey tour and watched every imaginable activity being carried out by these little women with great energy and patience. All the time I kept thinking, where are the men? Surely, they're out hunting somewhere. Shooting the birds or gathering eggs. Some man must have made the snare we found on the little duck's leg. Some man must have made the spider string and the stronger ropes that had bound Evan. Presently even that question was answered, for we came to a group of women making string. They had a huge spider in a wicker box, and were pulling its web from it through a crack and

174

winding it up on a spool. We even watched them spinning it into a thicker and thicker thread, but then Evan called us to come and we pressed on to other sights.

We seemed to be getting deeper into the jungle and also up against the mountain wall. We heard the roaring of a torrent and the trail crossed a deep ravine on a rough bridge made of a huge fallen tree. Below us was the river and ahead the face of the cliff. Then we saw that the cliff was dotted with many caves and the trail led up to them. Here in this fastness was the tribe's greatest treasure—the children. We heard their voices before we saw them. Then we came into a large cavern and there were dozens and dozens of children. They were of all ages and sizes, all dressed very much alike in the nondescript cloth made from the jungle plants. They were the first truly human things that I saw in that village, for they were running and shouting and playing as only children can.

We stood quietly to one side and watched them for a time, and then I became conscious of the numbers of little women passing silently among them, carrying the youngest, wiping a nose here or an eye there, ushering a group out the door behind us, or showing some little girls how to weave a mat. They were doing it with the same devotion and patience they had exhibited in clearing the jungle trails or winding up the spider's web.

It came to me that these were nurses, not mothers. The children were all being brought up by nurses. Where were the mothers? I said it aloud before I realized that I was speaking.

"Where are the mothers?"

"We come to that next," said Evan. "In the safety of the mountain."

"Come along, I'll show you," Flora commanded, and we all followed her out and along the mountain path till we came to more caves with rooms built into them and the greatest appearance of wealth and comfort that I had yet glimpsed among these people.

Looking through the door, I saw a number of women sitting about. They were all tall, like Flora, well formed and of good appearance; and they all seemed to be pregnant—all but an occasional mother with a very young child in her arms, who must only recently have given birth.

Evan stopped at the door and let Flora go in.

"This is forbidden for me," he told Menasi, "and for all men. But Mona has given you permission so that they can see what it was that frightened them and will no longer be afraid."

Tadessa and Menasi followed Flora into the room, but I stopped at the door and looked at Evan. Suddenly I could not leave him. What would they do to him, I thought, in this country that was practically all women? It's a conspiracy of the sexes, I thought, and something terrible is going to happen to Evan. I must stay with him until I can get him away. He was looking at me with his intense blue eyes and I felt that I must say something.

"I've seen enough," I told him. "It must be getting late. Where is this cave with the treasures? Is it one of these?"

"It is farther back," he told me. "Later I'll take you there. When they are feasting and dancing and there's no one about. Now you are right that it gets late."

He called through the doorway to Flora to hurry.

"The time is short. I will take her to see the bees and then to the feasting place."

He took my hand and pulled me after him, and we went back past the children's cave and across the tree bridge and along a jungle path.

"Evan," I said, when we were alone, "where are the men? There must be some men. Aren't they your friends? Where are they?"

Evan laughed. "Who can say where the men are? Now here, now there. They're enjoying themselves. Sooner or later we'll run into one. If not now, then at the feast. Where there's special food, you'll always find the men!"

"But don't they *do* anything, Evan? Like Tadessa. He's a doctor, as you know. Or Menasi, our leader. Or N'Gobi, who flies the airship."

"We don't have any airships. You know that. Sometimes we trap birds. I like to do that. I knew all the nesting places and when to find fresh eggs. I knew the jungle for miles and miles. No woman goes that far from the hive."

"Oh. So the men are all off hunting. Well, that's natural in a primitive society."

Evan repeated the word. "Hunting. You mean looking for eggs. Well, that's fun. As I told you, they're enjoying themselves."

"But hunting's more than looking for eggs. It's hunting animals."

"Animals? You mean spiders and such? Well, that, too. There's always something to eat in the jungle. And berries. Though not for you!"

He turned to laugh at me, and then pulled my hand. "Come on. I have more to show you."

I followed him at a trot along the trail until we came to another opening in the forest. As we approached I could hear the humming of a million bees. We came out into a meadow and spaced about were a dozen tremendous beehives. I might not have recognized them as such but for the streams of giant bees that were flying in and out and hovering about the meadow.

"There," said Evan, "you saw our treasure of children. This is our treasure of bees."

He stepped aside to speak to one of the little women, and I saw that she was standing alertly at the path we had just come from and that she held a weapon like a spear. I looked about and noticed more of these spear-bearers at every pathway into the jungle. Guards, I thought. As we place them around cattle. What are they guarding against? The bees won't wander off like cattle. Well, perhaps, if they swarm. What enemies could they have? Birds? Their own people? Another tribe? The idea of raiding these giant bees would seem like suicide to me. Perhaps they knew how to do it. They must have a technique for getting the honey when they need it.

I was roused from these thoughts by the sound of a deep voice calling, "Evan!"

A tall young man came bounding out of the jungle and seized Evan by the shoulder. In a trice the two men were clapping each other on the back and shouting at each other in the friendliest manner.

"Then it's true," cried the stranger. "I heard you were

back, but I couldn't believe it! And they say the strange thing that flew over us and made all the noise. . . ."

"Was a flying machine from the lands to the south!" Evan interrupted. "And here's one of the people who came in it. Amhara. This is my friend, Hu."

Hu looked me over with great interest, much as I felt Tadessa might look at one of his mares. "She's black all right!" he said at last to Evan, and laughed. "I never saw a black woman—or a black man either."

"You'll see one in a minute if you wait here," Evan told him. "Flora should be bringing them along."

"If you think it's surprising for me to be black," I told him, "I assure you it's nothing to the surprise we got in finding white people here."

Hu stared at me. "Why, she talks our language. But it sounds strange."

"It's not her own language," Evan told him. "She's learned ours—out of books, she says. They talk something quite different. I've learned a little of it myself."

"You did? What did you do that for? Say, I heard you'd been screened. How does it happen that you're back here? Aren't you supposed to be dead?"

"I would be," Evan said, without a trace of emotion, "but they set me free. Amhara and her friends."

"They did? But that's treason! What will Mona say?"

"I don't know. You'd better come to the feast and find out. I'm not staying long anyhow."

"If there's a feast, I'll be there. But say, did you hear about young Garth? He's being screened! He laughed at Flora and he talked back. They say he's for it this time."

"No, not Garth!" cried Evan. "But he was only a child!"

"Not as much of a child as you think. He's never followed the laws. I've talked and I've argued, but he wouldn't listen to me. He wouldn't listen to anyone, and now he's for it."

Before I could ask Evan for an explanation of this conversation, Menasi and Tadessa came out of the jungle, following Flora. They looked at the hives and the spear-armed guards and watched the huge bees flying about. All the time Flora bombarded us with statistics about how many pounds of honey each hive produced and the relative merits of each swarm of bees.

"Oh, yes," she finished, when Menasi complimented her on how much she knew about bees, "there is a great deal to learn from the bees. I was a keeper for several years before I became a mother."

"These people are not as primitive as you might think," Menasi whispered to me. "They have some things well documented. They showed us a place in the mothers' cave back there, where they have records of every birth, who the mother and father were, and how it turned out. They keep track of their genetic lines very carefully and the half-dozen females who do it seem to have a high rank in their society."

"There's something I want to ask you about that," began Tadessa, but Menasi cut him off.

"Later," he said, quirking an eyebrow at me. "Poor Tadessa's feeling frustrated because he can't follow everything she says. We'll thrash it out later on the way home. Now there's the first young man I've seen!"

"The first *man*," said Tadessa, "and he seems to be a friend of Evan's."

I was going to tell them about Hu, but just then Flora hurried us off and we were all too busy following the pigmy trail to talk. It is difficult to maintain a conversation when one is stooped over and in single file.

When we next came out of the jungle, it was evident that we had reached the feasting place. There was but one large shelter in the middle of the clearing, and in it was a long table with chairs at one end and benches down either side. The shelter was open on the side opposite the chairs. In the clearing, fires were burning and the pleasant smell of food cooking came to us.

Flora led us across the open place and into the shelter. The tribe was already assembling, and groups of the little women were converging upon the shelter. Here and there among them we glimpsed taller, fairer women with fewer signs of toil upon them, and these we judged must belong to the class of mothers. They had an air of independence and leisure about them that the others lacked. Often as not, walking with such a woman was a man. They were all young and strong and seemed not to have a care in the world.

We approached the feast-laden table and Flora introduced us to the woman who sat in the chair at its head. She arose to meet us, and I remembered at once the pictures in Don Ylma's books. For here was all the beauty and arrogance and pride that had so repelled me. This was Mona, and I did not need Flora's introduction to tell me so. This was the queen mother of the hive and her word was law.

She sat with an easy and royal grace that indicated her expectation that the best of everything would be served to her with blind obedience and unquestioning adulation.

I wondered how many perfect children she had managed to produce to reach this pinnacle of power. Certainly, she was the most gaudily dressed among her people, as though all the arts of spinning, weaving, and design surviving from a greater culture had been concentrated upon her costume alone. The working women we had seen wore ill-made, colorless clothing. Mona's robes, which fell about her in graceful lines, were made of a kind of silk that shimmered in iridescent hues. Another product of the spiders? Or was a different creature responsible? I had no opportunity to find out.

Her hair must once have been a beautiful gold. Now it was turning silver, but so gradually that it only seemed to enhance the gold. It lay in halo waves upon her shoulders, creating the illusion of another costly garment.

The whole effect would have been beautiful—and she must have been overwhelming as a young woman—were it not for the imperious look that flashed from her intense blue eyes. I knew she would brook no opposition, and I felt instinctively that I would not care to cross her.

Now she listened attentively as Evan explained who we were and where we came from. Then she addressed her remarks to me. At first I thought this was because I was acting as interpreter, but later I came to believe it was because I was the only woman, and in her society women ruled.

"This is indeed a great wonder," she said, motioning me to a seat beside her. "Not only that Evan has returned, but what he has brought with him. I have never, even from the oldest mother, heard of people like you. And this flying machine in which you came—I should greatly like to see that. Perhaps even to ride in it. How wonderful to be like the bees and mount into the sky toward the sun!"

I translated for Menasi and waited for his reply. He could follow her words in part, but in this important contact he wanted to be sure he got everything right.

"Perhaps we can arrange that," I told her for him. "But now our time is short. We are sorry we did not find you when we first arrived. But then the weather was bad. Now we must use the good weather to start for home. We will come again and hope there can be many profitable contacts between our people and yours."

Tadessa nudged me. "The wheat," he whispered. "Mention the wheat."

Menasi raised his eyebrows, and I could not be sure whether he wanted me to bring up the matter. But I made a stab.

"We noticed your grain that your women were tending. It is very small and weak. We have much better grain at home. We can bring you seeds."

Mona frowned. She seemed impatient of having me wait for Menasi's words, and kept trying to shut him out of the conversation.

"It may be," she said. "We shall think on it. But what have you brought now? This glass is much admired. Have you more gifts like this?" She brought out the mirror and studied herself in it.

"I'm afraid that's the only one we have," I said. "Our space was limited. However, we do have other presents. Show her the pickax, Evan."

Evan laid it on the table before her, after going through the motions of digging to explain its use. She handled it curiously.

"How heavy, and how smooth. Yes, I can see it is good to work with."

She made a signal and several of the little women scurried up, chattering and chirping among themselves. They seized my pickax and disappeared with it among the crowd.

Tadessa passed me the rest of our gifts. A good knife, a comb, and some ivory hair ornaments that Zulli had contributed. Mona seemed to like the ivory the most. She quickly appropriated them for herself, gave the comb to Flora, and the knife to the stern-faced woman on her right, who looked as though her childbearing had been done long in the past. Tadessa whispered to me that she was the chief keeper of the genetic records.

The men were delegating more and more of the negotiating to me as they realized that Mona expected me to be much more than the interpreter.

"I hope you realize," Tadessa muttered to Menasi in Afrian, "that the result of this bee culture has been to rule men out of the picture. The women are in the saddle."

Menasi chuckled, and I saw the slight quirk of his eyebrows. "That's the situation in the entire insect kingdom," he replied, "and remember, these people haven't seen any mammals besides themselves."

"But the men are practically nonexistent," sputtered Tadessa. "What do you suppose they've done with them?"

"I doubt that they eat them—like the spiders—if that's worrying you! Remember, the old cattle and horse cultures did about the same to women!"

"They certainly didn't kill them off! They couldn't have kept going."

"Well, they bought and sold them like cattle. Some of our marriage rites go back to that, don't forget. And they were kept hidden away from strangers and affairs of state. Don't worry! Let Amhara do the talking. She's making a good job of it."

On hearing this, I bent every effort on charming our hostess, who now was ready to dispense hospitality. At her signal, the little women began to bring up the food and drink. Huge trays and platters made of palm leaves and covered with ferns were carried to the table. Under the ferns were honey cakes and meats of diverse sorts. I thought I saw something that resembled roast duck, but perhaps it was only a disguised spider. In any case, I was not anxious to find out. I was beginning to worry about how we could put our food plan into operation and was glancing about to see what Tadessa and Menasi would do, when a terrific noise smote my ear.

It was the native orchestra tuning up—a variety of drums and horns and whistles—and it immediately centered everyone's attention on the clearing beyond the fire. I saw Tadessa and Menasi making a quick transfer of food from plate to pouch, and I made haste to do the same. Evan laughed at me while he stuffed his mouth with everything the table offered. He held out a mug to my brother.

"Honey wine. Very good."

Tadessa sniffed his mug that had just been filled by a passing woman.

"It smells potent enough," he said. "Probably knock you out. Don't really drink it, Amhara," he whispered.

"Do you think I'm crazy," I replied. "But I'm awfully thirsty."

"Drink up your canteen," Menasi told me, "and give it to Flora. You promised her, you know."

I did as he ordered, and Flora was obviously pleased. The canteen was passed around among those at the top of the table, but I was glad to see it got back to Flora before anyone thought of appropriating it. About then the dancing started and everyone forgot about the canteen.

I had to admit the orchestra had rhythm, but that's about all it had. Where was the fabled music of the white world, of which I had read so much and heard so little? Only a few pitiful fragments had come down to us, for music is the most perishable of the arts. I had to keep reminding myself that this was not the white world, but a very primitive world fighting for survival.

Then Menasi whispered in my ear, "Great Congo, Amhara! It's a bee dance! Look at the figure eights!"

I stared in fascination. A long row of the little people were dancing in and out and around in imitation of the dances that the bees perform on the comb. Round and round they went in tight circles to imitate the round dance of the bees. In and out, around and back again they followed each other closely in an approximation of the figure eights with which the bees communicate the distance and direction of a food supply. As they danced, a weird and eerie chant rose to accompany them.

The dancing and the chanting were hypnotic and I found myself going off into a contemplative trance, when Tadessa jabbed me in the side with his elbow.

"Get on with the transfer of food while no one's looking," he hissed.

I saw that he and Menasi had already completed the substitution and were busily eating their own provisions. I followed their example and soon was chewing hungrily on our dried meat and bread, which I did my best to conceal behind my hands. But my deception was unnecessary. All eyes were riveted on the dancers, and then Mona arose from her seat of honor and advanced to the edge of the hut.

She looked very regal in her flowing cloak of websilk and feathers and her pale hair curling over it all. She stood commandingly at the edge of the platform and made an imperious gesture. Probably some special dance she is ordering for our entertainment, I thought. Immediately, I was proved correct, for the wall of dancers opened and a young man came out into the circle they formed. He was tall and lithe and he moved irresistibly with the rhythm of the drums. He came straight to Mona and I saw that she held out a bowl to him, perhaps containing the honey wine that had been passing around so freely.

I was interested in all this symbolism and ritual, and I leaned forward to see better. Just then I heard a sigh from Evan. I turned to look at him and found that he was staring at the scene in fascination. It was hard to guess the emotions I read in his face. Excitement? Expectation? Yes, and also horror.

"What is it, Evan?" I whispered. "What are they going to do now?"

He hardly heard me. He answered only one word, "Garth!"

I remembered his friend who had mentioned this name to him. Here was a different young man. But what had the other said? "He's for it." Or something of the sort. I began to experience a feeling of foreboding and dread, and I knew instinctively that Evan was feeling this also. Only he seemed totally unable to move or speak.

I looked back at the dancers. The music, which had sunk to a low mutter while the young man drank, now swelled to a more violent tempo as he threw the cup aside. Garth began to dance, at first slowly and keeping his place directly in front of Mona.

"Did you see his eyes?" Tadessa whispered. "He's been drugged."

"Anyone who drank all that wine at one gulp could hardly help it," Menasi replied.

"No, no. Before. How he walked when he came out. Like Evan when we first met him."

"Do you really think so?"

They both leaned forward to be able to see better, and I, too, found myself unable to take my eyes off the dancer. He was obviously expert at it, and graceful. But it was more than that. I'll certainly have to write this up, I told myself.

The youth seemed unable to move away from Mona, as though directing all his gestures at her. Then, as the music rose to a peak, she suddenly seized a bundle of fern branches that had been standing at one side in an urn. She hit the young man over the head with them. She beat him upon the shoulders, the torso, the legs, as though determined to drive him away from her. As she did so, he began to chant in a high, wailing voice. Where had I heard that before? Among the rocks on the day we found Evan? The dancers closed in upon the youth, pushing him backward, away from the hut of feasting, out into the center of the clearing, where they left him. They moved aside into a giant circle so that he could perform alone his gymnastics, his incredible leaps and whirls.

Only then did I become conscious of a hum in the air. It must have been there before, but had been inaudible under the sound of the drums. Suddenly the instruments quietened and the ominous hum became a roar. The circle of dancers threw themselves upon the ground, covering their faces, while a black cloud seemed to whirl out of the jungle and envelop the unfortunate young man. In a second the dancer had fallen down, and only then I realized that he was covered with a mass of the giant bees, each one trying to insert her sting in some portion of his anatomy.

There was a terrible silence and then a sigh passed over the watchers. I could not repress a cry of protest.

"No! No!" I screamed, before I realized what I was doing.

Menasi turned to frown warningly at me, but Flora, who was standing behind me drew me aside, where I could no longer witness the cruel sacrifice.

"It will be over in a minute," she comforted me. Since my gift of the canteen, Flora had been very friendly and no doubt she thought me an unfortunate weakling who could not bear up under stress.

In spite of myself, I continued to plead with her to stop it.

"Once it is started, we cannot stop it," she said. "But it's quick, as you can see."

I sneaked a look toward the ritual and saw that the fallen youth was quite still.

"There's a story," Flora continued, "of a queen who changed her mind, and tried to stop the bees once they were released. In their fury, they turned upon her and her entire court and killed all who could not get away. That was long ago. We manage better now, but no one would dare to interfere once the bees are sent on target."

I turned away and looked for my companions. Flora's little story had given me time to collect myself, but I could see that Menasi and Tadessa were both moved. For once they had nothing to say and with set faces watched the termination of the ritual. Then Evan took my arm and led me to one side.

"Now is the time," he whispered. "The cave. They are all here and no one will notice."

"But Menasi and Tadessa?" I protested.

"It is arranged. We will meet on the way back. Come quickly."

He dragged me along with him, as I was scarcely able to collect my thoughts. I was worried about Tadessa and Menasi. Indeed, the vicinity of that diabolical dance did not seem to be a healthy place to stay. Even the interior of the feasting shelter could hardly be much protection if the maddened bees chose to detour in that direction. I said as much to Evan, but he shook his head vehemently.

"They are safe enough. I have told you and explained before. The bees attack those who have been marked. Didn't you see how Mona marked him?"

I saw it all right in my mind's eye. I shuddered, remembering Flora's story.

"I thought it was an honor," I said weakly. "Like being crowned with a laurel, or some kind of a symbolic ritual."

"Listen!" Evan said, holding up his hand so that we both held our breath.

Faintly, as though carried on a phantom breeze, we heard a high whining sound. Was it flutes? Or a whistle? It was so high that I almost missed it, and yet my ears felt it. Was it some strange sound that the bees made, and were they coming after us even now?

I seized hold of Evan, crying, "What is it?"

He only laughed and took the excuse to put his arm around me and steal a kiss.

"It is finished. Safe enough now. They are putting the remaining bees to sleep, and then they take them back to their hive."

"Take them!" I had a vision of those shrieking monsters bent on the kill.

"It's easy enough. When they hear the flutes they go to sleep and the keepers pick them up in their baskets and take them back to their hive."

Then I recalled something I had read about bees being lulled into inactivity by sound waves. Could these giants be as vulnerable as the bees of the ancients? I tried to remember the details—something about cycles and decibels. The figures escaped me, but Evan's people must have stumbled on the secret.

"I should think all of you would have one of those flutes, just in case," I told him.

But Evan shrugged. "It is the secret of the keepers. Besides, when the gods say that your time has come. . . ."

"The gods! Ridiculous!" I panted, climbing after him up the trail. "You mean, when Mona says. But why now and here, Evan? Why not later at the Rock of Sacrifice, like you?"

"It is the custom sometimes," he insisted. "It shows the power."

"It shows brutality!" I cried. "And senseless cruelty and waste!"

Evan only answered. "We are the drones. There's no other hive and outside the hive you die. Now nobody will talk back for many seasons. Garth always talked too much. She watches the records and she does not like a young man who says what he thinks."

Garth talked too much and perhaps fathered few children. And this was the outcome of their efforts to offset the unfortunate genetic results of the Disaster. Not so different from N'Gobi who likewise talked and was too light of skin. Two people facing the same aftermath of the Disaster, but in different ways. When you came right down to it, was it more ridiculous to condemn a man for the color of his skin or for his inability to improve the race with healthy offspring? My whole being recoiled from these barbaric customs. I was shocked by Evan's matter-of-fact acceptance. Yet, all the while, my mind ran on with comparisons and questions.

Then the trail came out upon a ledge part-way up the mountain's face. Below, spread out in the afternoon sunlight, was the clearing and the feasting shelter. I could even make out Tadessa and Menasi, exchanging pleasantries with Mona and her followers and going through polite leave-taking. I stared at them unbelievingly, for all evidence of the dance and the sacrifical murder had been miraculously cleared away, and I could almost believe it had been a dream. A very bad dream. A nightmare. Then Evan touched me on the shoulder and I turned to look behind us at the cave.

At first it seemed only an overhanging rock shelter that opened out upon the ledge we had just scaled. When we walked to the back, we found a small entrance leading to an inner cavern. It was closed with a strong metal door. Metal—with these people who were back almost to the stone age? I realized that it must be very ancient—pre-Disaster, in fact. Evan put his shoulder to the barrier and at last it gave before his strength. We passed through and found ourselves in profound darkness, so that we stood perfectly still, afraid to put one foot before the other. Then, gradually, the dim light coming through the door behind us showed our adjusted eyes that we were in a large chamber whose limits were lost in the shadows. Along the farther wall loomed shapes that appeared to be chests or heavily loaded shelves.

"We should have brought a light," I whispered, for the mystery of the place would not let me speak out loud. "I can't see where to begin."

"I've not been here since I was a child. It's very old and very holy. Forbidden. But I'll fix a light. No fire. It would be seen. You look at things over there. Take them to the door for seeing. I'll come back soon with light."

He rummaged in the debris near the doorway and came up with something that looked like a small cage. With this in hand, he hurried out along the ledge and disappeared into the forest.

I watched him go, completely baffled. Then I turned back to the cave and let my eyes grow accustomed again to the dimness. I moved carefully to the nearest chest and stretched out my hands. The chest was made of metal, too. Probably steel. It had stood up to the bombings and the centuries, and my reason told me that such a durable box must have been placed here to guard something of great value.

I strained to raise the lid. It had been opened by others before me, and the ease with which it came up made me fear that it had already been looted. I put my hand into the dark interior and felt—books! I seized hold of the first one that came to hand and crept to the cave's opening and out into the sunlight on the ledge. There I sat down to examine my find.

It was a book all right, and covered with the dust of centuries. The binding was crumbling, but all in all it was remarkably well preserved. I dusted it off and began to read. It was a scientific treatise and, as I had expected, in ancient Anglic. It was full of equations and things I could not understand. Whether it was material lost to us since the Disaster and therefore new to our scholars or only a duplication of some book locked up in our taboo files, I could not tell. Menasi would have known, but Menasi was now on the trail back to camp, and getting farther away every minute. As I looked back at the ancient and eerie cavern, I fervently hoped he would not get too far ahead of us. But the possible treasures of antiquity, piled in those dim recesses, held me.

I put down the book on science and went back to the chest and tried again. This time I was more fortunate. At least it was something I could understand. It was a book about art, a subject to which I had given little attention, save where it concerned the ancient civilization. As I sat in the sun outside the cave and turned the pages, the beauty that leaped out at me took my breath away. The reproductions of paintings, the cream of many centuries preceding the Disaster, were done in color and the steel chest had preserved them miraculously. I stared at picture after picture of the vanished glories of the white people. Under each was the name of the picture, the artist and his dates, and then an inscription: "Musée du Louvre, Paris," or "the Hermitage, Leningrad," or "Mellon collection, Washington, D. C." Not anymore, I thought. No more Washington; no more collection; no more painting. At least we have this. I knew it would make a sensation when I took it back to Har.

I had to make myself stop looking at the pictures and get back to the business of finding out what else was in the cave. I realized that I could only scratch the surface at this time, but if I could take back enough to impress the Wasan and the Council, perhaps we could send another expedition. I refused to let my mind dwell on the complications this might pose. Just get on with the work in hand, I told myself. Do as much as time allows.

I put the art book at one side of the cave, and after a moment's thought, I put the book on science with it. In short order I added two more art books, a book on music—happily including many scores—two novels of the period, and some bound medical journals that I knew would interest Tadessa. The pile was growing, and I was beginning to consider how much we could carry. Moreover, this was only the first box. There was no telling what might be in others farther back.

Now and then I paused to wonder about Evan. Where had he gone for a light? Why couldn't he hurry up about it? My hand closed over a fairly large book. I could feel that the binding had been expensive, although it was now practically in shreds. I wandered out on the ledge to look for Evan, and then my eye fell upon the title of the book: *The Collected Works of William Shakespeare*.

I stared at it unbelievingly and turned the pages in a daze. There were the plays I knew almost by heart: *A Midsummer Night's Dream, The Tempest*. The verses jumped out at me just as I remembered them. And here were the plays we knew only from fragments or from critical essays, and many more that I had not known existed. I ran down the index: *Hamlet, Macbeth, Othello*. I couldn't believe my good fortune. The thing I had wanted most of all to track down had fallen into my hands.

I sat down at the mouth of the cave with the book. Now I could satisfy my curiosity. How had the "To be or not to be" speech fitted into the play? What was it really about? All those references to ghosts and fathers in the old critical essays that set off such battles among our scholars! Now I could put an end to that silly controversy about Shakespeare and Bern-Shaw. Perhaps if I looked I could find a volume of the latter's work.

I began to read and I was in a different world—a world of kings and castles and conflict and all put together with such beautiful words. Words sang in my head, words I could never forget, words of such understanding and penetration it was no wonder they had lived from his day until the Disaster. No wonder that whoever had filled this cave with treasures to be preserved from the bombs had felt impelled to include this book among the highest accomplishments of the culture.

I leafed through the other plays, feeling that a door had opened and I had walked through into that ancient world of wealth and color and power, where man did not have to worry about mere survival till tomorrow. I have no idea how long I sat there reading, but I was still in that other world when Evan came back from the forest. I did not hear him when he spoke my name, and he had to put a hand on my shoulder.

I sprang to my feet, and when I saw who it was I fell into his arms.

"Oh, Evan!" I cried. "Look! You'd never guess! You couldn't possibly imagine!" And then I paused, for I realized that Evan indeed could not guess or imagine the importance of this find. He had never heard of Shakespeare.

"Look, Evan," I explained, trying to make my voice matter-of-fact. "This is a momentous discovery. I just happened to pick it out from the books in that chest. And I found some other good things, too. See, there." I pointed to the growing pile. "But this is the best. The greatest poet and dramatist your people ever produced, and his works have been almost all lost for five hundred years. This expedition will be famous for having rediscovered him."

Evan looked puzzled and pleased at the same time.

"You've found what you want? Very good. And I have brought light to help in the cave."

He held up the wicker cage he had taken with him into the forest. A dim glow seemed to emanate from it. I saw that it came from dozens of little worms. Not so little, either. The glowworms grew to giant size in this country, too. Still, how much light can a glowworm. . . .

"Come inside," said Evan. "You'll see."

I followed him into the cave, and he rummaged around till he had found several more wicker cages and divided his worms among them. I had to admit that in the darkness of the cave, which seemed to stimulate their efforts, the worms gave off a respectable amount of light. You could even read by them, a little. I opened my precious book and glanced down a page at random.

"Listen, Evan," I said. "I want you to understand. For this man was of your people, and your people read and loved these words for generations before the Disaster. If I take this book away with me, back to my country, it is only so that it will not be lost but will be known and read and loved again. Just listen a little:

192

> 'Oh mighty Caesar! dost thou lie so low?
> Are all thy conquests, glories, triumphs, spoils,
> Shrunk to this little measure?' "

I paused. From a thousand years in the past, the verses seemed to be describing the present. I turned the page to find the speech I remembered from a famous fragment.

> " 'Friends, Romans, countrymen, lend me your ears.
> I come to bury Caesar, not to praise him.
> The evil that men do lives after them;
> The good is oft interred with their bones.
> So let it be with Caesar.' "

I stopped again and looked up at Evan. I did not need to ask if he understood. In the dim light he stared at me and repeated softly.

"The evil that men do lives after them. But this evil has lived too long. I believe you, Amhara. I believe you now about my people. But surely there is a time to begin again. I will go with you to your country or to whatever place you lead."

He looked at me with his burning eyes, and then he was kissing me as from a great hunger, holding me with gentleness and devotion. At that moment I felt that everything was possible. A new start for both our peoples. A future of unlimited happiness and progress in spite of the havoc and destruction that had been visited upon our earth.

"We *can* start over again," I cried. "And you and I can help. Two people together. You'll see what love can mean. I promise."

As he kissed me, I knew that N'Gobi would say I was asking for trouble. Poor N'Gobi, who had endured so much and only wanted the best for me. But I was past thinking of such things and I closed my mind to his warnings.

It may have been a few minutes or a long time that we stood thus in each other's arms, and the world around us ceased to exist. I have no way of knowing. The next thing I heard was a scream from the doorway. It was an animal screech of pain and anger and hatred, as Mona burst in upon us, striking us both all over with her sinister branch of fern.

"Evil! Evil! Evil!" she was screaming. "Wicked! Vicious! Traitor! You know such love is forbidden! You know you were condemned a week ago, Evan. But here you are with this devil who defied the gods and is now breaking every law and sacred order!"

We were both so astonished and overwhelmed by her onslaught that at first all we could do was retreat farther into the cave. My first thought was how right I had been up to now to avoid tangling with a maniac like this. But my next reaction was to strike back.

"Your laws are evil!" I cried, pushing her away from us. "You'll have to change them. And if you won't, we'll make you. You're cruel and barbarous and disgusting and I don't believe it's even helping to improve your race. You're all horrible and there's no sense in it!"

I was getting very angry now, and I rushed her, trying to wrest the branch of fern out of her hand. But she saw what I was about and sidestepped me, retreating toward the door. In the dimness of the cave I did not dare run after her as I might otherwise have done, fearing to fall over some artifact or an unevenness in the floor. Mona escaped me and ran out of the cave, and I was so glad to be rid of her that I slammed the metal door shut and stood against it, feeling for some bolt or latch to lock her out completely. I could still hear her scolding from outside.

"So *we* are evil, are we? And *we'll* have to change? You'll find out! You won't get away this time! Breaker of laws! Flouter of authority!" She began to laugh, and presently her laughter went away and I judged she was going down the trail to the village, probably to get help in breaking down the door.

I turned to Evan and was astonished at what I saw. The man who had been so strong, so protective and hopeful five minutes ago, was crouched on the floor of the cave in an attitude of complete despair. What power that woman wielded, I thought! She had them all hypnotized. I could see that a big job of re-education would have to be done on Evan, and covering a lot more than reading, writing, and arithmetic.

"Come and help me with the door," I said. "There must be some way of locking it before she comes back with help. If we can just fasten it securely, the whole village couldn't break it down."

"What difference does it make?" Evan replied. "She has marked us well. We're screened. We can't get away this time."

I looked at him as the horrid thought began to penetrate. Certainly my mind had not been working about those ferns. I remembered now. They weren't meant for punishment at the moment. A beating with them inflicted little pain. It was the future punishment that they implied. They carried the dire odor to attract the maddened bees! I found I was beginning to tremble in spite of myself.

"But surely if we can keep the door shut. And if it's securely locked, an army couldn't break that metal. . . ."

"Don't be foolish. They won't try to break in. The bees won't come in the door."

As I stared at him incredulously, he led me to a corner of the cave and pointed out a dim recess in the roof where the light of day penetrated.

"Not big enough to let light down here, but big enough for the bees. And there must be other such holes."

"But surely," I protested again, for I was determined to prove him wrong in his defeatism, "the bees can't smell us out down here and we can hide in the dark."

For answer he put his arms around me and held me close, my head against his chest. My nose was tickled by the curly hair where his shirt lay open.

"Smell," he commanded.

It seemed to me that it was more than the hair that caused the tickling in my nose. Yes, undoubtedly there was an acrid odor, not noticeable at first but unmistakable when you looked for it.

"But it's so vague," I said.

"To us, maybe. But not to the bees. It arouses all their fighting anger, and they have been trained to seek it out. And as for the dark, that doesn't bother them. They live in a dark hive."

"Still, there must be some way to get rid of the smell. Discard our clothes. Wash it off."

I began rubbing my face and hands, but it was harder to detect the smell on myself than on Evan. He looked at me in a resigned and pitying way. Then he sat down on the floor and pulled me down beside him, putting his arms around me. Now, when there was nothing he could do to protect me, he had again become the comforter.

"We could of course take off our clothes," he said. "But didn't you notice that Mona took especial pains to strike us where we were not covered? It takes a good washing to get clean again. Such a bath as I had in the ocean. We don't have any such amount of water here. Just rubbing won't do." He drew me close to him, and for a moment I was inclined to forget our predicament in his sheltering arms. "My poor Amhara," Evan murmured. "Don't be afraid. It is a quick death."

At that I sprang to my feet. "I'm not going to sit here and wait to be stung to death by a lot of bees! There must be some way out. Think! Use your brains! That's the trouble with you. You believe everything those women tell you! I don't think you've ever used your brains in your life!"

Evan looked at me, surprised and hurt. "What good would it do?" he asked. "There's no way out."

"There must be a way. Get busy and look. We've just got to figure it out in time."

I began to prowl about the cavern with one of the glow-worm lanterns. In one spot there seemed to be an extension that went farther back.

"Evan," I called, "what's back here? There seems to be a passageway."

Evan did not move from where he sat. "Many passages in cave," he said. "No one knows where they all go."

"But they must go somewhere! Surely we can get out that way! I've heard of caves like this. Sometimes you can come out on the other side of the mountain. That way we'd be almost back at camp. Come on, anything's better than sitting here waiting to be killed."

To my relief, Evan began to shake off his despair and to show some interest.

"It might work. There's a chance. I've never been in the passages and it will be rough. We may never come out. But let's go. Hurry up before they come."

Now that Evan was convinced, he couldn't wait to start down the narrow tunnel. First we collected all the glow-worms and put them into two cages, one for each of us. I picked up the volume of Shakespeare, and Evan frowned.

"You're going to need both hands for climbing. You can't carry anything."

I fastened the cage to my belt, along with my food pouch, now full of Evan's rations. He, at least, would not starve. Whether I would be driven to try his food was something I didn't let myself think about. I looked long-ingly at my little pile of books, now never destined to see Har, but I clung to the Shakespeare.

"I know I can't take much," I said. "But I won't leave this. It's the chief thing I came for, and it's going back with me if I ever get back."

Evan smiled at my fervor. "The evil that men do," he muttered, and led the way to the passage.

We had to enter bent double, and before long we were crawling on hands and knees. We knew there was no going back. Evan pushed his light before him so that he could see a short distance ahead, and I followed right behind. When we had been crawling for what seemed hours and my knees felt completely raw, Evan called back encouragement.

"We're getting somewhere, Amhara. We're out at last. I mean, out of the tunnel. There's a big room here. There's also a big drop. Wait till I find the best way to go."

Presently he disappeared from in front of me, and I was able to stick my head out of the tunnel and see that we were indeed in a much larger cavern. Our tunnel came into it high up on the wall, and Evan was already making his way down to the floor of the chamber by means of precarious footholds. He called up to me and held out his hand. Soon I had let myself down the face of the cliff after him and we both stood on firm footing. We held up our lanterns, but their luminous glow could not reach to the limits of this room. All we could guess was that it was large.

Evan set off around it, hoping that there would be another exit at the opposite end. Now that I had roused him to action and instilled a slight hope, he could not move fast enough, and I was hard put to keep up with him. I knew he thought I should abandon the Shakespeare book in order to use two hands in feeling my way, but I would not leave it. He did not argue the point. He only urged me to hurry.

"Once they pick up our trail, they'll cover the distance in much less time than we have."

"It seems incredible," I gasped. "Do you think they're in the cave entrance yet?"

"I don't know," he answered. "I've lost track of time. Perhaps not. Mona would have to send to the hives and have the keepers bring up a swarm. Then they have to get the scent and become aroused. It takes a little time."

"It's the most fantastic thing I ever heard of. What idiot ever thought up the idea?"

"We have always trained them. As long as my people remember. What is it you told me? Five hundred years?" He rolled the number off his tongue as though proud of his learning.

"Oh, but they can't have been doing it for five hundred years. That was when the Disaster happened. Menasi was discussing it. He thinks your people must have been living in some secluded area, perhaps to the north or in the mountains, as happened with us. Some little spot that happened not to get bombed and to have stayed fairly free of poison. Not anywhere around here. Long afterwards, when this part of the country recovered a little, your tribes moved down here and then you found the giant insects and started to use them. After all, it took them a while to grow this big. But since insects have such a short life and so many generations, they developed quickly."

"You seem to know more about us than we do," Evan said.

"We don't *know*, of course. That's just a theory. The result of studying and thinking and using one's brain. It may eventually prove to have been quite different."

We had stopped to rest in about the sixth large cavern we had traversed, with a variety of tunnels, alleys, and passageways between, some of which branched in several directions. We had found a trickle of water and we paused to drink. Now I regretted having given my canteen to Flora. But we drank as much as we could and Evan ate some of his honey cakes. I looked at them longingly, but decided I could keep going for the present on just water. We were about to go on when Evan held up his hand.

"What is it?" I asked, but I already knew. There was an unmistakable humming from the tunnel we had just left.

With a sharp increase in sound, two of the monsters burst from the tunnel opening and swooped toward us. I had been positive and optimistic in my assertion that we could beat the bees back there in the first cave. Now that I saw two of the giants winging toward me, I was filled with panic, and turned to run. Evan laid a hand on my shoulder.

"Don't run," he said. "They'll get to you anyhow."

He put down his lamp and peeled off his jacket, deliberately laying bare a large expanse of flesh. As the bees descended, he swung the jacket, smashing it down to the floor of the cave. There was a shriek of angry buzzing from the bees, and then silence. I looked on in amazement as Evan cautiously unrolled his jacket to shake out the insects. The bodies fell down beside our lanterns. One was definitely dead. But the other suddenly came to life and with an angry buzz shot off and disappeared down the tunnel whence it had come.

"Damnation!" exclaimed Evan. "There goes our chance of safety. We'd have done better to let them both sting us. It would have been painful, but it would have been the end of those bees. Now that scout will have the whole swarm down this way in no time."

"You don't mean to say she'll go back and *tell* the others!" The whole thing got more incredible all the time.

"Of course. All bees tell each other about directions and distances and where the honey flowers are."

He looked at me as though astonished at this ignorance in one who was otherwise so learned. Then I remembered that I had read something of the sort about the ordinary bees back home. They did it with their dances. And if *they* could communicate, how much more these giants.

Obviously, I was an ignoramus about bees. I turned to Evan to see what we should do, but he merely pulled on his jacket, picked up his lantern and urged the greatest speed in getting out of there. Perhaps we would come to some more divisions in the way and thus might throw off our pursuers for a time at least.

After that it was a nightmare of stumbling and scrambling, jumping and climbing through one passageway or cavern after another. Some of the halls we went through held beauty to please the eye, but we were too hurried to pause and look. Great stalagmites reared from the cavern floor to be met by their opposite formation hanging from the unseen roof far above us, and forming strange and forbidding shapes. Sometimes we heard the sound of running water, and I felt sure we must be near a larger river where we could wash and get rid of the deadly smell, thus defeating the bees. Evan was sure there would not be enough water for the purpose and that we were only insuring our speedy death if we stopped to search.

We went on, running where the cave floor was smooth and level; climbing up and sliding down; crawling through the smaller passages. Sometimes we got to the end of a large hall only to find no exit where we expected one. Then we would begin a frantic search, each one exploring a different side with the dim lanterns, fighting against time to find a way out and onward. Several times we almost gave up, and I felt that here was where the bees would surely find us and we would die together and no one would know we were buried far underground in these dank caverns. I was ready to sit down and weep in exhaustion and frustration. Each time Evan kept on, going over every foot of wall and finally coming upon a small opening, sometimes high up in the side of the cave, where he would have to climb and then dig with my stone chisel to make the opening large enough for us to get through.

We lost all idea of time, and Evan would hardly let me rest after the experience with the scout bees. It all seemed a futile race against unbeatable odds. For all we knew, we were going in circles. We had no assurance that we would ever come out or that we would be on the right side of the mountain when we did. I felt that we had been struggling for days and I wondered at Evan's strength and endurance and at my temerity to have suggested this attempt in the first place back there in the first chamber.

At last, as I was about to give up and suggest that we sit down where we were and wait for the inevitable, Evan, who was searching a small cave for an exit, let out a shout.

"Light, Amhara!" he called. "I can see daylight! It's very dim and at the far end of this passage, but it must be a way out. Hurry up and let's try it!"

My spirits rose, and I staggered after Evan. He was already disappearing down the passage, and I could not see the daylight that beckoned him, because he completely blocked the tunnel ahead. I saw only the glimmer of his glowworm lantern, but I hastened after it, stumbling over loose rocks and sliding on a slippery spot. I thanked fortune that it was daytime and not night outside, or we would never have found this exit. But whether it was the same day we had started our flight or sometime the following day, I had no way of knowing.

Then all at once I saw the light of day. Evan had stepped outside, and the light flooded into the tunnel entrance, almost blinding me. I stopped for a moment and blinked, and then I crawled through the small opening and crouched on a hillside next to him, my mind grappling with the question of where we were and where we should go next.

Evan was jubilant. He hugged and kissed me, all the time babbling almost incoherently.

"We did it, Amhara! We did it! We're through the mountain! Look, there's the lake below us, and there's the camp and your friends down there! I can see the airship!"

I saw it then, all spread out before us. We had come out of the caverns through a small hole on the hillside above our camp. It was unbelievable after that night of terror to look down on our camp and pick out Menasi and N'Gobi and the others going about their accustomed tasks. I realized that it was early morning and later I learned that they were hurrying their preparations to fly in search of Evan and me. At the moment all I could think of was the joy and relief that sight brought me.

"You were right," Evan cried, kissing me again. "We did it. I didn't think it possible, but we got away."

"I didn't think it possible either, when I was back in there. It was all your doing. You kept us going. I felt like lying down and giving up."

Evan stood up on the hillside and began to shout, and our friends below heard him and there was a great commotion, running about and calling and pointing.

"We're coming!" I called. "We're coming!" But my voice seemed lost in the distance and it took Evan's great shout to reach them.

Suddenly the idea of breakfast, with hot tea and Zulli's bread and my friends about me seemed more than I could wait for.

"Hurry up," I said to Evan. "I'm starved!"

I picked up the Shakespeare that I had laid in the grass as I crawled from the cave, and looked for the best footing down the hillside.

Just then Evan took hold of me with a compelling hiss between clenched teeth. I stopped to listen and a chill came over me. Yes, I heard it, too. A humming buzz from the cave behind us. A growing roar, as when you approach a cataract and hear the boiling waters grow ever louder. Only this sound was approaching us, not we it.

Evan was pulling me frantically down the mountain without pause or consideration for the best footing. All he did was take the shortest path in the direction of camp. The beeline, I thought, with a certain irony. Well, the bees knew all about that, too. Even above the noise of the falling rocks and pebbles that we started in our rush down the incline, it seemed to me that I could hear the growing roar of the maddened insects, impatient to break out of the narrow passageway into the air and sunlight where they could get on with their war against us.

As Evan pulled me after him down the hillside, a sudden jerk dislodged the book I had carried for so long, clutched in my arms. It fell against a bush, its leaves askew, the remnants of its bindings crumbling.

"Wait, wait, my book!" I cried, and frantically pulled loose from Evan and ran after it.

Then a stone turned under my foot and I fell. As I

rolled to a stop an armslength from my treasure, I felt a sharp pain in my ankle. Now of all times to be injured! I gritted my teeth. I would have to ignore it till I reached the safety of the camp. Or would it be safety? Perhaps we were only bringing destruction upon the whole expedition. There was no time to stop and consider. The only thing in my mind was to reach the Shakespeare. I picked it up and rose to my feet and the pain in my leg almost threw me.

As I paused to collect myself, I heard an explosion behind me. The bees had burst out of the cavern. They were milling around in a dense cloud, more and more of them coming forth to join it, and giving out a noise that was terrifying even to the uninitiated. To me, who had seen a man struck down by them in a second, it was appalling.

The people in camp had heard and seen it, too. I had one frozen glimpse of them staring up at the swarm on the hillside, and then I heard Menasi issuing orders, and saw them all running for the ship. Evan had turned and was yelling at me. I sat down and began to slide crabwise down the mountain, doggedly holding the book in one hand and trying to forget the pain in my foot.

"Go along!" I called to him. "Hurry up! I'm coming! I'll get there somehow!"

The next moment he was back with me and picking me up in his arms.

"Grab hold!" he cried. "And drop that book!"

But I clung to it with one hand and to Evan with the other, while he raced down the lower slopes and across the clearing toward the lake and our airship with unbelievable speed, considering his extra burden.

"Evan," I cried, even as I clung to him. "Put me down. You can do it alone!"

Evan made no answer. I could hear his great gasping breaths and his pounding heart, and I knew he was exerting every ounce of strength in a final effort to outdistance the bees. And I heard those monsters screaming after us with an indescribable noise of insane frustration and fury.

Then we were in the camp and Evan, near the limits of his strength, dropped me for a moment, and with his arm about my waist, urged me toward the ship. I saw that all our friends had gone inside and closed the windows, but Menasi and N'Gobi were arguing near the hatch, and then N'Gobi pulled something away from him, and leaped down over the entrance ladder.

"Get her inside!" he yelled to Evan. "I'll cover you."

I saw that what he had taken from Menasi was the weapon of lightning, which he was aiming over our heads at the bees, now swooping in for the kill.

Then everything happened at once. The weapon exploded with a terrible roar and flash, so that even Evan jumped as he urged me up the ladder. I thought surely it must frighten the bees if nothing else. As Tadessa and Zulli pulled me into the shelter of the cabin, I turned and saw them falling like hail, knocked down by the terrible weapon of the ancients.

Perhaps of all animals evolved by nature in her millennia, bees are the most dauntless. When they sting they expect to die. When they attack they think of nothing but the kill. No reverses, no amount of slaughter can induce the still-living bees to consider their own safety. Instead, they press on where others have fallen, bent on nothing but delivering the one sting they possess for the defense of their hive and the annihilation of their enemies. This invincible defensive instinct had been forged into a weapon of attack and execution by generations of Evan's people.

When N'Gobi fired into the swarm it had the momentary effect of diverting the bees, so that Evan and I could both scramble up the ladder to safety. As we turned to help N'Gobi up, we saw the bees change their direction of attack, and before we could think or shout, they descended in a swirling mass upon N'Gobi, who was still firing steadily into their midst.

Before our horrified eyes, he became a black mass of stinging, maddened bees. And then there was silence from the gun and N'Gobi had fallen to the ground.

I was too stunned to think. My mind seemed frozen but I kept hearing Flora's voice saying. "In their fury they turned upon her. . . ."

Zulli was screaming. "Do something! Somebody do something!"

Then Menasi seized one of the blankets, which were piled to the side where they had been hastily thrown into the ship. He leaped through the hatch and ran to N'Gobi, wielding the blanket like a broom. The swarm of bees, their fury sated for the moment, were swept helter-skelter, and Menasi grabbed N'Gobi practically from under their wings and bounded back up the ladder. Someone slammed the door behind him, and the rallying swarm began to vent its spite against the ship and the window panes.

For a moment I wondered if there were any cracks in our cabin, like the crevice in the cave, through which they might creep to finish us all off. Menasi laid N'Gobi on the floor and began systematically killing off the bees that had come in with him. I turned with fear and horror to look at my cousin.

He was not dead, for he was breathing in rasping gasps. He was beginning to swell alarmingly all over, and there were still bees clinging to his body and his clothing that had not been knocked off when Menasi swung the blanket and dragged him into the cabin.

Tadessa was issuing orders in a steady voice.

"Don't move him. Leave him right there. Try to get the stings out, some of you. But don't pinch them with your fingers. That'll make it worse. Use a knife and scrape. Zulli, hot water. Hurry up. And adrenalin. All we have. Hurry up with the syringe."

By this time Menasi, Tadessa, and I were all working on N'Gobi, trying to scrape out the myriad stings before they could empty their venom into his body, and trying at the same time not to squeeze them in a way that Tadessa told us would only hasten that process. Evan watched us with such skepticism that my heart turned cold when I looked at him, and I hastily went back to work, while hoping that Evan did not know everything about bees.

At last Zulli told Tadessa the water was boiling, and he went to prepare his hypodermic of adrenalin. Soon after the first shot there was some improvement in N'Gobi and his breathing became easier. Tadessa directed Zulli to keep the water boiling and to prepare hot and cold cloths to apply to the stings.

Presently N'Gobi opened his eyes, as much as the swellings would permit and took in the situation. He tried to speak, but his throat seemed to close on the sound, and only his pathetic efforts to raise himself showed his wish to communicate.

"Take it easy," Tadessa urged. "Just lie quietly. We've got things under control." He reached for N'Gobi's wrist and told Zulli to prepare another injection of adrenalin.

As Tadessa expertly administered the drug, N'Gobi made a frantic effort and found his voice.

"Take her up, you fools!" he gasped. "Don't sit here till those things clog up the propellers!"

Only then did we become aware of what was going on outside the ship. The bees were swarming all over the cabin, flying desperately against the glass in a frenzied effort to get in at us. Menasi looked up at them.

"You know, I think he's right," he said. "I'll do it, N'Gobi. Just lie quietly and get better. Tadessa knows his job."

He rose and made his way to the pilot's seat, and there was a long moment before we heard the motors turn over, while N'Gobi stared past me at the furious bees outside the window. I knew he was hoping that the ship would not fail us now.

Then the motor started, the propellers began to revolve, and the great wind blew the bees away from the windows. As we felt the ship rise under us, I saw a look of tremendous relief cross N'Gobi's face. It was as though he had stood off all the gathering shades of death until he could be sure that his ship would take us home. Then he gave up the struggle. His eyes closed and he lapsed into unconsciousness.

Tadessa continued to work steadily, administering adrenalin and a heart stimulant and keeping Zulli running back and forth with hot and cold water. The ship bucked under us as we hit an occasional air pocket, but Menasi continued his course away from this inimical land. At last Tadessa turned from his close watch on N'Gobi and reached back to Zulli.

"Another shot," he said. "It's the only thing that seems to work."

"It's all gone!" cried Zulli. "You've used it all up!"

"Surely not. Turn out the kit. There must be another vial there."

"But there isn't. You've had it all. I've been looking and looking."

He seized the bag from her and tumbled the contents upon the floor, searching frantically for what wasn't there.

"Who would have thought . . . the one thing we needed! But they made us cut down on everything and I brought the antibacterials!"

He threw down the kit in a helpless rage, and I heard Zulli beginning to cry in soft, strangulated sobs. As for me, I was unable to cry. I was unable to think, beyond the strangeness of hearing Zulli cry for N'Gobi. I held my cousin's unrecognizable head on my lap and felt turned to stone.

Menasi called impatiently from up front. "What's going on back there? Isn't he responding?"

"The only thing that seems to help is the adrenalin and we've run out of that," Tadessa told him.

"But there must be something. Try something else."

"He's had such a massive dose of poison. It's beyond all experience."

"Well, ask Evan. They must have an antidote."

Tadessa looked at Evan with a sour expression.

"You ask him," he said to me. "You'll get further."

I could see why Tadessa looked sour. Evan had retreated into his defeatist attitude that I had encountered in the treasure cave. All his life he had been conditioned to the invincible bees. While we now worked to save N'Gobi, he sat as though waiting for the end. I forgot for the moment how he had carried me to safety. I shook him impatiently.

"Listen to me, Evan!" I cried. "There must be something! What do your people use? What's the antidote?"

"Anti? Anti what?"

"The cure! You must have a cure."

"There is no cure. You get a few stings, you get well.

You get a lot, you die. No one gets the whole swarm like that and lives."

But I wouldn't give up.

"Think!" I commanded. "Perhaps they never told you. Perhaps it's a woman's secret. But they must have worked out something. Try to think."

He put his arms around me and his voice was very sad.

"My poor Amhara. You don't understand. The gods were cheated when you spared my life. Now they have taken their due."

I would not believe it. His fatalistic acceptance of events repelled me. I pushed him away and turned back to N'Gobi.

"It's no use. He doesn't know anything," I told Tadessa.

My brother did not reply. He continued to work stubbornly with what little he had at hand, but we both saw that it could not offset the poison. It was as though a giant hand were about N'Gobi's throat, squeezing the life out; as though that insidious venom were creeping through his body to cut off and smother the action of his heart.

I watched in sick horror as Tadessa patiently felt his pulse and listened to his heart, yet his strangled gasping must have ceased for several minutes before I was aware that I was no longer hearing it and was instead listening to Zulli's sobs.

At last Tadessa stood up and put away his instruments. He spread a blanket over N'Gobi and gently urged Zulli and me into our seats. Then he went forward to talk to Menasi.

I had no way of knowing how long it had been since Menasi began to fly the ship at N'Gobi's urging. For me time ceased to matter as I watched my cousin's losing battle with death. Now I stared out the window with unseeing eyes, and it was some time before I realized that we were flying over dense forests. We might have crossed the Channel and might now be over the mainland of Europe. Presently, Tadessa came back and looked speculatively at Evan.

"Do you think you could fly the ship?" he asked.

Evan's face lit up, and I found myself envying him this opportunity to do something active and of service to the expedition, something that would keep him too busy to think of anything else. At the same time I marveled at N'Gobi's insight that had recognized Evan's innate ability and had trained him before he was needed.

Evan went up to the pilot's seat and I heard him talking with Menasi as our leader pointed out the position of the sun, and direction of flight and wind and other information. Then Menasi came back and sat down with the rest of us in the cabin. He bent over N'Gobi and raised a corner of the blanket as though to satisfy himself that we were not all deceived. At last he let it fall with a final gesture.

At this Tadessa burst out. "It's my fault! I should have known! Been prepared! I brought the wrong things. Not enough adrenalin. . . . To be beaten by an insect!"

"But what an insect!" said Menasi. "And also, it was aimed by humans. Don't forget that. And don't blame yourself. You could not have known."

"It was my job to know! To prepare for every possibility!" The words came out in a burst of frustrated anger that overrode the sorrow in my brother's face. I knew he felt he had failed us.

Menasi spoke quietly. "We all knew we faced hazards when we came on this expedition, but I never envisaged anything like this. I'd begun to think we'd get everyone back safely. It almost seemed too easy. I was mistaken. We have got to put our minds on getting the rest of us back. There is no time for the ritual of weeping or for the funeral customs. He will have to be buried somewhere here."

He glanced sternly at Zulli who had controlled her sobs a few moments, only to start in again at his mention of burial so far from home. Menasi frowned.

"We are now flying toward home," he went on. "Retracing our route as much as possible. We have no time for further exploring. I suggest that if the ship will do it, we keep going till we cross the sea and the mountains and reach the lake of the giant dragonflies. I think N'Gobi would like it there. I think we can leave him there in peace."

He looked at us for approval. No one spoke, but we all nodded. He glanced around the disordered cabin and his eyebrows began to rise in disapproval.

"We'll have to run this ship according to the rules," he said. "It will take constant watch and work by Evan and myself to make up the loss of N'Gobi. The women will have to keep us supplied with food, whether they feel like eating or not. That means clearing up here. Tadessa can help out all around. He'd better begin by looking at Amhara's leg. When it gets dark some of us can sleep, but enough must stay on guard to watch how the ship is flying. So get to work. That's the best medicine. Get busy."

He went back to the pilot's cubby, and the three of us began to do his bidding. We moved N'Gobi to the side out of the way; and Tadessa and Zulli gathered up the scattered contents of the medical kit and strapped up my injured ankle. Then it became apparent that the cabin was full of the bodies of dead bees, and Zulli began to sweep them up and dump them out the window, with a look of the greatest distaste on her face.

For the first time, Tadessa came to life and threw off the cloud of N'Gobi's death. He grabbed the blanket of dead bees away from Zulli.

"What are you doing? Throwing them out? You're crazy!"

"Surely you don't want to keep them? Nasty, murderous things!"

"Surely I do! I've few enough specimens as it is. How can I work out a defense if I don't have anything to work on . . . even dead ones? No, my dear, you collect every single one of those and guard them as your life!"

Zulli frowned, but she did as he told her and made a thorough job of collecting them all, no matter how damaged. Perhaps the idea of creating a defense encouraged her. Tadessa's words made me think. Were we to be only the first of our people to face the onslaught of these monsters?

I was interrupted in my thoughts by Tadessa poking me

in the shoulder. He held out the Shakespeare book. I had completely forgotten it, and now I looked at it with aversion. Had I traded this for N'Gobi's life? If I had left it in the cave; if I had not stopped to pick it up when I dropped it; if I had not then sprained my ankle; would we have reached the ship in time and N'Gobi not have been compelled to come out to our defense? I said as much to Tadessa.

"Put it away," I said. "I don't want to see it."

Menasi spoke from the pilot's hatch.

"You mustn't think that way. Anymore than Tadessa should reproach himself. Don't you suppose I regret that I let him take the gun from me and go out in my place? At such times we do the best we know how. We cannot stop to think and weigh the results. And do you think N'Gobi would be better served if we came home empty-handed?"

When I made no reply, he frowned. "What is this thing you were at such pains to bring back with you?"

Tadessa handed him the book and his brows shot up in astonishment.

"Well, Amhara, this find is likely to make you famous! Don Ylma will kiss you for this!"

I turned away and let him keep the book. It would be many days before I could read Shakespeare again without reliving N'Gobi's death.

Menasi leafed through the volume, and I could tell he was impressed. "So this was in Evan's cave!" he said. "What else was there? We've had no time to hear about your little jaunt with Evan."

I told them about it, and they listened in silence while I described the scene with Mona and our desperate flight through the unknown mazes of the cavern.

"I'd hardly begun to work," I finished. "I had some medical books put aside for Tadessa, but I couldn't carry them. And books on art and music. There was everything you could imagine there, but I had to leave it all."

Tadessa's eyes opened at the mention of the books he did not get.

"It's a treasure cave all right," he said. "The ancients must have stocked it when they saw the Disaster coming.

It's all there—and Evan's people can't use it. They've gone back too far."

When Menasi went to keep an eye on Evan and the ship's progress, he took the Shakespeare with him. Even though he had teased me about it that day in Don Ylma's garden, he could read the ancient language and appreciate the beauty of the words.

When he joined us later to eat what Zulli had prepared, he told me about the work he wanted me to do.

"This is a historic expedition, and the facts and knowledge we have turned up are unprecedented. You are best fitted of us all, Amhara, to write the report for the Council. Of course, I will write one, too, but I want them to hear your story in full. You know what is in that cave. You know what it is like to be white." He smiled at me as he said this, and shot a glance at Evan, bent over the controls. "And you know what it's like to face up to those bees. Stop thinking now of what's done. Think of what's to come and what we must tell the Wasan."

We put the ship down at last by the lake beyond the snowcapped mountains. Our craft had performed well, and it was time we rested and refueled. Long before we landed by that beautiful and peaceful lake, I had begun writing my report.

Menasi was right. With an effort, I took my mind off the tragedy, so that by the time we dug the grave beside the lake, I could face our loss with resignation. I could look upon Evan again with love and not think it had been paid for with N'Gobi's life. I could think about what we have learned and accomplished without counting the cost.

It is now two weeks since the successful return of the expedition. For two weeks we have sat in quarantine, while our Medics make sure we have brought back no contagious poison or disease. For two weeks we have been questioned and interviewed. The reports are in. The examinations are over. Why are we being held? Are they afraid to face the fact that we are not alone on the planet? Are they afraid to let the people see the reality of Evan? Are N'Gobi's gloomy predictions to be realized?

Our expedition went out with a divided personnel, but

it has come back with one mind and one purpose. As Tadessa puts it, "You are not looking for a disease to quarantine, but for an attitude of mind."

I have brought back a promise of lost arts and a great culture. It is there for our taking. But we must take them both—the culture and the people. We cannot benefit from their heritage unless we reach out in friendship to our white brothers. We cannot censure their peculiar barbarism while we condemn a man of N'Gobi's caliber for his color.

The way is open if we want to take it. We have sent in our reports to the Wasan, to the Council, to the people.

We are waiting to hear their voice.

ABOUT THE AUTHOR

A. M. LIGHTNER became interested in science fiction while her son Christopher was growing up, and she read him science fiction stories and books. Later, although her early writing interests had been drama and poetry (her poems have appeared in a number of magazines), she decided to try her hand at science fiction. Since that time her stories have appeared in several magazines, and she has written four other science fiction novels for young people: *Doctor to the Galaxy*, *The Galactic Troubadours*, *The Space Olympics* and *The Space Plague*.

Miss Lightner was born in Detroit, Michigan, and educated at Westover School and Vassar College, where she majored in music and English. After graduation she moved to New York to work on an engineering magazine and, more recently, on the house organ of a major advertising agency.

After her marriage, the author and her family spent summers on a small farm in Bucks County, Pennsylvania, where she developed a serious interest in the natural sciences. Her special hobby is the study of butterflies, and she works with a group centered around the University of Toronto, tagging the monarch butterfly for migration study. Miss Lightner has written a book for children on the subject, and she has published a number of articles on butterflies and animals. She is a member of the Lepidopterists' Society and the New York Entomological Society. She and her husband live in New York City.

OUT OF THIS WORLD!

That's the only way to describe Bantam's great series of science-fiction classics. These space-age thrillers are filled with terror, fancy and adventure and written by America's most renowned writers of science fiction. Welcome to outer space and have a good trip!

☐	THE TIME MACHINE by H. G. Wells	4063	50¢
☐	A CANTICLE FOR LEIBOWITZ by Walter Miller, Jr.	5423	95¢
☐	THE MYSTERIOUS ISLAND by Jules Verne	5439	75¢
☐	THE DAY OF THE DRONES by A. M. Lightner	5567	75¢
☐	THE MARTIAN CHRONICLES by Ray Bradbury	5613	95¢
☐	20,000 LEAGUES UNDER THE SEA by Jules Verne	5939	75¢
☐	VAR THE STICK by Piers Anthony	6948	95¢
☐	ALAS, BABYLON by Pat Frank	6991	95¢
☐	FANTASTIC VOYAGE by Isaac Asimov	7137	95¢
☐	RAGA SIX by Frank Lauria	7249	$1.25
☐	STAR TREK 10 by James Blish	8401	95¢
☐	COMMUNE 2000 A.D. by Mack Reynolds	8402	95¢
☐	STAR RIDER by Doris Piserchia	8408	95¢